The
Broken
Spine

The Broken Spine

Dorothy St. James

Berkley Prime Crime
New York

BERKLEY PRIME CRIME
Published by Berkley
An imprint of Penguin Random House LLC
penguinrandomhouse.com

Copyright © 2021 by Dorothy McFalls
Penguin Random House supports copyright. Copyright fuels creativity, encourages
diverse voices, promotes free speech, and creates a vibrant culture. Thank you for buying an
authorized edition of this book and for complying with copyright laws by not reproducing,
scanning, or distributing any part of it in any form without permission. You are supporting
writers and allowing Penguin Random House to continue to publish books for every reader.

BERKLEY and the BERKLEY & B colophon are registered trademarks and
BERKLEY PRIME CRIME is a trademark of Penguin Random House LLC.

Library of Congress Cataloging-in-Publication Data
Names: St. James, Dorothy, author.
Title: The broken spine / Dorothy St. James.
Description: First Edition. | New York: Berkley Prime Crime, 2021. |
Series: Beloved bookroom mysteries; 1
Identifiers: LCCN 2020035708 (print) | LCCN 2020035709 (ebook) |
ISBN 9780593098578 (hardcover) | ISBN 9780593098592 (ebook)
Subjects: GSAFD: Mystery fiction.
Classification: LCC PS3619.T245 B76 2021 (print) |
LCC PS3619.T245 (ebook) | DDC 813/.6—dc23
LC record available at https://lccn.loc.gov/2020035708
LC ebook record available at https://lccn.loc.gov/2020035709

Printed in the United States of America
1   3   5   7   9   10   8   6   4   2

Cover art by Anne Wertheim
Cover design by Sarah Oberrender
Book design by Alison Cnockaert

This is a work of fiction. Names, characters, places, and incidents either are the product of the
author's imagination or are used fictitiously, and any resemblance to actual persons, living
or dead, business establishments, events, or locales is entirely coincidental.

For the librarians
Those who inspire
Those who teach
Those who are the warriors
And for those who introduced me to the power of the story,
I'm forever grateful.

A (VERY) SHORT HISTORY OF BOOKS
By Trudell Becket, Assistant Librarian

Clay tablets were used in Mesopotamia in the third millennium BCE. In ancient Egypt, papyrus was used for writing. In Mesoamerica, information was recorded on long strips of paper, agave fibers, or animal hides, which were then folded and protected by wooden covers. Writing on bone, shells, wood, and silk existed in China long before the second century BCE.

Paper was invented in China around the first century CE. The first printing of books started in China shortly thereafter.

In Rome, parchment gradually replaced papyrus. In the Islamic world, paper had replaced parchment by the ninth century. Europe switched from using parchment to paper in the thirteenth century.

The first movable-metal-type printing was used in Korea in the 1300s. The Gutenberg Bible, the first major book produced in Europe with movable metal type, was printed by Johannes Gutenberg in 1455.

The 1930s ushered in the age of mass-market paperback books.

In 1998, the first dedicated e-book reader went on sale. In 2011, the sale of e-books outpaced the sale of paperback books for the first time at Amazon, a large online book retailer.

In 2014, the world's first bookless library opened in Bexar County, Texas.

In the present day, the Town of Cypress, South Carolina, became home to the nation's next bookless library.

And then civilization collapsed . . .

Or at least it did for me.

Chapter One

—◦—

No one in the moderately sized rural southern town of Cypress would ever suspect their stalwart assistant librarian of breaking into the library where she worked. Why would they? A bronze plaque hangs on my kitchen wall. It was personally presented to me by Mayor Goodvale. He declared me an asset to the town. I'd received the award because I always performed my job with the highest level of pride and professionalism. For the past thirteen years I put the town and library first, often to the detriment of my personal life.

An even bigger honor occurred a few years ago when Mrs. Lida Farnsworth, the town's head librarian, whispered (she always whispered) while we busily returned books to their shelves: "Trudell Becket, I couldn't be more pleased to be wrong about my first impression of you. I would have hired *any* other candidate for the position. But, alas, the only other person who'd applied was that drunkard Cooper Berry. I honestly didn't think you had it in you, honey. But, bless your heart, you've become the model of a perfect librarian."

And she was right. I was perfect. Until . . .

Well, let's just say someone needed to do this.

As a general rule, librarians don't speak in loud voices. Librarians don't exceed the speed limit when driving to work. And librarians certainly don't dress head-to-toe in black ninja-wear while attempting to pick the library's backdoor lock.

Yet, librarians can always be counted on *to get things done.*

"Don't look at me like that," I muttered to a lanky brown cat with black tiger stripes. It had emerged from the darkened back alleyway to stand next to the library's cool pearly-pink granite wall and watch me. "Someone needs to protect those books before they all end up destroyed. They're sending them to the landfill." The small metal flashlight clenched between my teeth caused the words to come out garbled. Both of my hands were busy working the lock.

A textbook for locksmiths that I'd borrowed from the library's reference section sat open to the page featuring a diagram of a lock. Since I didn't own a lockpick kit—why would I?—I'd improvised with a few sturdy paperclips bent to resemble the tools depicted on the book's previous page. Every little sound, every scrape and rumble in Cypress's quaint downtown boomed in my ears. I jumped at the soft cough of a car engine. And with that cat watching me, I felt an itchy need to scurry into the nearest mousehole to hide.

But I couldn't run. I had to finish what I'd set my mind to finishing.

After what felt like a million thundering heartbeats while I fumbled with the paperclips, the lock clicked. The door opened. I rose on shaky legs, gathering up the reference book and the stack of flattened moving boxes I'd brought with me. My gaze darted to the darkest corners of the alleyway before I slipped inside.

Just as the door started to close, the cat that had been watching with such a judgmental glare shimmied between my legs and into the library before the heavy metal back door clanked closed.

"Hey!" I called in a harsh whisper because shouting in a library simply wasn't done. Whispering seemed even more important in the middle of the night as I sneaked inside on my clandestine mission.

The brown cat ignored me. With a yeow loud enough to have me instinctively hissing "*Shhhh!*" the little beast darted upstairs and disappeared into the shadows of the stacks.

"Tru, you're in for it now," I muttered before dropping the stack of boxes. I sprinted after that darn cat.

Mrs. Farnsworth would have a heart attack if she discovered a flea-bitten kitty wandering among her books in the morning. I needed to get him out. The head librarian was already on edge with having to deal with the changes coming to the library.

If I didn't know the tough older woman better, I would have suspected she was busy plotting a murder. Every time she had to deal with the man behind the changes that were ripping apart both of our worlds, she'd grit her teeth and smile so tightly it looked as if her lips might crack open. But later, when she talked about him and his grand plan, her smile changed into something horrible that made ice tiptoe up my spine.

The trouble had started three weeks ago. Duggar Hargrove, the town's new and aggressive town manager, had made his way up the long run of steps and into the library's historic atrium. Dressed in a tweed suit and a pink tie that matched his bright pink complexion, he stood in the middle of the room with his round fists planted on his hips. The mayor and several members of the town council had followed him into the library's semicircular atrium and had gathered like a smiling army of suits around him.

Duggar, talking much too loudly for inside a library, called for Mrs. Farnsworth to stand next to him. Because she was both a southern lady and a librarian with the highest standards of comportment, she complied without question. The only sign of her displeasure was a slight shivering of the string of pearls that always adorned her long, elegant neck.

Although I grew up in the South and had attended the strictest cotillion classes in town, I had never mastered the art of masking my feelings. Those pesky emotions showed up on my face as clearly as a bright red hat sitting atop a lady's head. I could feel my brows wrinkling and my mouth twisting into a look of puzzlement as I stepped out from behind the front desk to watch as Duggar raised his beefy hands as if asking for silence. This struck me as silly since he was standing in the middle of a library where silence was the rule.

He cleared his throat and gave the mayor a nod before speaking. His voice rumbled like a car engine in need of a tune-up. "Thanks to my efforts . . . and those of our elected officials, of course, of course," he said, clearing his throat again, "the town of Cypress has seen unprecedented growth over the past year. We've welcomed industries that make auto parts, fertilizers, and tractor tires. They've invested in our town and in our people. It's all very good. Very good. But now is the time for us to start thinking bigger. And by bigger I mean high tech. We want companies who are on the cutting edge of technology to look to Cypress as their new home to grow."

The politicians standing around him all nodded in unison. Mrs. Farnsworth's pearls shivered again, and her dainty brows dipped ever so slightly toward her deep brown eyes. I felt for my boss. I knew how much she loathed surprises.

"In order to accomplish our goal," Duggar's low growl continued, "we need to become forward thinking. We need to modernize every aspect of our town. We need to be featured in the national media as a town of the future, a town that deserves to be watched."

When he'd finished, the politicians started to clap loudly. Mrs. Farnsworth shot them a sharp look, which put a quick end to that nonsense.

"What you are saying is uplifting and all, but why are you making this pretty speech in my library instead of at last night's council meeting?" she demanded in a hard whisper that made the skin on the back of my neck prickle. Her eyelids snapped with impatience.

Duggar flashed a full set of teeth. "I'm glad you asked, ma'am. I'm here because, with the full support of our council, we're going to invest in upgrading the library."

"*Finally*," I breathed. After years of budget cuts, the library no longer stocked the latest and most popular new releases. And none of the library employees had seen the cost-of-living raise we'd been promised for three years in a row now.

"Well . . . now . . . that's good news," Mrs. Farnsworth pronounced.

Duggar tugged at his tight collar. It was as if he knew what was coming next would be ill-received by the library staff and patrons. "Modernization of all aspects of our town is essential. And I'll need everyone's help. Even if change feels painful at first, I need each and every resident in the community to be a part of my team. Can I count on you?"

The mayor and town council all nodded. Mrs. Farnsworth rolled her eyes. Everyone else stood silently by, waiting to hear the changes Duggar and the elected officials had planned for our beloved historic library.

Duggar tugged at his tight collar again. I'm not sure what he was expecting. Cheers of agreement? Not in this library. Not with the stern Mrs. Farnsworth standing watch. "Well," he said, "the library of the future is a library with no limits. It's a library that brings the world to our small, rural town."

No one could disagree with that. For centuries, libraries, and the books they contain, have served as a ticket to the world and beyond. The books populating the stacks educate, inspire, and in some cases save lives. They had certainly saved mine.

"Just spit it out," Mrs. Farnsworth chided. "Ever since you were no taller than my knee, you'd talk and talk and talk and never get to the point. I'm an old woman with a busy schedule. I don't have time for this."

His pink face turned a shade pinker. "Fine." He huffed. "We're going to turn our library into a bookless library."

A what?

"A what?" Mrs. Farnsworth demanded in her haughtiest, most re-fined southern tones. She'd reached for the pearls adorning her throat, which showed how much his announcement had flustered her. She almost never clutched her pearls.

I sat down and rolled over to the computer at the reference desk and typed "bookless library" into the search engine.

As images of what looked like cybercafés—stark rooms filled with computers—appeared on the screen in front of me, Duggar explained to the crowd, "We will do away with all of these out-of-date books and replace them with computers and computer terminals. Patrons will be able to check out tablets with electronic books and references loaded onto them. Or they will be able to check out electronic books and load them onto their own tablets and phones. Instead of a static collection of moldy paper, we'll have the most up-to-the-minute resources for our community and for the industries that will come. We'll be the envy of our neighboring communities. We'll be educating the best and brightest with the best and newest information."

I glanced at the books behind me. Yes, some of them were out-of-date. Every spring we purged books that were no longer relevant. If the town council would simply give us a decent budget, we could refresh our collection on a regular basis.

Yet while some of our books might be old—*really* old—many of the titles in the stacks were timeless classics. There were first editions. A few were even signed.

"I must have misheard you," Mrs. Farnsworth said, her voice tight with emotion. "It sounded like you said that you planned to get rid of *my* books."

"Yes, ma'am. These old books will be replaced with state-of-the-art computers." When Mrs. Farnsworth scoffed, he added, "Your patrons will have access to more books than you can imagine."

"But what will the children do?" she said. "You cannot set a baby up in front of a computer."

"The babies and tots will use child-friendly tablets," Duggar was quick to answer.

The back-and-forth went on like this for a while. Finally, Mrs. Farnsworth held up her hands. "You can modernize with your computers while keeping our books."

He shook his head and turned to Mayor Goodvale for help.

"I am sorry, Lida." The mayor, a kindly man who had just a touch of gray on his temples, took her slightly bent hands in his. "I know this must come as a shock to you. And you needn't worry, your position is safe. We'll always need you to help curate our collection, even if it is online. But we only have enough money to purchase the computers, tablets, and subscription services for the various online media sources. We cannot afford to purchase printed books too. We're building a library of the future. There's no place here to shelve outdated books."

She yanked away from his touch. "This is a mistake. Abandoning books is not moving forward. It's a step back toward the Dark Ages."

I agreed with her. And I wasn't the only one. In the days that followed, several of our long-term patrons complained about Duggar's dramatic announcement. Letters were written to the editor. But nothing anyone said or did stopped Duggar's plans for modernization.

As each day passed, I worried more and more about Mrs. Farnsworth. On the surface, she was acting as if nothing was happening to her beloved library—a place where she'd worked for more than fifty years. Practicing the perfection she expected from others, she never complained. She never questioned the rules. She went along with the town's plan to convert the library into a futuristic technological center. *An abomination.* All the while her slender seventy-nine-year-old body grew tauter and tauter. Her adhesion to the rules, and her requirement that everyone else within her sight also strictly follow those rules, grew more and more stringent as the days passed.

She'd scolded young Timmy Cho for breaking the spine of a popular picture book with such a firm whisper that tears had flooded the eight-year-old's eyes.

She'd ejected Betty Crawley, the local newspaper reporter, from the stately old building for interviewing library users about what they thought about the coming changes to the library. Not only that, she told the sputtering Betty that she was banned from ever coming back.

And she'd given strict instructions to the library staff that we could no longer waive fines for books returned late. "If the citizens of Cypress cannot return their books on time, they're going to have to *pay the price*," Mrs. Farnsworth had whispered ominously. A worrisome gleam darkened her rich brown eyes as she emphasized "pay the price."

Despite her determination to pretend the library wasn't getting a hideous overhaul, changes had started to happen. A newly hired technology specialist imported from Silicon Valley showed up one morning and took charge, ordering everyone, even Mrs. Farnsworth, around.

Anne Lowery looked like she should still be in high school. The purple streak running through her inky black hair only added to her youthful looks. I would have suspected she was lying about her credentials if not for the bright spark of confidence in her glittering green eyes and the way she took charge without hesitation.

Change was coming. Whether we liked it or not, the books were going to be replaced by computers and tablets. A mainframe computer system had already replaced the employee lounge, and the children's section was slated to become a café.

As the renovations entered their last stages, the library closed its doors to the public. The staff had spent our days pulling our collection from the shelves and packing up the books in cardboard boxes.

"I don't understand why we have to get rid of all the books," I'd given my last plea for sanity two days ago to Duggar, who'd been on hand every day to oversee the changeover. "Isn't there some way we can keep at least some of the books as a special collection? Some of these books are worth the world to our residents."

"We're not getting rid of the books," he'd explained as if I were an idiot. He pointed toward the employee lounge, which was now filled with computer equipment. "They'll still be in there. On hard drives and in the cloud on the Internet. And more books will be joining them."

"Yes, but some of our patrons—"

"It might take a while for our citizens to get used to the new way of doing things," Duggar had cut me off to say. "It's normal. Soon everyone will be raving about the ease of accessing information from the library. No one will even have to come into this building. Everything will be accessible online."

"Not everything," I'd grumbled. Not the escape from a family that was falling apart when my parents were heading toward divorce. Not the refuge from the chaos of living a divided life between two households in the aftermath of the divorce. And certainly not the friendships I'd forged as a lonely teen wandering through the stacks, running my fingers along book spines, and stumbling upon steadfast friends within the pages of timeless classics written by great literary voices such as Daphne du Maurier and Georgette Heyer. I found the justice I felt was lacking in my home life within the pages of novels written by Agatha Christie, Dorothy L. Sayers, and especially Carolyn Keene.

How would a child facing similar challenges find such a lifeline in the keywords of a search engine?

"This is a mistake," I'd told Duggar.

He'd patted my head and chuckled. "Scores of people once worried about switching from carriages to automobiles. It's progress. I'm leading the way for our community to attract the kinds of jobs that raise the standard of living for all of us. It might seem difficult now, but you'll see. One day you'll understand."

I'd thought and thought on what he was telling me. I knew that nearly ten percent of the residents in Cypress were out of work. Many of them had long given up hope of ever finding a position that would put healthy food on their family's table. These were good people in tough situations. They deserved better. We were at least an hour-and-a-half drive to the closest city. And Duggar was right. Jobs in our rural corner of the world were both low paying and scarce. But destroying the books? That didn't seem like the answer.

Which was what had brought me out here on this moonless night. I flicked on the flashlight. Its light bounced around the empty stacks. The stray cat was nowhere to be seen. The books had already been packed into cardboard boxes very similar to the flattened ones I'd brought. The only media allowed to remain on the shelves were the DVDs, music CDs, and audiobook CDs.

The newer books and the children's board books were going to be shipped to a third-party resale company. The older books, the ones that had served as lifesavers and friends for generations in Cypress, were slated for the landfill. Just thinking of dumping those books with the everyday garbage made the acid in my stomach churn. I had to save them.

Thanks to Mrs. Farnsworth and her dedicated attention to order and detail, all the boxes were cataloged and numbered. In a way, this made my job tonight easier. But it also complicated matters. Once I was done here, if anyone opened the boxes, they would know which books were missing.

I knelt down beside a box labeled 31A and peeled open its lid. The heady smell of leather and paper filled my nostrils. I ran my hand over the spine of *The Secret of the Old Clock*, a 1930s edition of the first Nancy Drew Mystery, and sighed.

I continued working in the dim glow of the security lights, pulling classics out of the boxes bound for the landfill and carefully repacking them in the boxes I'd brought. I left the boxes that were going to the book reseller untouched. About an hour into my work, a metallic tap, tap, tap sounded.

Finally, they were here.

With a smile, I hurried downstairs to the back exit in the basement. I quickly unlocked the door and threw it open. When I saw who was standing there, the smile froze on my face.

"Who are you?" I demanded. My heart pounded in my throat. Had I just been caught in the act of saving my books?

The man standing on the other side of the threshold was a stranger. A very tall, very menacing stranger. I was in trouble.

Chapter Two

He was dressed in a dark suit and looked like a television-show FBI agent, his blank expression speaking of power and determination. His eyes, hard as black onyx, seemed to know everything about me, while I knew nothing about him. I was struggling to come up with a reason to explain what I was doing, here, in the middle of the night, when he spoke.

"I was invited," he said in a voice as hard as the rest of him.

"Not by me," I countered and started to close the door.

"Tru, don't be rude." Tori Green, my best friend ever since preschool, jogged up from the shadows of the alleyway. "I invited him."

"Are you crazy? Who is he?" I demanded, not daring to take my eyes from the stranger, who with a word to the wrong person could ruin our mission and—I swallowed—cause us to lose our chance to save these books from the trash heap.

"He's my new friend." She grabbed his arm and, pushing me aside, pulled him into the library. "Charlie, meet Tru. She might be tense now, but I promise you she has a heart of gold. Charlie just moved to town. He loves books nearly as much as you do."

Tori, in normal Tori fashion, had ignored my suggestion that we wear black. Instead, she was dressed in a bright flamingo pink sundress. The neckline dipped low in a flirty manner. Her blonde hair was twisted into an updo that accentuated her high cheekbones. The heels on her sandals added at least five inches to her already tall frame. And yet, she still wasn't as tall as the man she'd decided to invite along on our caper. Why on earth did she invite him?

One look between the two of them and understanding dawned.

"You brought a date? To . . . to our undercover, super-secret rescue mission?" I didn't want to believe my friend capable of doing something so irresponsible. But we'd been friends since forever. I knew her better than I knew anyone else in my life. This was exactly the sort of thing she'd do.

"Don't be such a worrywart." She ran her hand up and down his arm and smiled. "He knows how to be discreet."

"Discreet?" I squeaked. How did she know that?

I was about to send them both on their way when the bright headlamps from a passing car turning a corner on Main Street seemed to sweep through the alleyway like a searchlight. I grabbed both their arms and dragged them farther into the library, slamming the door closed behind them.

Tori had always been the brave one of our duo. Even at a young age, her good looks allowed her to get away with nearly anything short of murder. During high school, she'd been cheerleader captain and homecoming queen. She never lacked for a date. She'd been voted most likely to succeed. She laughed quickly. And rarely took anything seriously.

"You need to take this seriously," I whispered as I pulled her away from her date. "If he tells anyone what we're doing, we can get into terrible trouble."

"He's fine," she whispered back. "He recently moved into town from Las Vegas. Isn't that exciting? I have good memories from Vegas. I married Mr. Number Two in Vegas, remember? We started talking a few hours ago at the coffee shop and—"

"Wait, wait, wait. What? You just met him *a few hours ago*?" I must have said that too loudly. Charlie's brows rose as he watched us.

"Listen, Tru. He's here. He already knows what's going on, so you might as well let him help us with the heavy lifting. We need someone with strong arms." She finger-waved at him and then sighed happily. "He has muscles and then some."

"You're already thinking he could be Mr. Number Five, aren't you?"

She shrugged. "I just met him. But since you mentioned it, I don't know . . . maybe. Not tonight, though. Let's get busy."

I hesitated. "He looks like a cop." The number of reservations I had against including him could fill an oversized notebook. "He looks dangerous."

"Yeah, he does. Isn't it delicious?" Her pretty blue eyes sparkled even brighter. "Stop worrying so much. The books won't wait forever."

Resigned that I was stuck with this new guy who might ruin our chances to save the books, I started back upstairs and toward the boxes I'd been repacking. I'd barely made it to the first step when someone tapped on the metal backdoor again. I jumped.

"That'll be Flossie," Tori said, flashing that perfect smile of hers. Not at me, mind you, but at her new "hunk of the month."

Tori opened the door before I could. She was right about who had knocked. Our friend Flossie was waiting on the other side. Unlike Tori, she'd followed my instructions and dressed in black pants and a gauzy black shirt; she'd even donned a black felt hat with a small, but dramatic, black veil.

Flossie Finnegan-Baker had attended high school with Mrs. Farnsworth, but that was where the comparison between the two older women ended. While the head librarian wore conservative dresses and pearls to work every day, Flossie wore tie-dyed dresses and an oversized moonstone necklace that she claims was blessed by the Dalai Lama. She'd left Cypress for decades, traveling the world with her husband. After he went to "claim his great reward in the hereafter," she returned to her hometown and started writing books. She'd been coming to the library to write in a quiet environment for the past seven years. She never lets anyone read what she taps into that purple laptop of hers. It must be good, though. She used her latest royalty check to buy a bright red Corvette complete with hand controls for the gas and brakes and a high-tech accessibility package for her wheelchair.

"Why are y'all just standing around gaping?" she complained as she wheeled herself through the door. "And who the devil are you, young man?"

"I'm Charlie, ma'am," he said in a deep voice. Tori quickly stepped in and performed proper introductions.

Flossie looked over at me and mouthed, "Number Five?"

I shrugged.

We didn't talk much after that. The task of digging through the books, packing them up, and carrying them down to the basement proved to be a bigger undertaking than I'd anticipated. I hated to admit it to Tori, but I was glad she'd brought a date with strong arms. He had strength enough to carry three boxes at a time down the narrow back staircase.

During World War II, the town had built a bomb shelter in the far corner of the library's basement. The shelter is a dark vault with double metal interlocking doors that are a foot and a half thick. Cypress used to store rations, cots, water, and radios down there in case of an enemy attack. By the mid-eighties, the shelter had been emptied out and largely forgotten. The overhead lights flickered and buzzed as we worked. I made a mental note to figure out how to get the lighting updated without attracting undue attention.

Shelves that had once held canned beans and tinned meats lined the walls. This was where we started putting the books. I would have liked to bring down a few of the shelving units from the main library to put in the middle of the room. But the oak shelves were so heavy that even with Charlie's incredible strength, we couldn't manage it.

Hours passed. Gradually, our secret bookroom started to take shape. Flossie worked the lower shelves, while I handled the higher ones. Tori and Charlie worked as a team, packing up the boxes and carrying them down the back stairs.

I had just shelved a book from the latest box Charlie had delivered, when a loud crash sounded from directly above our heads. I glanced at the ancient gray institutional clock hanging above the vault's door. It was already half past nine in the morning. How did that happen? It was late.

It was very late.

We were supposed to be done and out of the building before eight o'clock. The library staff arrived at nine, which meant they'd already come in. If any of them came down to the vault or happened to notice one of my new "assistants" packing and carrying boxes away from the main part of the library, my plan to open the secret bookroom wing of the library would be ruined.

The crash worried me. Had either Tori or Charlie run into trouble upstairs? With that upsetting thought circling my mind—and a host of explanations I would need to give to Mrs. Farnsworth to keep the stickler from firing me or having me arrested—I exchanged a worried glance with Flossie.

"Go," she said.

"Already gone." I dashed out of the ancient bomb shelter and into the basement hallway. There, I passed Tori. She had a look of surprise on her face.

"Find Charlie and get him and Flossie out of here," I hissed as I hurried up the stairs.

This morning, the historic library had an odd feeling to it. With the books removed from the shelves, it felt as if the old building had died. Which was a silly thought. Buildings weren't living creatures. They couldn't die.

I kept running to where I thought the crash had come from and skidded to a halt in the media section. One of the tall wooden shelves that had held hundreds of DVDs had toppled over. Movies from the past twenty years were scattered throughout the area.

That was where I spotted a pair of finely polished leather shoes.

I stepped closer. My heart shuddered in my chest. There were legs attached to those shoes. The shelf had fallen on someone.

"Help!" I screamed as I frantically tried to lift the shelf. It was too heavy. I couldn't move it by myself. Library or not, I kept shouting at the top of my lungs for help.

"What are you—?" The hissed rebuke died in Mrs. Farnsworth's mouth. She moved quickly and, with a strength that surprised me, helped me lift the heavy wooden shelving unit from the person it had fallen on. Together, we managed to slide it to one side. Plastic DVD boxes crunched under its weight as it landed with a heavy thud.

"Him," Mrs. Farnsworth said, as if the sight of the body we'd uncovered had caused a bad taste in her mouth.

Yes, him. The man lying motionless on the ground was the very man Mrs. Farnsworth would have liked to have killed. Duggar Hargrove.

I knelt down next to him and put a finger to his pink neck, searching for a pulse and finding none.

"He's dead," a voice behind us gasped.

I turned to find Mayor Goodvale and his adult son, Luke, standing not ten feet away. Their wide-open eyes made them look like cartoon figures.

"Yes, he's dead," Mrs. Farnsworth repeated the mayor's pronouncement in her whisper-soft voice. She didn't sound upset, not in the least. Rather, she sounded almost triumphant.

Chapter Three

———•———

Nancy Drew would never find herself in a knot of trouble this tight. The teen sleuth knew how to figure her way out of such a bind without experiencing even the slightest twinge of worry. I, on the other hand, kept glancing over at the three boxes that Tori and Charlie still needed to carry downstairs. What if someone noticed that those boxes weren't the same style as the others? What if someone started asking why no one had seen me in the library this morning until the time I'd found Duggar's body?

Despite the library's constant cool temperature of sixty-five degrees, a bead of sweat trickled down my back. While I was still crouched beside Duggar, I half expected to see the man get up and start accusing me of tampering with his grand plans for the library. But the dead are eerily still.

As the mayor called his office, I rose from Duggar's side and took step after step, backing away from the scene, hoping the building's old plaster walls would swallow me up.

"I didn't see you come in this morning," Mrs. Farnsworth whispered as she followed me in my retreat. "You didn't sign in on the timesheet either."

I blinked at the proper older lady and drew several deep breaths, hoping I could calm my pounding heart. "Didn't I? But I always sign in."

Gracious, my voice was quivering with guilt.

Mrs. Farnsworth raised an eyebrow at that.

Before she could accuse me of any wrongdoing, I added quickly, "Since the library is closed this week, I wasn't sure that we were following normal protocol. I came in and continued work on getting the boxes organized. I suppose I forgot about the timesheet." Without realizing what I was doing, I gestured toward the boxes that Tori and Charlie had failed to carry down. The brown cardboard stood out in stark contrast with the library's neatly cataloged white packing boxes.

Mrs. Farnworth's eyebrows traveled a bit higher as she zeroed in on the damaging evidence. "Tru? What are—?"

"Nobody move. I need everyone to remain where you are while we figure out what happened," a man's voice boomed through the high-ceilinged library.

Mrs. Farnsworth sucked in a sharp breath and whirled toward the art deco bronze and glass double front doors. The police chief, who was as lanky as the tabby cat that was still lurking somewhere in the library, had the doors pushed open. The coroner and several police officers were pouring into the space.

The last man to come through the door made me want to crawl under the nearest table. I hadn't seen him since high school graduation. I'd heard he'd recently moved back home, but I'd kind of hoped the town would be big enough that we could avoid each other forever.

Tall, with an arrogant, jutting chin, Jace Bailey was dressed in khaki pants with a dark blue blazer slung over one arm. His white shirt looked crisp, almost as if it'd never been worn before. He'd been the quarterback and a track star in high school. Unlike some of our classmates, he'd kept in shape since graduation. And as in high school, his slightly too long dusty blond hair still needed taming. With a nod from the police chief, who was heading over to talk with the mayor, Jace took over, directing the other officers, the coroner, and her staff.

Once he'd finished giving orders, his gaze headed in my direction. I had to grab hold of the nearest chair to keep from making a mad dash toward the nearest exit. It was bad enough that Duggar had died in the middle of my scheme to save the books and that I was going to have to answer all sorts of questions for the police while not letting on that every bone in my body was trembling with guilt. Having to deal with Jace was going to break me. I shivered when his roaming blue eyes paused and his gaze touched mine.

Heavens, my heart thundered in my ears just as it had the last time he'd looked my way all those *mumble-mumble* years ago. I suddenly wished for a natural disaster (any kind of natural disaster would do) so I wouldn't have to face him. At the same time, I hated myself for having those feelings, for letting what he did to me—oh, heck, it was nineteen years ago—still hurt me.

What felt like a million years lasted less than a second. His gaze moved on without showing any sign of recognition. Not even a twitch of his mouth or a crinkle of his brow. Odd.

"Detective!" the coroner, an older lady with pinkish-white hair styled into a tight corkscrew perm, called to Jace as she crouched down next to Duggar.

"Be right there!" He said something to the uniformed officer standing next to him before hurrying over to Duggar's body to find out what the coroner wanted.

"Shh!" Mrs. Farnsworth hissed several times before rushing over to where the police chief and Mayor Goodvale were talking.

Not sure what I should do, I stood still as if my feet had been glued to the terrazzo floor. My hands were still locked around the back of the wooden chair in front of me as I watched the crime professionals while they worked.

My father liked to call the local police department "The Barney Fife Club." But the officials that had arrived on the scene moved with confidence. They measured. They used modern-looking electronic equipment. And they were writing everything down. No bumbling Barney Fifes here. They were professionals who seemed determined to discover what had happened in the library this morning, which only made more sweat trickle down my back.

The police chief and the mayor moved to stand next to Duggar's body while Jace and the coroner worked. Jace's gaze hardened as he studied the heavy oak shelf Mrs. Farnsworth and I had tossed aside. He drew a long, slow breath as he rose to his feet. "This wasn't an accident, sir," he said to the police chief. "There's no way something like this would fall over without help. Someone pushed the shelf over onto the decedent."

"The decedent, Detective?" I'd never heard Mayor Goodvale's voice sound so tense. "Duggar was our town manager. He lived in Cypress his entire life. He was my friend."

"I meant no disrespect, sir," Jace said as he studied his shoes. "I was only—"

"Don't mind the boy none," Police Chief Fisher said as he thumped Jace on the back. "The NYPD taught him to talk like he's on one of those police drama shows. But as I was telling you, Marvin, he's determined to prove his salt to us."

"Can he?" the mayor asked, as if Jace were not standing right there. "This is an important case. We can't hand it off to a wet-behind-the-ears whelp with a history of—"

"I ain't handing nothing over," Chief Fisher drawled in his thick backwoods accent while Jace, a little red around the ears, started to jot notes in his casebook. "I'll be overseeing every step my officers take, especially with him. Now Krystal, what are your preliminary findings?"

The coroner, who was crouched beside Duggar's body, shook her head. "Based on my initial examination, the impact flattened him. Like a pancake. A body can't survive something like that."

"So it *is* murder?" Mayor Goodvale's voice trembled with what sounded like fury. "In . . . in my town?"

Jace flicked a glance in the police chief's direction before answering, "I'm afraid so, sir. Someone had to have pushed that shelf over onto the . . . er . . . Mr. Hargrove."

Murder? Although I'd suspected it all along, hearing the word said aloud only made Duggar's death seem that much more horrible. My gaze flew straight over to where Mrs. Farnsworth stood next to an empty bookshelf, her back ramrod straight. A look of satisfaction curled up one corner of her mouth.

"We'll need to question everyone who was at the library when this happened," Jace said to the mayor. He sounded apologetic, unsure almost. After what the police chief had said, I didn't blame him.

Mayor Goodvale frowned. "Son, don't you think you should call in the state folks and let them handle the investigation? This isn't a robbery or a fraud. It's important that we do things correctly."

Jace's jaw tightened as he turned a questioning look in Fisher's direction. "Chief? What do you want me to do?"

"Of course we'll call in the boys from the state. They have resources we can't afford. But we'll also play a part in the investigation. Can't hand over all the power to a bunch of outsiders."

Jace nodded. "It is important to take statements now before our witnesses start forgetting things," he said. "Sometimes it's the seemingly insignificant details that break a case wide open. If you don't mind, sir?"

The mayor waved a shaky hand. "Of course not, son. Do your job. You can hand over your notes to the state folks and let them fill in the holes and connect the dots."

With a huff, Jace turned toward me. "You're one of the librarians?"

"I am." There still was no hint of recognition in his eyes.

He gave me a curt nod. "If you don't mind," he said and motioned over toward a large wooden table. "I need to ask you a few questions. Shall we sit down over there?" He then called to Mrs. Farnsworth, "I'll need to talk with you as well, ma'am."

"Shh," Mrs. Farnsworth answered.

I sat across from Jace. He clicked his pen open and closed a couple of times before drawing in a deep breath. Finally, he looked over at me.

"Name?" he asked.

I stared at him.

"Please, ma'am. I understand this might be upsetting, but I need your cooperation. Name?"

"Trudell Becket." He'd honestly forgotten who I was?

"Hmm . . ." He wrote my name on his pad of paper. Underlined it and frowned. "Trudell? That's an unusual name. In high school, a fellow student by that name had tutored me in math." He looked up at me. "A relative, perhaps?"

"She tutored you in English," I corrected. "And that tutor was me."

His mouth dropped open. His cheeks took on a pink hue as he quickly looked down at my name written in his notebook and underlined it three more times. "Oh. Sorry. Let's get back to going over what you saw."

Oh? Sorry? I wanted to scream. *After how you humiliated me in front of the entire high school, that is all you have to say to me?*

But I didn't scream. I didn't even raise my voice. This was a library, after all. High school was ancient history. So instead of doing anything foolish, I focused on getting this awkward situation over as quickly as possible. "I didn't see anything. I heard the bookcase fall. I ran into this area and found him." I gestured toward Duggar's body. "Mrs. Farnsworth helped me move the shelving off him. I then checked his pulse while Mayor Goodvale called town hall."

Jace gave a tense nod as he jotted down some notes. After a moment he asked, "Do you know who was in the building this morning?"

"I didn't—" How did I explain that I wasn't really "at work" when Duggar was murdered without endangering the books we were working so diligently to save?

"Yes?" he pressed.

I quickly looked down at the table. "I didn't see anyone until after finding Duggar's body. As I've said, Mrs. Farnsworth came when I'd shouted for help. She helped me move the shelf. And then Mayor Good-vale and Luke Goodvale were in the room. I . . . I don't know who else might have been around."

"You didn't see anyone in the library before the murder?"

I crossed my fingers below the table. "We've been buried in books. Boxing them up. Getting them ready to be shipped out. It's a big job."

"A big job?" he echoed.

I nodded. It was a jerky motion. Most mornings I would see nearly everyone who was already in the library when I'd pass through the front entrance. Not only did the staff generally enter at about the same time, but we'd often chitchat around the front desk before disappearing into the stacks.

Jace leaned forward. "There's something you're not telling me."

There was an entire bucket packed full of somethings. And no, I wasn't going to tell him any of them. "I'm upset," I admitted instead.

"Of course you are. But there's something else."

"Yes, there is something else." I drew a steadying breath. "You."

His cheeks turned pink again. But unlike before, he didn't look away.

"That's not it." He tapped his square chin with his pen. "It troubles me, this something you're not telling me. I'm going to find out what it is. That's my job now."

I glanced down at the floor, picturing the partially organized book-room just below our feet, and then back at him. He'd followed my gaze.

He sat back in the old wooden chair and crossed his arms over his chest in a show of determination. I echoed his body language.

He had a murder to solve. I had a community to save. The residents of Cypress needed those books I was working so hard to protect. They needed the lifeline the stories contained in those pages provided. Nothing, not a murder and especially not Jace's arrogant glare, would discourage me from saving this town I loved so much.

Chapter Four

The next morning, after a restless night, I arrived at the stately old library to find Mrs. Farnsworth sitting at her desk in her office. As always, she was impeccable in a somber blue dress trimmed with white lace. She tapped the toe of her polished dark blue pumps as she spoke on the phone in low tones. The pearls adorning her slender neck shimmered in the overhead fluorescent lights.

For a brief moment, the day felt like a normal day. But it wasn't. The shelf in the media section remained toppled exactly where Mrs. Farnsworth and I had left it. The old movies were still scattered across the terrazzo floor. And Duggar was still dead. Not that his death had accomplished anything. The library would remain closed as the conversion to a bookless library continued. The books that belonged on the shelves would remain boxed up.

Anne Lowery, the library's young IT tech, wearing a long raincoat and carrying the biggest mug of coffee I'd ever seen, stomped through the front door. She mumbled a hello before disappearing into her computer mainframe hub, which used to be the employee lounge.

Not sure what I should do, I brewed a cup of tea and then searched for the stray cat that was still at large somewhere in the building. After an hour, I gave up on finding him. I sat down at the front desk to start work on a project of my own.

"You argued with Duggar." That was how Detective Jace Bailey greeted me about a half hour later. His too-handsome blond brows were furrowed as he seemed to study me. He sounded suspicious, accusatory almost.

Gracious, how much time did he spend every morning getting his hair to look perfectly disheveled like that? The one time I tried out a stylishly messy hairdo, over a dozen patrons asked if I'd overslept.

"Half the town had argued with Duggar. He wanted to take away all the books." I gestured to the empty shelves that filled the once grand space. "He was making a mistake."

"A mistake?" Jace leaned his hip against the circulation desk. He was wearing khaki pants again. But instead of the blue blazer and starched white shirt, which really had been too warm for the sticky August weather, he was wearing a light blue polo shirt with Cypress's town crest stitched over where one imagined his heart should be.

"Yes, mistake. You don't need to look at me like a spider watching its dinner fly into its web." I hadn't forgotten how he'd practically accused me of lying to him yesterday. He'd made me feel as guilty as if I had actually committed a murder. "And please don't sit on the counter. It's against the rules."

He looked around. "The library isn't even open."

"Still, Mrs. Farnsworth is a stickler about these things." Which was the truth, but that wasn't the only reason I wanted Jace to back up.

Seeing him again after such a long absence, while smelling the same sandalwood-scented aftershave he'd worn in high school, brought back too many memories. I really didn't want to be transported back to that awkward time when I wore braces and had bad skin. And I didn't want to remember the crushing humiliation I'd suffered thanks to him and my own stupidity.

Jace appeared determined to crowd my space until he spotted Mrs. Farnsworth. She'd left her office and was now standing at the opening to the media room, where Duggar had died. Her hands were on her hips as she stared at the toppled shelf and disarray of DVDs still littering the floor. As she turned toward us, Jace jumped up as if the circulation desk had suddenly caught fire.

The disarray in the one room that wasn't slated for renovation should have ruffled our head librarian—pushed her over the edge, even. After all, she'd been as snappy as a hungry alligator leading up to the library's conversion. For weeks she'd walked around with her lips pressed so tightly together that the vivid red lipstick she wore had completely disappeared from view.

But today, her lipstick looked as red and bold as ever. In fact, Mrs. Farnsworth looked as if she was holding back a smile, which was ridiculous. Why would she smile at the sight of such disorder in the middle of her library?

I shivered and wondered once again if Mrs. Farnsworth had been the one who had pushed the shelf onto Duggar. Had that been her plan for saving the library?

I have to admit that I had hoped yesterday that Duggar's horrible death would result in something good, like the mayor canceling the library's renovation plans. It hadn't. Mayor Goodvale had given a statement last night to local newspaper reporter Betty Crawley, which had run in the morning edition.

He'd told Betty how he was all the more determined to move forward with Duggar's plans for modernizing the town. "It's what my dear friend Duggar would have wanted," he'd been quoted as saying in the front-page article. Betty had noted that tears had filled the mayor's eyes as he'd made his impassioned speech.

Had Mrs. Farnsworth not seen the article? Did she believe that the city crew wasn't still scheduled to come and transport the older books to the landfill this afternoon?

Just thinking about it made me want to kick something. Unfortunately, the nearest something was the detective. And even though I dearly wanted to, kicking him would cause more trouble than I needed.

Since my hopes for an eleventh-hour reprieve had been dashed with the newspaper's morning edition, I had planned to work all morning on my rescue scheme for the books. I hadn't expected to have a police detective peering over my shoulder while I did it.

"What are you doing there?" Jace asked as he leaned over and attempted to read the typed note cards spread out in front of me on the desk.

I pushed the cards I'd been sorting into a manila file folder and then slapped my hand over it. "Just library work."

"I thought the library was going all digital. Why in the world are you typing? Are those cards for an old-fashioned card catalog? The library doesn't still have one of those, does it?"

"We are going digital, and yes, as you should know, the card-catalog system went the way of the dodo bird long before we started high school." I tried to keep my expression bland.

He was too perceptive. I *had* been sorting the catalog cards I'd created for the secret bookroom's library catalog.

Since our basement vault library didn't yet have the funds to purchase a small computer for the space, Flossie had suggested we utilize an old-fashioned card-catalog system to keep track of the library books. I liked that idea. We were, after all, protecting and celebrating the tactile analog world.

While poking around in the maze of rooms below the first floor,

Charlie had literally stumbled into a discarded card-catalog cabinet made of sturdy oak. He'd complained how the antique had bruised his thigh until Tori had promised to kiss it later.

"Then why are you—?" Jace started to ask.

It was a question I didn't want to answer, so I blurted out, "Are you sure that shelf didn't fall over by itself? Are you sure Duggar's death wasn't the result of a horrible accident?"

"The bolts securing the shelving unit to the floor had been removed." He gave me a meaningful look.

Did he think I already knew the bolts were missing? I had to force myself not to look away or do anything that made him detect the guilt gurgling around in my stomach like battery acid.

My parents had instilled in me a strong sense of right and wrong. So of course I felt horribly guilty about taking the books that were slated to be removed from the library for my basement library without permission. I felt guilty about sorting the catalog cards during work hours. And I felt guilty about not telling Jace that Flossie, Tori, and Charlie had been in the library at the time of the murder.

If Duggar's death had been accidental, wouldn't that alleviate much of my guilt? Sure it would.

But that wasn't the only reason I wanted Jace to tell me that Duggar hadn't been murdered. I loved this small town of mine and had a difficult time believing that anyone in Cypress—especially the steely Mrs. Farnsworth—could be capable of taking another person's life.

"Perhaps the bolts were removed as part of the library's renovation project? Perhaps Duggar leaned against it and accidentally knocked it over on himself," I said, hoping Jace would agree with me, hoping that the professionals, in the shock of the moment, had made a grave mistake.

"If he leaned against the shelf, it would have fallen away from him, not toward," he pointed out. "Someone had planned for him to die."

"I don't like it," I said.

He leaned slightly closer. "What don't you like? That I'm here investigating?"

"That too." Jace made me uncomfortable. "But mostly I don't like the thought that Cypress might not be the idyllic paradise it appears to be. It kind of feels like we lost part of our innocence yesterday."

He inhaled a slow breath. "I agree. It does feel like that. I came back here because I needed . . ." Instead of telling me why he had moved back to Cypress from New York, he shook his head.

I wasn't surprised he didn't explain himself to me. We weren't friends, and I wasn't someone he trusted as a confidant. No, I was a suspect. Everyone who was in the building yesterday was a suspect.

Well, not *officially* everyone. Jace didn't know about Flossie, Tori, or Charlie. Another sharp twinge of guilt pinched me in my gut.

But none of my friends were killers. I was fairly certain of that. Sure, I didn't know Charlie. He was a stranger to the town, having only recently moved here from Las Vegas. What reason could someone like him possibly have for pushing a heavy shelf over onto our town manager?

None that I could think of.

"Let's get back to this disagreement you had over Duggar's plans for the library," Jace said. "I heard from some of the other library employees that you'd been angrier than a rabid raccoon ever since the town manager announced the modernization plans. One witness even said"—he pulled his casebook from his pants pocket, flipped through the pages, and then read to me—"'Tru loves these books in the library and would go to any lengths to protect them.'"

He snapped the notebook closed and waited with his brows raised expectantly for me to answer the charge.

"That's true," I admitted.

"Is it now?" he asked slowly.

I nodded.

I couldn't say he looked pleased at my admission. He didn't. He gave me the impression that he was disappointed. Had I said something I shouldn't have said?

Wait a minute. Had I? My mind replayed the statement he'd just read to me. I wondered some more about why his expression had suddenly hardened. Why his eyes had darkened. I bit my lower lip. He didn't really think that I could have—?

My heart beat a little faster.

"You don't think—? I . . . I mean, I . . . I didn't—" I stammered. "Everyone was upset over the changes to the library. Just look at—"

My hand shook as I gestured over toward where Mrs. Farnsworth was standing with her hands fisted on her hips. At that moment Anne emerged from the computer mainframe room, where five oversized computer servers that she called the "heart of the new library" were kept.

The younger woman was dressed in flip-flops, ripped jeans, and a dark gray T-shirt with "Ancient Alien Theorist" written across the chest. I sucked in a sharp breath as I watched her walk right up to Mrs. Farnsworth.

Anne wore a guileless grin on her adorably rounded baby face. That grin was about to be crushed. Her outfit broke just about every single one of Mrs. Farnsworth's dress codes.

The one time I'd worn open-toed sandals to work, Mrs. Farnsworth had lectured me mercilessly for nearly an hour on the kind of image every employee was expected to present to the reading public. According to Mrs. Farnsworth, librarians were expected to look professional and as plain as an old brown shoe. Librarians should never distract from the serious reading and research that happens within these hallowed walls.

Mrs. Farnsworth's widening gaze traveled from the slap-slap of the young tech's flip-flops to the bright purple streak in Anne's raven-black hair. Her shoulders tensed for only a moment before her expression softened, transforming her face into the picture of elegant beauty. She placed her hand on Anne's shoulder.

Jace and I were too far away to hear what she was saying to the techie, who was as giddy about destroying the only library within a sixty-mile radius as Duggar had been.

"She was in the library yesterday morning," I mused aloud. "But I didn't see her come into the media room. Everyone else"—save for my friends—"had come running to see what had happened. But she didn't. I wonder why."

"Who?" Jace asked.

"Anne Lowery. She's in charge of the computers that are replacing our books." I tried, but I couldn't keep the note of disdain from my voice. "I guess that makes her the most important person in the library now."

"You don't sound like a fan," he said.

"I suppose she's a nice person." I shrugged. "Mrs. Farnsworth sure is being friendly with her this morning." Which made absolutely no sense. Mrs. Farnsworth had refused to even speak to Anne the first week the computer tech had started working at the library. She'd given me the fun job of following Anne around, answering all of her questions, and helping the young woman figure out the best (and swiftest) way to gut one of the town's best assets. It'd been an agonizing exercise. Anne's obvious excitement about tossing out all the books in favor of a computer system didn't help endear her to me.

Jace watched as Mrs. Farnsworth continued to chat with Anne. He then turned to frown at me.

"You'd been arguing with Duggar." Gracious, he simply refused to let that go. "You found an enemy in your newest coworker. And you clearly disapprove of how Mrs. Farnsworth has taken a liking to a new employee who has a job that clearly outranks yours."

"Now, I wouldn't go that far. Her job is completely—"

He held up a hand and plowed on with his grim speech. "Tru, it's written on your face like words in a book. You're carrying around heaping piles of anger. Plus, you're obviously hiding something from me.

Tell me what I should think." He opened his notebook again and flipped through the pages. "I need you to tell me again what you were doing yesterday morning." He tapped a pencil on the blank page in front of him. "You can begin by telling me exactly what time you arrived at the library, who was already in the building when you arrived, and who might have seen you."

"What time?" I repeated back as I groped for answers. I couldn't tell him the truth. I certainly couldn't tell him that I'd broken into the basement back door a few minutes after midnight and that no one had been in the building at the time.

My neck burned—a sure sign that my skin was turning red and blotchy. If that didn't suggest guilt, I didn't know what would.

Should I tell him the truth? Nancy Drew would instinctively know what to do. I'd read and reread all of her books from cover to cover while dreaming that one day I'd encounter an adventure and, yes, a little danger in my life. The teen sleuth had made these kinds of moral decisions seem so easy, so straightforward.

Now that I had my chance to step into a real-life mystery, nothing felt right. I didn't know what to do. None of this felt easy.

If I told Jace about the secret bookroom, he'd have to report what I'd done. Those books I'd so lovingly rescued would be put back with the others waiting to be hauled away.

But what choice did I have? Tears filled my eyes as I opened my mouth to confess all.

This was it.

The library would die today.

Chapter Five

There . . . there is something I did, um, something that—"
I stammered just as Police Chief Fisher sauntered through the front
entrance. An older gentleman with a bristled mustache and salt-and-
pepper hair that had been cut so short his scalp showed through, walked
in beside him. The new man was wearing a dark navy suit and swag-
gering like a sheriff in an old Western movie.

The sight of the two lawmen heading straight for me made my
mouth turn drier than Aunt Sal's Sunday biscuits. "Honest! I'm not
guilty of murder," I had an urge to shout. Shouting, however, would
only make me look suspicious. Besides, Mrs. Farnsworth would never
abide such behavior. And she was already looking at me differently ever
since I'd found Duggar's body.

To rein in my jangling nerves, I gripped the edge of the desk.

Jace cocked one eyebrow as he took note of my whitening knuckles
before turning his attention toward the police chief and his companion.

Fisher gave me a quick, dismissive nod before catching hold of Jace's
arm. "Son, I'd like you to meet Detective Gregory Ellerbe from the

state's Regional Investigative Unit of SLED. He's going to be helping us figure out what happened."

So this was the expert from the State Law Enforcement Department that Mayor Goodvale had demanded, the expert who would take charge of the investigation?

Jace had schooled his features and showed no sign of resentment as he welcomed Ellerbe to Cypress. He even smiled as he shook the man's hand. "I've been looking forward to your arrival, sir. I'm anxious to go over my notes and theories with you. Right now, I'm questioning one of the librarians who was working in the building at the time of the murder and who had reason to—"

"Splendid, boy," Fisher interrupted. "I was telling Ellerbe how you've taken this bull by the horns, so to speak. He's here to interview the librarians. He wants to begin right away." Fisher's gaze flicked toward me again.

I held my breath, not looking forward to having not one, but three officers of the law pick apart my teensy-tiny lie. I fully expected to be the first one in the hot seat. Perhaps even the only one.

But Fisher had apparently looked straight through me. He pointed over toward Mrs. Farnsworth. "There's the head librarian and her new assistant. You'll want to talk with both of them."

I wasn't completely surprised that Fisher had ignored me. All of my life, people have acted as if I had nothing important to say. I'd been talked over and my ideas disregarded more often than I cared to remember. And yes, it bothered me to no end because I did have opinions and could be passionate about things that mattered to me, especially books.

But at that moment I wasn't the least bit upset. For the first time in my life my plain-Jane looks and plain-Jane personality were paying off. Without realizing how suspicious it might seem, I let out a long sigh of relief.

Unfortunately, eagle-eyed Jace noticed.

When Fisher and Ellerbe circled around the front desk and headed toward Mrs. Farnsworth and Anne, the young detective didn't budge.

"Aren't you coming?" Fisher asked. "It might be instructional to watch how a professional manages a murder investigation."

"I'll be there in a minute," Jace said, without shifting his troubled gaze away from me.

Fisher shook his head with a look of consternation, but he left Jace behind without another word.

"I know you've been lying," Jace whispered. "Things are going to go sideways for you, and really quickly, if you don't start telling me what happened yesterday. Tell me what happened, and perhaps I can help get you a plea deal."

"A what?" I said too loud.

"Shh," Mrs. Farnsworth admonished.

"What?" I whispered. Jace couldn't be saying what I thought he was saying.

"Was it an accident? Or was it something you did in a fit of rage? I can't imagine you meant to hurt anyone," he continued.

I would have protested. Heck, I did start to protest, but before I managed to do much more than mutter a few incoherent sounds, that brown tabby cat stepped out from wherever it'd been hiding and stood behind the detective. It stared at me with its round, almost accusatory emerald-green eyes.

"Umm . . ." Mrs. Farnsworth would take one look at the cat and assume right away that I was the one responsible for letting it in. She always seemed to assume I caused trouble, like stray-cats-roaming-through-libraries kinds of trouble. I didn't know why. I'd only made a few mistakes during my time working here. Like the time I'd accidentally locked myself in the bathroom. Or the time I'd accidentally deleted the entire online card-catalog database.

Both of those things had happened years ago, when I'd first started working for her. I'd spent every day of the past thirteen years trying to convince her I wasn't a royal screwup, that I could be trusted to unlock the library in the morning and lock it up at night. I couldn't let a little thing like an uninvited cat derail all my hard work. "Excuse me." I skirted the counter and chased after the stray, which had dashed away the moment I moved toward it.

Jace chased after me. "Why are you running? You can't run from this. We all know where you live."

"I'm not running. I need to get something from the stacks in the reference department," I called over my shoulder, totally forgetting that all the books had been removed from the shelves.

"Shh!" Mrs. Farnsworth shushed us with even more force. "Detective," she said in her commanding, whispery voice that somehow carried across the room, "I think you should hear this too. Anne, here, has some information about yesterday."

I was tempted to join them. I wanted to hear what Anne was telling them, but that cat twitched its tail, darted around my legs, and ran directly toward the conference of librarians and police. With a quick sprint on my part, I was able to scoop up the cat and whirl toward a wall in time to hide it.

Hugging the skinny stray to my chest, I rushed toward the back stairs.

Ignoring the call to join his colleagues, Jace caught up to me.

"He's my cat." I don't know why I stopped my mad dash to tell him that. I hugged the wiggling, growling beast even tighter to my chest. "He's not supposed to be here. Mrs. Farnsworth would murder me if she found him." I winced. "Sorry. Poor choice of words."

Jace folded his arms across his chest. He looked amused.

The darn cat growled like a bobcat and dug its claws deep into my arm. But I was determined. I refused to let the beast go. "I'd appreciate it if you didn't tell anyone he's here."

I simply needed to hold on to the spitfire just long enough to get him to the back door. What I didn't need was a nosy detective following me downstairs, where he might stumble across the secret bookroom.

"I should have known," he said with a rueful shake of his head.

"Known what?" The cat sank his teeth into my arm. I gritted my teeth to keep from letting out a yelp.

"That this is your big secret. Of course someone like you would be mixed up with something like this—a cat."

"Someone like me?" What did he mean by that?

"And here I thought it was something more—" He looked up at the tall ceiling. It was a coffered tin ceiling decorated with delicate rosettes.

"Yes, Detective?"

"Nothing." He chuckled. The sound of his I'm-better-than-you laugh made me feel two inches tall. I might as well have been transported back to high school, back to that day when he'd crushed me as if I were no more important than a gnat in the middle of a crowded hallway. "You didn't want anyone to know about your cat."

"That's right," I said. I was smart enough to agree.

I shouldn't feel insulted that he looked at me and pictured a lonely (slightly crazy) cat lady. For one thing, he was only half off the mark. The one thing missing from my life as a lonely cat lady was a cat. And I was holding on to an exceptionally lively one right now. Besides which, letting him assume that I collected cats like my mother collected pig-shaped buttons seemed to convince him I wasn't responsible for Duggar's death. I could live with that.

"I didn't want anyone to know the cat was in here," I confessed.

Instead of leaving me to deal with the hissing stray alone, Jace moved closer to me. "I've never seen a cat with such unusual markings on its head. Those stripes come together to form the shape of a skull, don't they?"

"I've never noticed." I glanced down at the tabby and was startled by what I saw. My goodness, he was right. The black tiger-stripe markings on its head formed what looked remarkably like a skull. "I suppose it might resemble something like that." Instead of waiting to be dismissed, I jogged toward the stairs that led down to the basement.

"What's his name?" he asked as he followed me. "Or is he a she?"

I could think of several names I wanted to call this feral beast that seemed intent on clawing and chewing its way through my arm. But I really couldn't say any of those aloud.

"Dewey," I blurted.

"Dewy? Like water on the grass in the morning?"

"No, as in Dewey Decimal." I pointed with my elbow to a set of Dewey Decimal numbers listed at the end of the bookshelf we were passing. "His name is Dewey Decimal. But we all call him Dewey."

"Ah." He kept following me. "Why is your cat growling?"

"He doesn't like to be picked up. He's a former stray." I hurried down the stairs.

"I bet you have a house filled with strays."

"What's that supposed to mean?" That I don't have friends? That I'm a lonely woman?

"That you have a good heart." He held up his hands. "Honest."

"Oh. Sure." Why, oh why, did he insist on following me? And why was he wearing that amused grin that was both devastating and irritating?

I reached the back door, but I couldn't simply turn the cat out, not with Jace watching.

"I . . . I'll put her in here," I said, hurrying over to a storage closet where the maintenance staff kept their mops and floor cleaners.

"I thought you said the cat was a boy," Jace replied.

"Um . . . I probably did."

"What's that supposed to mean?"

"Dewey is a new acquisition. That's why I brought her, or him, to the library with me. It takes a while before a stray feels comfortable being inside. And I haven't had the chance to get Dewey to the vet. So, I don't know if I should be calling him a him or her a her."

Jace nodded as if he'd followed what I'd just said, which was a good thing. I wasn't sure I had.

When I tried to shift the kitty around so I could open the door to the maintenance room, Dewey dug its claws deeper into my arm. "Um, could you help me?"

I thought Jace would help by opening the door for me. But he didn't. He slipped his hands around the little cat and carefully pried its long nails and sharp teeth from my skin.

"Don't let it get away!" I warned.

Needlessly.

The cat snuggled against the detective's chest as if it had landed in a safe, warm bed.

My jaw dropped.

"Cats like me," Jace said with a shrug.

"Why am I not surprised?"

He chuckled.

I quickly opened the door to the maintenance room. "Please, put Dewey in there."

He carefully lowered the cat and released it into the small but clean and well-lit room. I slammed the door closed before Dewey could dart back out and disappear into the library again.

"Be sure to put some water in there," Jace said as we climbed the stairs.

"I will."

"And food. I've never held such a skinny cat. It needs to eat."

"I will," I promised.

"And a litter box, unless you want to have a big mess on your hands."

"Yes, yes, I'll get it all done."

He smiled at me. "I know you will. And I'm glad your big secret is that you're taking your cat to work with you and not that you killed the town manager."

"Of course I didn't kill anyone." Thank goodness for a skinny stray cat. I suddenly decided to buy Dewey a can of the best tuna I could find.

I rubbed the bloody scratches on my arm. Did I need to get some kind of shot to ward off cat-scratch fever? If the books were still on the shelves, I would have known exactly where to go to look up what I needed to do about the injuries.

At least I knew one thing for certain. Without the cloud of suspicion hanging over me, I could keep silent about my secret bookroom project.

The police chief's voice boomed down the stairs. "Detective, is Ms. Becket with you?"

"Shh!" Mrs. Farnsworth's whispery voice followed.

"With all due respect, ma'am, if what your assistant here is telling us is true, I need Ms. Becket to answer some very important questions."

Jace looked at me. "What is Fisher talking about?"

"My cat?" While I'd sounded confident, my insides trembled. What did Anne tell the policemen? Had she seen my friends packing up the books and carrying them into the basement?

Picturing Nancy Drew in my mind's eye, I straightened my shoulders. Worrying solved nothing. I'd find out what was going on soon enough.

I marched with a pragmatic gait up the stairs, more determined than ever to untangle myself from the web of this particular murder mystery. I could do it, even if it meant I'd have to prove I wasn't Duggar's murderer by catching the killer myself.

Chapter Six

As soon as Jace and I returned to the library's main floor, Ellerbe directed me to sit in a comfortable armchair in the reading room. The older detective from the state law enforcement agency took a nearby seat, propped his elbows on his knees, and leaned toward me.

"Are you okay, Ms. Becket?" he asked, sounding honestly concerned for my welfare.

"I'm perplexed," I said, and nudged my glasses up my nose. "Police Chief Fisher said I needed to answer some very important questions. This is regarding Duggar's death, I assume?"

He briefly glanced over his shoulder to where Police Chief Fisher and Jace were standing on either side of a pillar, watching. "Nothing too serious. Nothing to worry about." He touched his arm. "You're bleeding, though. That's what I was asking about."

I slapped my hand over the dark, wet stains on my blouse's sleeve. "Just . . . just a few scratches. Nothing serious."

"Serious for the blouse. It's likely ruined." He spoke so kindly. He reminded me of my father.

After a moment of quiet contemplation, Ellerbe sat back and tilted his head to one side. He talked about the town, the weather, and his favorite football team before asking why I had failed to sign in yesterday morning. We chatted a little more before he asked why no one had noticed my presence in the library until after the town manager's murder.

He then leaned forward again. "If you weren't around all morning, how did you manage to find Duggar's body before anyone else?"

"I don't know." It was the truth. "Anne should have been the one to find Duggar. Why didn't she come running when the shelf toppled over? And where was she when I'd called for help? She's always working with her computer servers. And those servers are located in the room adjacent to where he died. Where was she?"

Ellerbe looked thoughtful before crossing his arms over his chest. "Hmm. That is a puzzle. But we're not talking about her right now. We're talking about you. Why were you in the media room? You had no reason to be in there. The plans were to leave that room untouched. So you had no reason to be there unless . . . perhaps . . . you were the one to push over the shelf."

"I wasn't in the room when the shelf fell," I corrected.

"Then why were you the first one to find the town manager? The crash of the shelf must have been loud."

"It was," I said. "Startlingly so."

"And yet no one else heard it?"

"They should have." My brows crinkled. "They all should have heard it."

Ellerbe stroked his bristly mustache. "But no one else claims to have heard the shelf that killed the town manager fall. You're the only one. How can that be possible? Are you sure you weren't in the room when it happened?"

"I wasn't there."

"Perhaps you forgot? Finding the town manager like that must have been quite a shock."

"I didn't forget where I was when I heard the crash. I'll never forget it."

He smiled. "Where were you, then?"

"In the basement. Where was Anne?"

He sat back in his chair again. "Ms. Lowery only recently moved to Cypress from California," he said. "And the town manager had personally hired her and had been one of the biggest proponents for the work she was doing here. What motive could she possibly have to kill him?"

"What, indeed?" Anne's lack of motive didn't explain why she claimed she didn't hear the shelf's loud crash. She must have been in the next room, for heaven's sake. She practically lived in there.

After a long span of silence between us, Ellerbe dismissed me . . . for now.

I walked out of the reading room feeling as if I were leaving the principal's office. The three lawmen watched my exit with varying degrees of concern written on their faces. Fisher seemed to be seeing me for the first time. Jace looked fretful. And Ellerbe's expression remained disturbingly neutral.

For some reason, that neutral look worried me most of all.

"I can't believe this place doesn't serve Coke," Flossie complained when I met her during my lunch break less than an hour later. She was dressed in a cotton dress in varying hues of peacock blue.

"It's a coffee shop," I pointed out after kissing her cheek. I joined Flossie at a table in Tori's popular coffee shop, Perks. The table was near the front door and in quite a busy location.

In the past, the three of us would usually meet at the library. Flossie spent most of her time at the library, especially when pushing herself to meet a publisher's deadline. The library's temporary closure had forced her (and us) to change our meeting place.

I liked Tori's Main Street coffee shop. The two-story brick building had served as the town's only feed and seed store for as long as anyone could remember. When old Brantley retired and handed his family's legacy over to Junior, his oldest son, Brantley's "golden boy" promptly sold off all the shop's stock and put the building up for sale. Tori had used the divorce settlement from Number Three to buy the building and renovate it into a cozy coffee shop. She'd scavenged old feed ads and put them in rustic frames as a nod to the building's history. A plump brown hen pecked away at a pile of corn as the sun rose over a red barn in the illustration hanging near our table.

Flossie glanced at the happy hen. She shook her head slowly. "I tell you what, when I was your age, every place sold Coke. Even the feed store."

"You could order coffee," I said.

"I already had a coffee this morning."

"We can go somewhere else," I said. "I'm sure Tori would understand."

"No, no, we're already sitting down." She pulled a reusable water bottle from her leather purse. "I'll just sip on this."

I looked at my triple mocha with whipped cream and caramel sauce dripping down its side and felt bad that Flossie didn't have anything to drink other than a bottle of warm water. "Are you sure you don't want to try something else? They also sell teas and milkshakes."

"I had my heart set on a Coke. They have everything else. I cannot believe a coffee shop like this doesn't offer Coke."

"Perhaps because it's unhealthy."

She narrowed her gaze as I took a sip from my tall, frothy drink. "And that's health food?"

"Yeah . . . um . . ." I bit my lower lip.

"I have a grandchild. I visited her in Athens last year."

"She lives in Greece?" I'd never stepped foot out of the South.

"No. No. Athens in Georgia. She'd go to a coffee shop like this one and drink coffee after coffee as she worked on her computer. She pictures herself as a budding screenwriter. But she's really a salesclerk at the downtown department store. I told her that she needed to get herself a husband and family. And she told me that I was old-fashioned."

"She sounds like she wants to be a writer like you," I said.

"I had a husband. He was my everything. I don't know why your generation is so set against marriage."

"I'm not against it." Flossie was starting to sound terrifyingly like my mother. So I made an abrupt conversation change. "I can't believe the town council is moving forward with converting the library to a bookless monster. Duggar is gone. Dead. Why didn't his plan die with him?"

Her eyes widened just a bit. "You'd better hush. Saying things like that makes you sound guilty as sin."

"You know I'd never . . . that I could never."

"Honey, of course I know better. But I'm smarter than most around here. You need to watch your words. They have power, you know. You have to use them with care, or else you might find yourself in a situation you can't handle." She leaned toward me and whispered, "You've already bent the law by stealing all of those books."

"I was saving them."

"By stealing them."

"Not technically. They haven't left the building."

"Let's not dwell on that." She took a sip of her bottled water.

"I agree. What we need to do instead is find out who killed Duggar."

"So we can give him a medal?" Tori asked. She plopped down in the chair next to mine. Today she wore her hair in a high ponytail. She was dressed in a pair of cutoff jean shorts and a black crop top with "Perks" blazed in red across her chest.

"No, of course not," I said. "We need to catch the killer."

"We're not the police," Tori pointed out.

"I know that," I answered.

"We'd look horrible in those uniforms," Flossie added.

"Speak for yourself." Tori gave her gorgeous blonde ponytail a toss. "I happen to know from firsthand experience that I look quite fetching in—"

"We don't want to hear about what you do when you go out on dates," Flossie said.

"I do," I said eagerly. "But perhaps later?"

"Later it is." Tori gave me a wink.

Flossie cleared her throat. "Right now we need to make plans for the secret bookroom. I've typed up some more cards for the card catalog from the list you provided." She looked furtively around the room before sliding a manila envelope across the table.

I wondered again if Flossie wrote thrillers. She seemed well versed in how to be sneaky.

"Thank you," I said. "But—"

"And we need to figure out how to invite the public to come browse the books without exposing the secret," Tori said.

"That's true," Flossie agreed. "Opening the library will be tricky. We'll have to—"

"Before we do any of that, we'll have to convince the police I didn't kill Duggar," I blurted out.

"Honey, why in the world would they think that?" Flossie narrowed her eyes at me. "Have you been saying things around them like what you said to me?"

"No, I've not said anything," I said.

"Then I don't see the problem." Flossie pulled out a pad of paper filled with notes concerning our basement library.

Tori nodded in agreement. "You're as tame as a kitten, Tru."

"Kittens can be feral." I rubbed the scratches on my arm. "Anyhow,

Chief Fisher brought in a detective from the state to head up the investigation."

"Oh, I bet that is sitting like a burr in Jace's pants," Tori said. "Please, tell me he was twisting around in pain."

"I don't think Jace intends to step aside." Ellerbe's arrival hadn't stopped Jace from following me around the library, questioning me.

"The young man does bring a local perspective that the state investigator could never have," Flossie pointed out. "He grew up here."

"He also moved away right out of high school. He's as much of an outsider as anyone," Tori countered. My two friends rarely agreed on anything. "He knows much more about crime on the streets of New York than life in Cypress."

"That may be true. But he knows Tru, doesn't he? Y'all were all in high school together."

"We were," Tori agreed. "And everyone knows Tru is as straitlaced as they come."

"Thanks for that," I said dryly. "I wish you were right about him knowing me, but you're not. He barely remembers that I'd tutored him. He didn't remember the humiliation he caused me in high school. And he sees my passion for the library as motive."

Tori snorted. "He's a man. They need more time than women to figure basic things out."

"It's not just Jace. Detective Ellerbe questioned me just now. He seemed to be very interested in why I'm the only one who heard the shelf fall over. It felt as if he didn't believe me when I told him that I was in the basement at the time. I got the impression that he wanted me to confess that I was in the room with Duggar when he died. The way he looked at me afterward made me worried that he thinks I killed him."

"That is a troubling development," Flossie said.

"I'm not worried," Tori said. "Jace will eventually come around and see the truth, and so will that outsider from the state."

"Will they?" Flossie swallowed some more water. "The police don't have the full picture. And unless you want Tru to go to jail for her heroic act of rebellion, they will never have the full picture of what was going on that morning."

Tori's face fell. "I hate to admit it, Flossie, but you're right."

"Don't sound so surprised," Flossie grumbled. "I'm right about nearly everything."

"This is serious." Tori plowed on. "Unless Tru tells them the truth about what she was doing in the basement vault, which would ruin everything, the police won't be able to adequately do their job. No one knows we were in the library. And, heck, the killer could have been any one of us."

Flossie patted one of the arms of her wheelchair. "Not me."

"Oh, really?" Tori shot back. "You might be sitting in that chair, but I know your arms are as strong as an ox's."

"Don't be ridiculous. Oxen don't have arms," Flossie said.

"That's not what I meant. And you know—"

"Of course none of us killed Duggar." I put up my hands to stop them from arguing in circles for no reason. "But someone did, and we need to figure out what to do about it. With our combined know-how, we can do this with our eyes closed." My heart thumped with excitement.

Flossie winced. "Going after a killer on our own could stir up more trouble than we're willing to take on."

"As you already so aptly pointed out, Flossie, if we don't do this"— Tori put her arm over my shoulder—"Tru might find herself in a heap of trouble. The police are set on making an arrest, and from the sounds of things, Tru has gotten herself caught in their crosshairs."

Part of me agreed with Flossie. Investigating the murder could be dangerous. The police were the professionals. They'd eventually find the true killer. That was their job.

But another part of me pooh-poohed the idea of putting my fate into someone else's hands. Wasn't this the moment I'd dreamed of ever since I'd discovered my first Nancy Drew mystery in the children's section of the library? I'd been eight years old at the time.

"We need to do this," I said. This was my opportunity to prove I wasn't a mousy, simpering miss jumping at my own shadow. This was my chance to stand up for myself and—as sure as the sun rises in the east—I wasn't going to run away from it.

It wasn't as if I was taking on a murder investigation on my own. My gaze went first to Tori (my friend since forever) and then to Flossie (a constant companion at the library with an encyclopedic mind). With their help, I knew we could accomplish anything.

"Someone removed the bolts that kept the DVD shelf screwed to the floor," I told them. "Before my lunch break, I checked every shelving unit in the library. Every single bolt was in place, as one would expect in Mrs. Farnsworth's library. And yet, the bolts for the shelf that killed Duggar are gone. They weren't just removed and set aside. They're gone. Missing. If we find them, I bet we'll find the killer."

Flossie nodded. "That gives us somewhere to start."

"It does." And we could do this. "We were all there when it happened. We might have seen something that we don't even realize is important. Who is better equipped to solve the crime than we are?"

"No one!" Tori jumped up from the chair. "Before we start hashing out the details, I need to get more coffee. Can I get y'all anything?" she asked as she hurried toward the counter.

"Nothing for me until you start selling Cokes," Flossie yelled after her.

Chapter Seven

When I returned to the library after lunch, I felt pleased with the progress Flossie, Tori, and I had made. We'd filled a small blue notebook, now tucked inside my purse, with potential suspects and possible motives.

Correction: motive. Singular.

I was convinced that whoever pushed that shelf onto Duggar had done it because he (or she) wanted to stop the library's modernization plans.

My lead suspect was still Anne Lowery, although I couldn't figure out why she'd want to stop the work she'd been doing. Both Flossie and Tori disagreed with including Anne in our list of suspects. *For now.* They'd come around to my way of thinking after we gathered more information.

Out of everyone who was at the library, Anne's behavior was the most suspect. Why hadn't she come running when the shelf had fallen on Duggar? Why did she go out of her way to convince the police that I was their prime suspect? Did she do it so they wouldn't look too closely at her actions?

Sure, all I'd written in the place for potential motives under Anne's name was a bunch of question marks. She was perhaps the only person in town (save for Duggar and the mayor) who was actually excited about tossing out all of our old hardbound books.

But I was confident that, with a little digging, I could figure out why Anne killed Duggar. Everyone had their little secrets.

Even me.

That last thought made me giggle. Shy Trudell Becket, a woman of mystery? Well, why not? I'd lived so many adventures in the pages of my precious books, I was more than ready to start some in my real life.

My first assignment, as stressed by both Tori and Flossie, was to find out what Anne had told the police. I wasn't looking forward to confronting Anne, but my friends were right. I wouldn't know what I needed to tell the police to explain my behavior yesterday morning until I talked with Anne.

"A city crew will arrive in an hour to take away the boxes," Mrs. Farnsworth announced as soon as she'd noticed my return from lunch.

"Oh." Her reminder hurt like a sucker punch. I pressed a hand to my chest. "I'd figured that with what had happened yesterday, the police would want us to put the renovation plans on hold."

"The mayor is insisting we let nothing delay the renovations." Mrs. Farnsworth fixed her gaze on the front doors. Was she plotting to do something to stop the men from hauling the boxes to the landfill? If so, I wanted in on it.

I stepped closer to her and whispered, "So what are we going to do?"

The question seemed to take her completely by surprise. Her head jerked back slightly. She looked at me the same way Police Chief Fisher had after Anne had apparently accused me of killing Duggar. It was as if she was seeing me in a new light.

"*We* don't do anything," she said. Her delicate brows furrowed into a deep V. "You need to stay out of the workers' way while continuing on with your job."

"Yes, ma'am." I locked my purse in the bottom drawer of the circulation desk and then headed toward the small maintenance room in the basement to check on Dewey. I hoped he had liked the tuna lunch I'd given him and had known what to do with that litter box.

As I passed through the empty stacks and the boxes of books that would soon be headed to a trash heap, I felt a strong tug to rescue more of them.

It would be risky.

I could be jeopardizing the books we'd already saved.

But it was something that needed to be done.

If she wasn't such a stickler for the rules, Mrs. Farnsworth would want me to rescue those books. I headed straight for the children's section and toward one particular box containing several timeless adventure books that would please any boy or girl.

What I found stopped me midstride.

It was Mayor Goodvale's backside. An unmistakable sight. No one else in town still wore seersucker suits. He was on his knees on the floor, his head nearly buried in one of the boxes.

No, not just one of the boxes, he was digging around in the box I wanted. It was a box that was already half-empty from our earlier rescue mission.

We'd liberated all the Nancy Drew and Hardy Boys books from that box. Those books had topped my list of ones to save. Many of them had been in the library and loved by children since the 1930s. The mysteries, which had been puzzled over by earlier generations, were still being devoured by their grandchildren and great-grandchildren.

What was Mayor Goodvale doing pawing through that box? There were hundreds of boxes in the library we hadn't had time to touch. Why couldn't he have picked one of those to riffle through?

"Can I help you, sir?" I said as neutrally as possible.

He jerked up in surprise and nearly toppled over as he twisted around to look up at me. "Oh, Miss, um . . . !"

"Becket," I supplied.

"Yes, Becket. You startled me."

"I'm sorry." I linked my hands behind my back. "Can I help you with something?"

He looked at the box and then back at me. He spread his hands and smiled. "You caught me."

"Caught you? What do you mean?"

"I was looking through here to find a few of Luke's childhood favorites to take home with me. My boy has just moved back to town."

"Yes, I know. He was here with you yesterday." And he wasn't a boy. He was nearly thirty years old.

"Terrible. Terrible. I hated for him to see that. The boy was quite shaken up. Duggar was like an uncle to Luke. We were going to have lunch with him later in the day to discuss my son's future. Luke recently lost his job due to company cutbacks." He shook his head. "Duggar said he might have some contacts with the tech industries that he'd been courting. But now . . ." He shook his head again. "It's all so tragic."

"Luke was working in Nevada, wasn't he?" Everyone had been talking about how the mayor's son had moved home with nothing more than a small carry-on suitcase.

The mayor frowned. "He was working with computers or something. He's told me more than once what his job was about, but he's much smarter than I am. All that techno mumbo jumbo just goes right over my head."

"Mine too." I gazed lovingly at the boxes of books I wanted to snatch up and run away with. "I'm much more interested in things that I can touch, things I can hold in my hand."

"We're part of a dying breed. The future is digital. Cypress will wither like a diseased vine if we don't take steps now to move our town into *this* century."

"I don't see why we can't both preserve the past, like keeping these books, while also investing in our future."

"Funding, my girl. It all comes down to funding. We're stretching our coffers thin with the hopes of a big payoff on the other side."

"If money is such a big issue, perhaps we should slow down just a bit." I couldn't stop myself from making a last-minute pitch for the books.

"It's too late to slow down now. The money's been spent. We have to keep pushing and making sure word gets out to the major media outlets about how we're setting ourselves up to become the Silicon Valley of the South. The *new* South, that is."

It sounded like a campaign speech. He was good at those, which was why he was currently serving his ninth term as mayor.

"Anyhow, with Luke back in town after such a successful time out in the big world, he's living with me and Mrs. Goodvale until he regains his bearings and finds work locally. I was hoping to snag a few of those Hardy Boys books he'd loved so much as a teen to help make him feel more at home. He used to always have one checked out of the library and tucked in his backpack." He tapped the box's lid. "The label says a few of the Hardy Boys books should be in this box. But they don't seem to be in here."

"Oh." I flicked my hand as if a few missing books were no big deal. "You know how it is. We might not have been as careful as we should have been in packing up the boxes. All of this is going to the landfill. It's not as if any of the seagulls that live at the dump will care if a book is in one box or another."

He snorted a short, unhappy laugh. "Of course. Shoddy work."

His words stung.

"Please don't tell Mrs. Farnsworth." I tried to sound casual, but my voice cracked a bit as I made my plea. "If she knew how we'd rushed through the packing, she'd order me to unpack the boxes and repack them correctly. And she'd expect me to get it done before the city crew arrives in an hour."

He closed the box and rose from the floor. "It'll be our secret. If you happen to find those books, though, could you set them aside?" He brushed imaginary dirt from his pant legs.

"Consider it already done," I said.

"Thank you. Well, I suppose I should go. The paperwork back at town hall waits for no one." Even as he said this, he still didn't move. "I can't believe what happened here yesterday. It feels like a bad dream."

"It does," I agreed.

The mayor's frown deepened. "Duggar was a good man. I considered him one of my closest, most trusted friends."

"I am sorry, sir. I can't imagine how hard it was for you. To be here, I mean. When it happened." My heart raced. This was my chance to do a little sleuthing. "It must have been terrible to hear the crash as the shelf came down."

"Hmmm . . . The sound echoes in my mind even now." He shuddered. "It chills me."

"Where were you at the time?" Why hadn't he come running? Why had he ignored such an awful crash in a usually silent library?

"I was here, in the children's section, like I am now. Luke was with me. We were reminiscing about those old books I was looking for just now. Didn't think much about the sound at the time, not until I heard you screaming for help."

I nodded, but what he told me only added to my confusion about the murder.

By all accounts, Anne had been the closest to the media room. She should have been the one to have found Duggar's body. The mayor and his son, in the children's section, should have arrived shortly after. I'd been in the basement, for goodness' sake. I should have been the last person to arrive on the scene.

Gracious, no wonder the police were looking at me funny. Nothing about Duggar's death made a lick of sense.

Chapter Eight

I now understood why it was rare to find an amateur sleuth outside the pages of a mystery novel. Clues didn't come with instructions for what do to with them . . . or even if they meant anything.

While I felt unprepared for the role I'd undertaken, that didn't mean I was going to give up. I was, after all, a librarian. I'd spent the past thirteen years tracking down obscure bits of information for patrons. I'd figure out why the mayor and his son had ignored the sound of the shelf being pushed over.

In the meantime, I knew I needed to go talk to Anne and find out exactly what she'd told the police. I also needed to hear her excuse for not running to the media room when the bookcase fell on Duggar. But the books still trapped in those horrible boxes kept calling out to me. After making sure Mayor Goodvale had indeed left the building, I grabbed the box he'd been looking through. I tossed open the lid and started to pack it full with books from neighboring boxes.

Books about teen angst, books about cars, and biographies of notable historical figures that rarely get covered in school. Two nights ago,

I'd been discerning. I'd thought about the secret library and its limited space and what books would best serve the public. Right now, with the city workers due to arrive at any moment, if the book had a spine—even a broken one—it ended up in my keeper box. When that box was filled, I started on another. And then another.

I'd started to pack a fourth box when I realized I needed to get the books I'd already set aside to the basement. I managed to pick up two of the boxes stacked one on top of the other. (While books are heavy, librarians are strong.)

I was almost to the back stairs when I heard someone calling out to me. "Tru, hold up."

Clearly, the person asking me to wait had never carried a box filled to the top with books, much less two of them. The muscles in my arms shook a bit as I turned and peered around the boxes in front of my nose.

"Charlie?" As he had when we first met two nights ago, he looked dangerous. His dark onyx gaze seemed to see right into my soul. "What are you doing here? How did you get in here? The library is closed."

"I walked in. The front door wasn't locked. And no one stopped me." He was dressed in a dark suit. Too warm for the weather. But he didn't look the least bit wilted. He hurried over to me and immediately pulled one of the boxes from my arms. "*You're saving more books?*" he whispered. "*Let me help.*"

Not one to turn away free muscle, I let him follow me down to the basement. "But why are you here?" I asked.

"I love old books," he said.

"So Tori told me." I set down the box to open the thick double doors that led into the basement vault. "But why did you come to the library?"

"Well, she told me that the books were being carted off to a landfill today." He clicked his tongue. "That's wrong. Perhaps not as dramatic as the burning of the Library of Alexandria in the third century or the burning of all the Aztec and Mayan manuscripts in the sixteenth century, but still just as wrong. Wrong for this town."

"That's some impressive book knowledge there. Where'd you get it?" I asked.

"Oh, here and there," he said, with the same look people usually got when talking about their children. "Books have long been a passion of mine."

"Is that why you're here, then? To help me carry more books down into the basement?" I set the box in the secret bookroom.

Charlie placed the box he'd carried next to mine. "Well . . . no. That's not why I'm here. But I will."

"Then what are you—?" We had started back up the stairs when I heard a plaintive *mew*. "Wait a minute. There's something I need to take care of."

Even though I'd told him to wait, he followed me to the maintenance closet where I'd left Dewey. I opened the door a crack. Giving a horrible screech, Dewey jumped out.

Luckily, I'd been expecting him (or her) to do something like that. I caught the kitty and held on to the squirming beast with an iron grip. Unlike this morning, the skinny stray didn't try to tear through my arm or growl or hiss. In fact, he seemed happy to see me.

"I don't think he likes being locked in that room," I said.

"At least the room isn't dark and damp like most basement closets. He has food, a bed, and a clean litter box," Charlie said as he peered into the room filled with brooms and mops and cleaners neatly arranged on high shelves. "That sure is an interesting-looking cat you have there. Is that a skull on its head?"

"If you close one eye and squint, I suppose it might look like one. He's a stray that let himself in. I've been feeding him and trying to keep anyone who might take him to the pound from finding our little stowaway."

"Why don't you put him in your basement library? It's bigger than this room. And it'll soon be filled with happy booklovers, who are often also cat lovers."

"You know what? That's a good idea." Charlie seemed to be filled with helpfulness. I could see why Tori was so taken with him.

He smiled broadly. "Of course it's a good idea. That's the only kind I have. Here, let me help you move his bowls."

"And his litter box, please."

Charlie groaned, but carried the litter box and helped me get little Dewey set up in the secret bookroom. The lanky tiger-striped cat sauntered around the room, crouched low as if expecting some fearful monster to jump out of the shadows. He flicked his tail several times, sniffed a few of the books already on the shelves, and then leapt into one of the empty boxes. He circled around several times before settling down.

"Looks like he approves," Charlie said.

I crossed my arms and smiled. "He'll make a good mascot. I'd like to get some more books. If you can spare the time, I'd appreciate your help."

His dark eyes sparkled, and he suddenly looked much less dangerous. "A worthy endeavor. I'm glad to be put to work."

On our way to the reference section, we passed Mrs. Farnsworth. She was pacing the library atrium while complaining that the city workers were running late. "Punctuality is one of the cornerstones of civilization," she told us.

We quickly piled books from the reference section into more boxes. I made sure to include several books on cat care. We were carrying two boxes apiece toward the back stairs when someone else called out to me.

"What now," I mumbled and pretended not to have heard. I recognized the voice.

"Ms. Becket. Tru," called the persistent detective. Heavy footsteps followed us.

"As you can see, I'm busy," I said without slowing my stride.

"I'll come with you," Jace said.

I don't know why I expected him to say anything else.

I stopped.

"*Go on without me,*" I whispered to Charlie.

"*You might need me,*" he whispered back before moving to stand right next to me.

In Jace's defense, he did jog over to where we were waiting. He also asked if he could take one of the boxes. I politely refused.

"Is there something I can help you with?" I asked in my chilliest librarian tone.

"Yes, but—" he started to say and then turned to Charlie. "I don't believe we've met. Do you work here, I mean, for the library?"

"No to both. I'm Charlie Newcastle. And you are?"

"Detective Jace Bailey," I said before Jace had a chance to answer. I wasn't sure why I felt the need to handle the introduction. Perhaps I'd picked up something about southern hospitality from all of those hours and hours of cotillion classes after all. Or perhaps I was worried that Charlie might say something that would make this particular police detective even more suspicious of my actions.

Crazy, right?

It wasn't as if the two of us were doing anything suspicious at that moment—like carrying boxes of books down to the basement to put in my unauthorized collection.

A nervous laugh escaped. "The detective is investigating what happened here yesterday," I explained.

Jace looked at the boxes we were carrying. His gaze narrowed with suspicion. "What are the two of you doing? I thought the city staff was coming to take these boxes away this afternoon."

"That's why I'm here," Charlie said, completely nonplussed. "Do you mind if I set them down? Many people don't realize this, but books are wicked heavy. Never pack your personal library into large boxes when you move your collection. You'll never be able to get them into the room where you need them without unpacking the boxes at the front door, because that's where the movers will drop them." He set the boxes on the floor. "Don't ask me why I suddenly know that."

Since this was turning into a long conversation, I set the boxes I was holding on the floor as well.

"You still haven't explained what the two of you are doing." Jace propped his hands on his hips.

"Well, we . . . um . . . were—" I stammered.

"Didn't I?" Charlie said at the same time. "How forgetful of me. It must be the time change and the move and all the work I've been doing on opening my new shop."

"A shop?" Jace asked.

"Oh, yes, didn't I already mention it? I'm opening a used bookstore right here on Main Street. It has always been a dream of mine, but one I hadn't been able to manage until now. The rents on commercial storefronts in Vegas are prohibitively high. But then I heard about Cypress and how the town is working hard to grow into a center for innovation. I thought to myself, *Why the heck not*. So I sold everything in Nevada and bought the Tupper Building for practically nothing."

"That doesn't explain what you're doing here," Jace said.

"Doesn't it?" Charlie smiled kindly. "I'm opening a used bookstore," he repeated, speaking slowly, as if perhaps he thought Jace couldn't understand Charlie's flat accent. "Mrs. Farnsworth gave me permission to go through the books the library is disposing of and take whatever I wanted for my shop." He tapped the boxes he'd set down with the toe of his leather shoe.

"Oh," Jace said.

Oh, I thought to myself. Charlie was an expert liar. I wouldn't have been able to come up with such a reasonable explanation for carting off so many books. But there was a problem with his lie. A *big* problem that would soon become *my* problem.

"What brings you to the library this afternoon, Detective?" Charlie asked. "Have you returned to search for more clues? Are you still questioning witnesses?" He spoke with the excitement of a man who watched too many mystery shows and had no personal attachment to our unfortunate town manager.

"Nothing so serious. Actually, I'm here on a personal errand." Jace looked at me as he spoke.

I don't know why that made me even more nervous, but it did. Perhaps it was because his brows were still slightly furrowed. Was he trying to puzzle out the flaw in Charlie's lie?

"And what kind of errand would that be?" I asked.

"This." He held up a small toy mouse. "I brought it for Dewey. How is our kitty doing? Did he eat?"

I felt the blood drain from my head at the sight of the toy mouse. He would want to see the cat. I couldn't let that happen. Why had I moved him out of the maintenance closet?

"Thank you," I said and snatched the mouse from him. It was made of wool and smelled kind of minty. "I'll see that Dewey gets it."

"How is he doing?" Jace reached down and picked up one of the boxes. "I hope he didn't fuss about being locked up in a closet. Cats don't like to be locked up."

"He's fine. I . . . um . . . I found him a bigger room in the basement. You don't have to carry that."

"I don't mind."

"It's not your job." I managed to wrestle the box away from him. "Thank you for the mouse. I'll let you know how he likes it."

Jace looked as if he was about to protest. But Charlie said something about wanting to get the books to his car and that he was then going to take me out to lunch as a thank-you. That last bit—another lie—seemed to do the trick.

Before walking away, Jace picked up the second box I'd been carrying and placed it on top of the first one in my arms. I stood there and watched with dread as the detective headed for the atrium, where Mrs. Farnsworth was still pacing. At the same moment, the city crew arrived to carry away the boxes.

Neither Charlie nor I said a word as we descended the steps. We remained silent as we set down our heavy loads. Once relieved of my burden, I crouched down and dangled the toy mouse by its long, woven tail over the box where Dewey had been napping. He reached up a sleepy paw and batted at it.

"I've already taken my lunch break. And you shouldn't have lied to Jace about what we were doing with the books," I finally said, watching Dewey repeatedly swat his paw at the mouse. "I'm sure Jace is asking Mrs. Farnsworth about your story right now. And with this murder investigation going on, he'll think any lie anyone tells is suspicious."

"It wasn't a lie. Mrs. Farnsworth did tell me that I could take whatever books I wanted for my store."

"She did?" I looked up at him. "That doesn't sound like her."

He was walking around, looking at the books that had already been shelved with an appraising eye. "I'm a charming guy. Women tend to say yes to me."

"Perhaps too charming." I didn't like how he seemed to be mentally putting price tags on the volumes he occasionally pulled off the shelf. "You can't have these books."

He picked up a copy of *The Maltese Falcon* and whistled while his eyes widened with surprise. He pushed the book back into place, glanced at me, and quickly schooled his features. "Of course not. I'd never dream of taking any of these gems from you. As I've already told you, I'm honored to play a role—no matter how small—in helping preserve your town's printed library. I'm on your side, Tru."

After he'd left, I stayed and dangled the toy mouse for Dewey. I stayed hidden away longer than necessary, even though I knew I should have gone in search of Anne to question her. But I didn't want to watch as the city crew carted off the books. Nor did I want to watch as Charlie picked through the boxes like a vulture in search of carrion.

Dewey had flipped over on his back and was going after the mouse with all four paws when a loud crash from above my head shook the room.

Not again, I thought before I took off running.

Chapter Nine

I shot upstairs at a record pace. My heart beat triple-time.

"What . . . what happened?" I demanded as I skidded to a stop in the reference section.

Charlie, who was on his knees as he dug through a box, jumped up. Anne frowned in my direction. And the city crew, who were loading boxes onto trollies, ignored me completely.

"Shh!" Mrs. Farnsworth scolded. She had positioned herself in the middle of the room and was directing the crew. "Decorum, Ms. Becket."

"What happened?" I asked again, this time my voice pitched low, nearly a whisper.

"Everyone is doing their jobs," Mrs. Farnsworth answered tersely. "Where have you been?"

"I . . . um . . . I was organizing the storage areas downstairs in case we wanted to store some of the furniture that won't be used in the renovation."

"Well, then." Mrs. Farnsworth looked surprised. "That's a good idea. But why are you storming in here like a schoolchild who has had too much sugar?"

"I heard a crash, and I was worried that . . ."

Mrs. Farnsworth clicked her tongue. "Those workers are careless. She pointed to a second crew of workers over near the media section. Boxes were scattered all around a tipped-over trolley.

"It's just boxes. Thank goodness." I breathed a sigh of relief.

"Thank goodness?" Mrs. Farnsworth bristled. The pearls at her throat shivered. She stopped herself before scolding me for, well, for whatever she thought I'd said wrong. "I suppose it doesn't matter how they treat the books now. It's not as if they're ever going to be read again."

"Sad, isn't it?" I said.

"It is," she agreed.

For a brief moment, Mrs. Farnsworth and I seemed to connect in a way we had never been able to before. As equals. As booklovers. As two people mourning the loss of a good friend.

"As you can see, there's nothing amiss here." Mrs. Farnsworth cleared her throat. "You may go back to clearing out the downstairs. I'm sure we'll soon have plenty of furniture that will need to be stored."

"Yes, ma'am," I said. But instead of returning to the basement, I veered over to where Anne was pacing the length of the reference section with a clipboard in her hand.

"How's it going?" I asked.

"Uh, Tru!" She pressed the clipboard to her chest and backed away from me. "What are you up to?"

"I've been working in the basement. I came up to check on things after hearing a crash. It was just the handcart toppling over, but I was afraid that, well, after yesterday that . . . you know . . ." I said with a grimace. "And you?"

"I'm checking on locations for wiring." She pressed the clipboard even tighter to her chest.

"Wiring." I'd spent hours with patrons in this area of the library, helping friends and relatives research genealogies, look up medical information, or calm frantic teens in search of source materials to include in term papers due the next day. "What's this room going to become again?"

Anne's eyes lit up. "This will be our makerspace."

"A maker-what?"

"There will be state-of-the-art 3D printers over there, web-connected sewing machines along that wall, and long worktables down the middle of the space. Walls will go up over there to create four additional rooms. One will be for digital photography and movie production. Another will be used for audio production. The third space will be used for robotics. And the fourth space will be a hacker's lab."

"A hacker's what?"

"I know. Everyone reacts that way when they hear the word 'hacker.' It sounds shocking on the surface, but if we don't teach kids the ethics of hacking when they're young, we'll lose them forever. It's like encouraging a young Lex Luthor to use his genius for good instead of evil."

"Lex Luthor?" None of the kids who came into the library even remotely resembled a super-villain. Sure, there was Berry Jamison and his tendency to try and steal the graphic novels instead of checking them out. But I tried to cut him slack. His parents had misspelled his name on his birth certificate and had never gotten around to changing it from Berry to Barry. And being called Berry in middle school would be difficult for any boy.

"Did you not understand my example?" Anne said with a look of concern. "I tried to pick a vintage archvillain so you'd know what I was talking about."

"I'm not that much older than you," I pointed out.

Her tan cheeks turned a deep red. "I thought that you were . . ."

"Yes?" I said when her voice faded away before she tried to guess my age. I was disappointed. I truly wanted to know which dinosaur era she thought I was from.

"You do know who Lex Luthor is, don't you?" she asked instead.

"I may have heard of him a time or two. I am a librarian. Locked in my head are references to the characters of Beowulf, Jane Eyre, and all of Hemingway's classics, as well as the heroes and heroines appearing in both the DC and Marvel universes and the major manga comics. It is my job to know all of these things. And when I don't know, I can find the answer. I'm the female equivalent of Doctor Strange."

"Oh, I didn't realize."

"People rarely understand what librarians do."

"Well, you won't have to keep that kind of information in your head anymore." She sounded so chipper, as if she were about to tell me something I would love to hear. "In the new database, a patron can look up books using nearly any keyword, including character name, setting, or even a memorable line from a book. All you'll have to do is show people where to sit at one of the terminals and turn them loose."

"I see." Where would a librarian's skill fit in with all of this computerized madness? Our collections were going to be subscription-based, curated by Mrs. Farnsworth with Anne's help. Anne had also been given the task of maintaining the makers' labs and equipment. And I'd given myself the task of cleaning out the basement, which would be completed in a few days. After that? Where would my skills be needed in this hyper-technological library? I was afraid the answer would ultimately be "nowhere."

"I love how you're removing the personal touch," I said sarcastically. "Heck, we could shut our doors completely and simply let people access books from their phones at home. There'd be no need for anyone to ever leave their home."

"That's the goal," she chirped.

She must have noticed the unhappy look on my face. She quickly dampened her enthusiasm.

"I just don't understand all this fuss about these library books." Anne pointed to a box that one of the city workers was lifting. "Printed books are relics. The production of paper is an environmental disaster. What I'm doing here is part of the green revolution." Her eyelids snapped as she blinked excitedly. "In fact, I don't even read. I listen to podcasts and stream videos. That's the future anyhow. No one has time for reading, or for books."

I had to bite my tongue to keep myself from saying what I thought of that. Oh, I dearly wanted to argue with her. I wanted to tell her that she didn't know everything. I wanted to shout that she was wrong. Dead. Wrong. More than ever, the world needed printed books.

But I didn't shout.

My future job security or my anxiety about what technology was doing to communities wasn't what I needed to talk with Anne about. I mentally straightened my imaginary sleuthing hat, narrowed my gaze, and said slowly and calmly, "What did you tell the police this morning?"

Anne spun away from me. "I don't know what you mean."

"Please, don't be coy with me. Everyone heard Chief Fisher shout to Detective Bailey that I needed to answer some very important questions based on what you told them about me. All I want to know is what you told them. Certainly, it's not a big secret."

When she turned back to me, her eyes were as wide as saucers. Her voice trembled when she said, "I don't want trouble."

She was frightened? Of me? No one had ever been frightened of me, not even the little hooligans I'd once caught shooting spitballs onto the library's tray ceiling. And they should have been frightened. I'd threatened to call their parents.

"I'm not angry, Anne. I simply want to understand what's going on."

"I don't want trouble," she repeated.

"What do you mean? How could I cause trouble for you?"

She swallowed hard. "Everyone knows how angry you've been about the plans for the library."

"Yes, I haven't been happy," I agreed.

I would have said more, but a couple of city crew members picked up some more boxes of books around me. These particular ones were filled with local historical documents. I felt a moment of panic. "Wait," I said. "Don't take those."

"Ma'am, our instructions are to haul off all of the boxes."

"Yes," I said, thinking fast, "but these are for Charlie. Mrs. Farnsworth told him he could take whatever he wanted for his used bookstore. I'm pretty sure he wants these."

The men gave me an odd look, shrugged, and left without the boxes. I started to breathe a sigh of relief, until I noticed Anne hurrying away from me.

I hadn't learned anything from her other than her disdain for books and reading in general.

"Please," I said as I followed her. "I'm not trying to cause trouble. I'm as worried about what happened yesterday as you are. People don't get murdered, not in Cypress. We're a small, friendly community."

"You weren't around yesterday morning," she whispered as she continued to rush away from me. "You're always around." She was heading for the computer mainframe hub, the room that was filled with servers and all sorts of computer equipment with mysterious red and green blinking lights.

"I was at the library," I said.

"I know." She stopped and turned toward me. Her body trembled. "We all knew you were here. With Duggar. And you acted so upset to see him on the floor like that. But that's what you wanted, wasn't it? You wanted him dead."

"No, I wouldn't wish anyone dead. And if you knew I was in the library, why would you tell the police I wasn't around?"

"Don't you see? You're always around in the morning, like in our face. You greet everyone with a smile that has no business being that big that early in the day. You rush off and start the coffee brewing. When I came in yesterday, you weren't anywhere to be seen. The coffee maker hadn't been touched. And yet, you were somewhere in the library. And you were angry."

"Gracious, that does sound suspicious," I agreed.

She backed up a step, as if regretting that she'd led me to a room where I was blocking the only escape route. "Like I said, I don't want trouble."

I held up a hand. "No trouble. But how about I give you an explanation?"

"I don't see how you can—"

"There's a cat." I'd lowered my voice even though I was already speaking at a near whisper. "It was loose in the library. He ran in when I opened the basement door the other morning. And that's why I wasn't around. I'd spent the entire morning in the basement searching for where he was hiding. I finally found him."

I pushed back the sleeve of the sweater I'd put on over my ruined blouse and showed her the scratches.

"A cat?" she said, carefully forming each word.

I nodded. "He's a skinny little thing. Brown with black stripes." I smiled, remembering fondly how he'd batted at the mouse Jace had given me. "I named him Dewey Decimal. If no one is missing him, I think I'll keep him. I mean, I'll put up notices around town that I found him in case someone is missing him. But if no one comes forward, he'll have a home with me."

The tension drained from her face. She shook her head and laughed. "I should have guessed it was something like that," she said with a great deal of relief.

Even though that was the reaction I'd wanted, it sounded too much like Jace's smug laugh after learning about Dewey. "What's that supposed to mean?"

"It means simply that. I imagine you spend most of your free time rescuing stray cats and making sure they are comfortable," she said, echoing Jace's comments.

"Dewey will be my first." My parents had never let me keep a pet. They told me after the divorce that it wouldn't be fair to the animal since I was constantly being shuttled from my mom's house to my dad's house and back again.

"Good for you," Anne said with a patronizing grin.

"So, are we okay?" I asked.

"As long as you don't try and sabotage my work," she said and pushed her way out of the computer hub room.

My first attempt to question a suspect wasn't the blazing success I'd hoped for. Sure, I'd been able to find out what she'd said to the police to make them want to question me, which was helpful. But I still needed to find out why she—a relative stranger in town—would want to kill the town manager. He was one of the few in Cypress who agreed with her about the destruction she was wreaking in the library.

There had to be a reason she'd want him dead. Didn't there?

A little voice in my head reminded me how scared she was of me just a moment ago. That wasn't the behavior of someone with a guilty conscience . . . unless that person was worried I might figure out her secret.

"Anne, you're from out west, aren't you?" I asked as I chased after her. "Have you experienced much of a culture shock? I would imagine things are quite different here in the South."

"Not really," she said with a shrug.

"I've never been west of the Mississippi. I've always imagined life in the West to be as foreign as traveling to a different country."

"Well, I may have been raised in California, but I've been coming to Cypress my entire life. My aunt has a cabin on Lake Marion."

"Oh, I didn't know. Lake Marion is a great place to spend vacations."

The northern town limits of Cypress were bounded by a large man-made lake. Built in the 1930s to produce electricity, Lake Marion has become a fisherman's paradise. Summer cottages line the shoreline. In the summer, the town's population swells to nearly double its winter numbers. While all that sounded good and should have meant Cypress was a thriving community, the reality was that the service jobs associated with the tourism economy were low-paying and seasonal and the cute boutique shops that sold antiques and lake-related household goods barely survived from year to year.

Despite that, the town was ridiculously proud of the lake and its natural beauty, myself included.

Anne nodded. "When Duggar came out to Silicon Valley to sell his idea of developing a southern Silicon Valley and to research how best to attract start-up companies, I acted as liaison for him. I introduced him to executives and made sure he attended all the most important meetings. And when this position opened up, I was the first person he contacted. With my favorite aunt living nearby and the chance to be at the forefront of a transformation that will obviously receive national attention, I jumped at the opportunity." She leaned toward me. "And I'm not going to let anyone get in the way of making this a success."

"What do you mean?"

"What I mean, Tru, is that I'm not going to let you or anyone else derail my plans. I'm going to drag this library into the twenty-first century." Her painted purple eyelids snapped angrily. "And I'm going to make sure I get the credit for making it happen."

Chapter Ten

———— o ————

I brought Dewey home with me after work because I couldn't imagine leaving him in the library alone all night. When we entered my small house, he stepped out of the tote bag that I'd used as a carrier and sniffed everything in the living room, especially the books, before moving to the kitchen, where he jumped up on the counter and nudged the can of cat food that I'd set there.

I had just started to open the can when the doorbell rang.

"Surprise!" Tori said when I opened the door. She'd come with an extra-large veggie pizza and a rom-com DVD. "It's a cheer-up gift, because, you know, you need to be cheered up after everything that's been going on at the library."

But instead of distracting me from my worries, Tori ended up talking about books and the biblioclasts who destroyed them, and about Duggar's death and our investigation.

"What Anne told you isn't proof she murdered Duggar," she argued.

"No?" I said as I spooned the can of cat food into a small soup dish. "I don't see why it isn't proof. Duggar loved being the center of attention. I'm sure he'd planned the library's renovations so we'd become a national spectacle not only as a lure for tech companies but also to shine the spotlight on himself."

Dewey butted my leg with his head. He gave me a look that seemed to say, "Stop talking and put the bowl of beef stew down already."

"Sorry, bud. Here you go." As soon as the bowl touched the ground, the little kitty started to gobble the food.

Tori slid the pizza box to the middle of my secondhand dining room table and flipped open the lid. The table wobbled. "And you think Anne killed the town manager because—?"

"Because she wants credit for the work she's doing at the library, and as long as Duggar was alive and breathing, no one would have ever known she existed. He was going to be the one to talk to the media. He was the one who was going to bask in the spotlight." I drew in a deep breath. "I kind of feel sorry for Anne."

Tori made a face and started to say something, but the doorbell rang again.

"I'll get it." She jogged toward the front door.

Who, other than Tori, would drop by my house unannounced? I grabbed a piece of pizza and followed.

Flossie, wearing a bright red tie-dyed dress, was at the door with a towering cake in her lap. "I thought chocolate was in order."

"You thought right," Tori said, sounding suspiciously chipper.

I crossed my arms over my chest. "What's really going on here?"

But before either of my friends could answer, Charlie came bounding up to the porch and peeked around Flossie.

"Since we're celebrating our modern-day Saint Wiborada, I brought wine," he said, holding up an old, dusty bottle. He'd changed out of his suit. He looked fashionably causal in a pair of neatly pressed khaki pants and a crisp short-sleeved button-up shirt with green and blue stripes that was open at the neck.

"Saint who?" Tori demanded.

"Oh! That looks like a good wine," Flossie gushed.

"Saint Wiborada, the patron saint of libraries and librarians," I said with a frown. "I'm not—"

"In the tenth century, Saint Wiborada saved more than one Christian library in Switzerland from rampaging pagan Hungarians." Charlie tossed his arm over Tori's shoulder.

"That's our Tru. Standing like a warrior that no one has ever heard of against a wave of invaders." She laughed and then swung the door open wide. Flossie rolled in. "I was wondering when you'd get here, lover boy," she said. Tori brushed a kiss on Charlie's lips as they followed Flossie straight through my living room and toward the kitchen in the back of the house as if they lived there. I smiled and shook my head, thinking how lucky I was to have Tori and Flossie in my life. And even Charlie.

My plans for the evening had been to type up more cards for the card catalog while trying not to think about those boxes of books rotting away in the landfill. Or about the fact that it was supposed to rain tonight.

When I reached the kitchen, I pulled Tori aside. "I was wondering why you brought an extra-large pizza for just the two of us. How many people did you invite?"

"Just Charlie and Flossie and, well"—she skirted away from me and hurried over to where Charlie was uncorking the wine bottle—"Jace."

"Detective Bailey?" I cried with dismay. "Why would you do something crazy like invite him, of all people, into my home?"

"Didn't you tell me that he's not going to rest until he knows you're taking good care of Dewey? Honey, if that's the case, we need to pull off that Band-Aid and get him over here—or did you want him to visit Dewey in your basement library?"

"No, you know I don't want that." She was the expert when it came to handling men. "Still, I wish you'd warned me. This place is a mess."

I wasn't simply talking about my house. After work, I'd changed into a pair of old running shorts (not that I ever went running) and a dingy white T-shirt that was a few sizes too big. The outfit would have been fine for a night in alone with Tori. But this was turning into a party. And the thought of Jace seeing me like this—

I yelped and ran down the short hallway toward my bedroom just as the doorbell rang again. Dewey scooted into my room with me.

"What should I wear?" I asked my little kitty as I tossed half the contents of my closet onto my bed. He batted the hem of one of my dresses. I considered it for a brief moment. But no. The black dress seemed too dressy. The jeans were too warm for this time of year. The sundress was too similar to what Tori had on. I didn't want to look like her less attractive sister.

In the end, I pulled on a pair of dressy black shorts and a white tunic shirt that had pink roses stitched into the scoop neckline.

I traded my comfortable fuzzy socks for a pair of strappy sandals. With quick motions, I hastily applied a pale pink lipstick that matched the roses on my tunic and a dusky brown eye shadow. Finally, I dabbed a thick coating of cover-up onto my arm to hide the angry red scratches.

My fine-textured brown hair was impossible to tame in the South's humidity. By the end of the day it was a frustrating mix of both kinky and limp. The best I could do with it was pull it back into a high pony-tail like Tori's.

I took one last look in the dresser's mirror. A few stubborn tendrils of hair had escaped to curl around the crown of my head, making me look fuzzy. I sprayed some hairspray on the top of my head and patted everything down.

Once I'd finished, I drew a deep breath and said to Dewey, "Now remember, kitty, the detective—no matter how handsome he looks—is not our friend. So be careful around him."

My kitty meowed as if he understood. But I suspected he was simply tired of being closed up in the bedroom with me.

"You're right. Enough stalling. We can't hide in here all night."

I emerged to find the party had formed around the kitchen table. Tori was pouring the wine. Charlie and Flossie had their heads together in conversation. They both were laughing. And Jace was standing off to one side looking around as if he were still on duty and in search of a murder weapon.

He'd come dressed in worn jeans and black T-shirt, which made him look like the living definition of hot cop. Put a picture of him dressed like that on the cover of a romance novel, and it would hit the best-seller list in an hour.

"Um, hi there," I said, hoping to sound causal.

Tori spun around and splashed half the wine in the glass she'd been pouring onto the linoleum floor when she saw me. "What did you—?" she started to say, but stopped herself.

"You look nice." Charlie lifted a glass in my direction.

I glanced down at myself, pretending to notice for the first time what I had on, trying to act cool, and pretending that wearing makeup to hang out at home was a normal thing to do.

"Thanks," I said. "I hope y'all are eating the pizza. Tori brought enough for an army. And, Detective, I'm glad you could come by."

"I'm off the clock. Call me Jace." Off duty or not, he was drinking water instead of wine unlike the rest of my friends. "How's our kitty doing?"

As if on cue, Dewey sauntered into the kitchen with his tail held high, its tip shivering with happiness.

Jace crouched down and made a shushing sound. Much to my dismay, Dewey rushed right over and rubbed up against the detective's outstretched hand while purring loudly.

"He's eaten two cans of stinky beef stew since we've gotten home. And he's been carrying that mouse you brought for him everywhere," I said. "So I think he's happy."

"Don't know that I've ever seen a cat look happier," Jace agreed as he stroked Dewey's petite back. "Is he smiling?"

"Cats can't smile," Flossie said from across the small room. "Their facial muscles aren't built that way."

"I don't know. This one sure looks like he's smiling," Jace said. "He wasn't grinning like this when Tru caught him and stuffed him into the maintenance closet this morning."

I rubbed my arm. The deep scratches still stung. "Have you had pizza yet? Tori bought this monster pie, and I don't want leftovers."

"Thanks. With everything that's going on with the investigation, I forgot to eat lunch." He'd forgotten to eat lunch, but he'd taken the time to buy Dewey a toy? My heart softened a little toward him.

I smiled.

He smiled back.

It felt like the start of a Hallmark movie.

But when he stood up, his gaze drifted over to the far wall to where my grandmother's old china cabinet was standing. His smiled dropped. His shoulders tensed.

The only thing out of place on the china cabinet was the screwdriver I'd left on the cabinet's top. Why would the sight of a screwdriver make Jace put his police game face back on?

"I was trying to fix the kitchen table," I explained and then demonstrated how the table's top wobbled. "But that was the only screwdriver I could find out in the shed. Not too helpful, right?" I'd set the screwdriver on the surface closest to the back door, intending to return it to the backyard shed the next time I went out that way.

Oh, dear. It suddenly hit me. That was what was wrong. The screwdriver I'd found in the shed wasn't a common screwdriver, but the kind with a hex head. It was the exact kind of screwdriver that had been used to remove the bolts that kept the shelf that had killed Duggar from tipping over. I knew what they looked like only too well, since I'd spent the morning studying the bolts keeping every other shelf in the library from tipping over.

"Let me take a look," Charlie said. Without waiting for permission, he crawled under the table. "You need a Phillip's head to fix this, not a hex."

"Too bad it isn't a flathead screw," Tori said. "I use a butter knife to loosen and tighten those."

"I might have what you need in the trunk of my car," Charlie said.

"Isn't he handy?" Tori gushed.

"And so well read," Flossie added. "Charlie, you're quite a step up from the idiots Tori usually dates."

"Oh, hush," Tori fussed. "I don't go on that many dates."

"Glad you consider me a higher-class idiot," Charlie said with a laugh.

Everyone in the room was talking and laughing at the same time, all except for Jace.

"My mom borrowed my toolbox several months ago and hasn't returned it," I said to him. "Actually, I don't think she will. I'm going to have to buy a new set of tools. But the previous owners of this house, a sweet older couple, were moving into a retirement community and had left me pretty much everything they had in their shed: the lawn mower, trimmer, and an odd assortment of tools."

"I see," he said, his voice curt.

I had no idea what I could do to loosen the tension between us. He wasn't my friend. I wasn't a killer, and it still surprised me that anyone might think I was. "I spoke with Anne this afternoon," I blurted. "I explained to her about Dewey being loose in the library and how I'd spent the morning searching for him. She seemed to understand." *And you should too*, I left unsaid.

He looked at me. And I mean really looked. He leaned toward me and gave me a hard once-over that felt like he was peeling my skin open. "It's killing you what's happening to the library. And that worries me. I might not remember everything from your tutoring sessions, but—"

"Like what subject I was trying to teach you?" I interjected.

"Exactly, but I do remember how passionate you were about books even then. You always had a library book in your hand. You called them your best friends. Who does that? Books are books. They're not people."

"Booklovers do that," I said. "*All* booklovers."

But he continued to frown. He obviously didn't see books the same way I did. I suspected they were simply words on a page for him, which I found incredibly sad.

He mumbled something about repeating past mistakes. "I shouldn't be here. I've got to go," he said louder. "I'm sorry, Tru. I need to take this." He picked up the screwdriver on his way out. "It might be evidence."

"What was that about?" Flossie asked when she noticed he'd left.

"Oh, I don't know," I said with a groan. "Hopefully not more than twenty-five to life."

Chapter Eleven

Tori pushed a glass of wine into my hand and told me to drink. According to her, I needed to put some color back in my cheeks.

"No one is going to arrest you," Flossie declared. She slapped her hand against the arm of her wheelchair as added emphasis. "I won't let that happen."

"I don't see how you can stop it. The police seem to be doing a bang-up job of building a case against me." I took a long, slow sip of the wine Charlie had brought. The deep red flavors swirled in my mouth. It was smooth and not at all like the tangy wine we usually drank at our girlfriend parties. Gracious, I couldn't remember ever tasting anything quite like it. "This is good," I said to Charlie, holding up the glass.

"It should be. It's a 1961 Château Pétrus Cru Merlot from France," he replied. He'd just climbed out from under the table with a Phillips-head screwdriver in hand. He gave the table top a wiggle. It didn't move. "It was an excellent year for grapes in the region. I'm glad you like it."

"It's amazing, really. I'll have to be sure to remember the name and ask for it the next time I'm at the grocery store," I said as I jotted down the name onto my shopping list.

He smiled warmly. "You do that."

"You're not going to find that at a grocery store," Flossie teased.

"Oh, right." I blushed. We'd never had wine at one of our girls'-nights-in that didn't come from our local A&P. To cover for my blunder, I thanked him for fixing my table. Tori gushed again about how handy he was. She gave his arms a squeeze. And Flossie ignored us while she continued to make plans about how to keep the police from making me into a convenient scapegoat.

"Enough of that," Tori fussed. "We're supposed to be distracting Tru, not giving her a panic attack."

"You're the one who invited the detective to our party." Flossie wagged her finger at Tori.

"It had to be done." Tori waggled her finger right back at her. "Besides, who could have guessed he would have gotten all weird over the sight of a screwdriver. Like, who doesn't have a screwdriver in their house?"

"A hex-head screwdriver? Sitting out on a china cabinet?" Flossie said. "Honey, that's not an everyday thing."

"Well, what's done is done," Tori declared. "We have wine to drink, pizza and cake to eat, and a movie to watch. I say let's get this party started."

I carried the box of pizza. Charlie picked up the bottle of wine. Tori had the DVD. And Flossie carried Dewey, who'd decided her lap made the best perch in the house. We made our way into the living room and were all settling into our spots when someone sang out, "Knock, knock."

There was only one person in my life who'd sing "Knock, knock" instead of actually knocking on a door.

"Maybe she's returning your tools," Tori said.

"Yeah, and maybe the library books will grow legs and walk back into the library tonight." I opened the door and smiled. "Hey, Mama. We were just sitting down to watch a movie. Do you want to join us?"

My mom, Edwina Trudell Becket (Mama Eddy to my friends), matched me in height. She was neither exceptionally short nor exceptionally tall. But that was where the comparison between mother and daughter ended. Unlike me, everything else about my mom was exceptional. She had platinum blonde hair that didn't have a spot of gray, despite celebrating her fifty-eighth birthday this year. She never stepped foot out of the house without a full application of makeup. And through even the leanest of financial times after the divorce, she managed to keep her wardrobe filled with the most fashionable dresses by saving every spare penny and scouring secondhand shops.

Even by our southern town's high standards (which had produced more than our fair share of Miss South Carolinas), my mom was considered quite an uncommon beauty. A little more than a year after the divorce, an artist visiting our town to paint lakeside landscapes had stopped her on Main Street. He'd been so taken with her refined features, he'd begged her to let him paint a portrait.

It'd happened on a weekend night in the summer. The street had been crowded with locals and tourists. The residents had talked about it for weeks. I'd been an awkward preteen at the time. Her stunning beauty awed me. People noticed her. I'd dearly wanted that for myself.

Her beauty still awed me. And although I'd long ago accepted that I'd never be considered beautiful, I still secretly ached for someone to see me and be inspired.

Tonight, Mama Eddy was dressed in a pale purple silk pantsuit with a white silk scarf artfully wrapped around her neck. She swept into the house and brushed a kiss on my cheek as she passed by. She took a few more steps into the living room before coming to an abrupt stop.

Her attention zeroed in on the pizza box propped open on the coffee table.

"Pizza?" She crossed the room and snatched up the box. Only after she had it in her clutches did she remember her manners. "Good evening, Flossie. The yellow in that sundress is a lovely color on you, Tori. Um, hello, I don't know you."

Charlie jumped to his feet. "I'm Charlie Newcastle, ma'am. I only recently moved to Cypress."

Mama Eddy, who has helped teach the local cotillion classes for the past fifteen years, was clearly impressed that Charlie had showed proper manners. He stood up before speaking to her, for instance.

She quizzed him about his parents, because that's what people did around here. You might be a decent person, but we still needed to find out about your family before we could pass judgment. He must have come from somewhere that was similar, since he didn't seem to find this line of questioning odd.

"Y'all stay here and enjoy the movie," Mama Eddy said, once she was satisfied she knew enough about Charlie's past. "I'll go whip up some proper dinner food."

"What are you doing?" I asked as I followed her into the kitchen.

Before I could stop her, she smashed the pizza box, with the remaining pizza still inside, into the trash can. "Do you know what all that fat will do to your veins? You can't eat dairy or saturated fats. No one in our family can. Uncle Frank has had two heart bypass surgeries and is heading for a third. Do you want to be like him? Or do you want to be like Grandpa Phil? You know, dead?"

"Phil was *your* grandfather," I reminded her. "And if he were still alive, it'd be a miracle since he'd be well over 110 years old."

She wasn't listening. "Do I need to remind you how he had a heart attack and died while playing water polo?" she said.

"He was ninety-seven years old and playing water polo. I hope to be that lucky."

"That's beside the point, and you know it. He had a heart attack. And you will too if you keep eating garbage like this." She sucked a dramatic breath through her clenched teeth. "Or this." She pointed an accusing finger at the tower of chocolate cake sitting on the kitchen table. "You shouldn't allow anything like this into your house." She rummaged around in the cabinet next to the stove and pulled out a large frying pan. "I'm going to make all of y'all a nice, healthy meal."

"*M-om-ma.*" I drew out the word, hating how I sounded like a whiny teen. "*Please,* my friends are all here. This isn't even your house."

She jerked as if I'd struck her. "Oh? So I'm not welcome here? But your father cooks you dinner on Wednesday night, and you don't complain?"

"It's not like that." For one thing, he hadn't appeared at my door unannounced, or tossed out my pizza.

"You've always loved your father more than you loved me."

"Okay," I said, calmly. "This isn't about the pizza. Or my having dinner with Dad." And that worried me. "What's really going on? Why are you here?"

She turned to me and took both of my hands in hers. Tears swam in her eyes . . . a second reason for me to worry. She made it a point to never cry since it messed up her makeup.

"*My beautiful daughter,*" she whispered. She started to say something else, but she seemed to notice something on my face. She touched my cheek. "You're . . . you're wearing makeup?"

"I put on a little," I admitted.

She gave my hand a squeeze. "At least you're doing something right. Makeup is a woman's best armor," she said with a sob in her voice. "Always remember that."

"What's going on? Why are you so upset?" She was seriously starting to scare me now. "Are you sick? You can tell me. Just spit it out."

She shook her head. "It's—"

Dewey chose that exact moment to spring into the kitchen. With a sharp *meow,* he went straight for my mom's legs and started to rub against them in what I was starting to recognize as a kitty hug. Mama yelped.

"What is that?" she squeaked.

"Come on. You've seen cats before. Stop stalling and tell me what's bothering you. I'm seriously concerned." Terrified, really.

She shook her head while keeping her gaze glued to Dewey. "Did one of your friends bring it over with them? That's not very polite. Those things get hair all over everything without even trying."

"I found Dewey at the library. I brought him home today. He needs to put on weight. But he's a cute little guy, don't you agree?"

She dropped my hands. "You have a cat now? Who said you could get a cat? Your father?"

"I didn't discuss this with Dad. Besides, this is my house," I gently reminded her. "I am an adult. Been successfully living on my own for more than fifteen years."

She wasn't impressed. "I don't think you're ready for a cat. Taking care of another life is a huge, *thankless* responsibility."

"And I do thank you for taking me on," I said. "Please, forget about Dewey for a moment. Tell me what's wrong." Did she have cancer?

She looked away from the little stray tabby. Her teary-eyed gaze met mine. She whispered, "*You. I'm worried about you.*"

She frowned at Dewey again.

"Me? What? I'm fine," I said.

"Are you? Everyone is talking about the town manager's demise. He was well liked, you know. Affable. Came from a good family. His great-grandfather owned a mansion in Charleston."

"I may have heard something about that," I said with a great deal of confusion. What did Duggar's great-grandfather have to do with anything? "His murder is shocking. Things like that don't happen in Cypress. But you don't have to worry about me. Despite what happened, the library is a safe place to work. I promise. It's safe."

She grabbed my hands again. Her grip tightened so much, I was worried she might snap a bone. But I didn't pull away. I couldn't until I made her understand that she didn't have to be upset.

"You had dinner with your father on Wednesday night," she said. This was the second time she'd mentioned it, which was odd. I'd never seen her act this jealous over the time I spent with my dad.

"I'm sorry if that hurt you. We can have dinner next week."

"That's not what's wrong. But, yes, I'd love to have dinner with you next week. I hope I'll be able to." She took a shuddering breath. "Your father, you know, was always the passionate one, the impulsive one. That's why things didn't work between us. I needed someone to be my rock." She stifled a cry of distress. "I . . . I should have never let you spend so much time with him when you were young and impression-able. You'd always come home from his house acting even more impul-sive than he ever had. And now, now, the day after you had dinner with him . . ." A fat tear tumbled down her cheek. It traced a line in her carefully applied foundation.

"The day after I had dinner with Dad . . . ?" I prompted.

I had dinner with Dad on Wednesday, which was two days ago. Yesterday was Thursday, the day Duggar was—

Oh!

She didn't think—?

"You don't think that I, that I—?" I stammered.

My own mother thinks I'm capable of murder?

"That's what everyone is saying, dear."

"What is everyone saying?" Tori asked as she entered the kitchen with several empty plates balanced in her hands. "Oh, you tossed out the pizza. Why am I not surprised?" She gave her head a rueful shake. "Mama Eddy, you look even younger than the last time I saw you. Are you using a new beauty cream?" Tori set down the plates, peeled Mama's hands from mine, and gave her a great big Tori hug, which is awfully like a bear hug—only bigger . . . and longer.

"Don't Mama Eddy me," Mama said, not falling for Tori's charm. She wiggled out of the embrace.

Tori gave me a look and a shrug as if to say, "I tried." She then poked at the cabbage my mom had dug out from the back of my fridge. "You're not seriously going to cook that. It's Friday night. Certainly, cabbage is a Monday or Tuesday night dish."

"It's the only healthy piece of food my daughter has in this place." Mama Eddy opened the refrigerator and grabbed what was left of the double fudge pudding cups I'd bought earlier in the week. She waved them around in an accusing manner.

"It's been a stressful week." I pushed the bags of candy bars that were sitting out on the counter behind the bread box.

Of course she noticed. "When you're stressed, you need to be even more vigilant about your health."

"I'm going shopping tomorrow," I said.

"In your daughter's defense," Tori said, "it was a veggie pizza. And I'm sure you'll be glad to hear this: she even had a man come over. He came to visit Dewey. But it's a start."

"A man?" That news did cheer Mama up. *Goody.* "Who?" she demanded, not of Tori (who had no reason not to be reckless with information) but of me (the one who had to endure her badgering). She was determined to nag me into marrying soon and presenting her with not one, but a passel of grandchildren.

"Jace Bailey. You remember him? Back in high school I was his English tutor." Not that my lessons had made much of an impression.

"That Bailey boy? Isn't he the one who just moved back from serving on the NYPD?"

"Yes, that's him," I said.

"He's a police detective. You let a police detective into your home?" Mama's voice kept rising in volume. "Without a warrant?" She'd once dated a retired police officer. After the experience, she considered herself an expert on police procedure. Watching police dramas with her was . . . not fun. "You know he can use whatever he sees in here as evidence against you?"

"I know." That stupid screwdriver—if only I'd put it back in the shed.

"Just . . . just . . ." Fresh tears welled in Mama's eyes. She grabbed my hands in her crushing grip again. "Tell me, Tru, that you didn't do it. Tell me you didn't do something rash."

"How could you think that I—?"

"Because you have your father's personality," she nearly shouted. "Rash. Passionate. Quick to argue."

"No, that's not who I am."

"See. There, you asked me for my opinion and then shout that I'm wrong."

"I didn't do anything." I twisted away from her and picked up the cabbage before she could get her hands on it again. "Please, Mama. I appreciate your concern. Truly, I do." I shoved the cabbage back into the fridge, where it belonged.

"I'm going to hire you a lawyer first thing in the morning," she declared. "Gary Larsen. We went out a few times. He's got a sharp wit. And I heard he got Maggie Fenton's daughter out of trouble when she went on that bender and crashed her car into a tree. That family has a history of, well, you know. It's amazing that he was able to help that girl at all. I'll call him."

"I'm sure that's not necessary—" I started to say.

But she wasn't listening. "No matter what you do, promise me you won't talk to the police again without your lawyer by your side. Especially not with that Bailey boy. I heard from Gwynne Hansy how that boy came back to Cypress with his tail tucked between his legs. He did something that got him into all sorts of trouble with the NYPD. Gwynne didn't know what, but she did know that that boy is set on proving himself. You don't want to be the one he runs over to show he's not a screwup."

"Can I help with anything?" Charlie asked as he came into the room with a glass of wine. He winked at Tori before handing the glass to my mother. She took a sip of the amazing wine, smiled, and gave me a nod of approval.

"I'm going to make the four of y'all a proper meal," Mama said with a twinkle in her eye. "You know, something that'll actually go with this wine."

"Wine is a forgiving drink," Charlie said. "In fact, I know a brand of champagne that pairs perfectly with popcorn."

If I'd said something like that, Mama would have lectured me on the importance of keeping an eye on fat and sodium content. With someone as handsome and *male* as Charlie, she laughed her flirty laugh.

"Popcorn." She swatted him on the arm and gave another tinkling laugh. "Now where is that cabbage?"

Tori blocked the fridge while I tried to maneuver Mama back toward the living room. "Watch the movie. It's a rom-com. You love those."

Charlie had started to join us in trying to talk Mama down from her health-food mania when his phone chimed. He frowned at the screen. "I'd better take this."

He stepped out the back door.

"Mama, I'm not letting you cook for me. It's Friday. It's time to relax. Besides, we already ate enough pizza to keep us full until tomorrow night."

"That's what I'm afraid of," she said with a huff. "And I'm still not convinced that you didn't push that—"

"That was the police." Charlie returned to the kitchen with his phone still in his hand and a look of confusion on his face. "Someone has broken into my bookstore."

Mama gasped loudly. "Murder *and* robberies? What is happening to our town?"

"I don't know," I said. I wondered if Duggar's murder and this robbery were somehow connected.

How could they be connected? a snarky voice in my head hissed.

Charlie was shaking his head. "The police officer said the shop's front window had been smashed and the boxes of books that I'd taken from the library were all emptied out."

"I knew it!" Actually, I didn't. But I clapped my hand against my leg anyhow. "There's something about those old library books that we don't understand. Perhaps something worth killing over."

Chapter Twelve

———o———

Cypress's library remained closed to the public over the weekend and into the next week while workers put up new walls, ran new wiring, and installed all sorts of electronics and computer terminals. It was all cutting-edge technology and took time to set up.

I spent the time in the basement vault going through the boxes of books we'd saved, searching for a clue as to what about them might drive someone to kill and to steal. All I could figure out was that they were priceless books, at least in my mind. Was there someone out there who shared my passion for them? Someone who wouldn't think twice about killing? Someone like Mrs. Farnsworth?

Charlie had reported to us on Saturday morning that none of the books at his shop had been taken during the break-in. They'd simply been tossed out of their boxes.

"Could someone be looking for a piece of paper that had been slipped into one of the books?" Flossie had wondered the following Monday as we all worked together in setting up the secret bookroom.

I'd sneaked my friends into the library through the basement's back door. "It could be an incriminating letter or a—"

"Treasure map!" Tori exclaimed. She pulled a book from one of the shelves and started leafing through it.

"Don't be ridiculous. Why would anyone put a treasure map in a book around here?" Flossie scoffed. "We're not near the ocean, and there's no history of pirates within a fifty-mile radius of this place."

"It doesn't have to be a pirate map. It could be a map that has been handed down through the generations and hidden right here under our noses." Tori pulled another book off the shelf to look through it. "Tru, didn't Mama Eddy say Duggar's family once owned a mansion in Charleston? If it were a pirate map, there are plenty of tales of pirates associated with that historic city."

"She did say that," I said thoughtfully. "And there were pirates in Charleston."

"But why would anyone stick a priceless map into a book here?" Flossie said. "This place is public. It's even in the name: Town of Cypress *Public* Library."

"Maybe the killer was hiding the map from Duggar or from someone else who knew about it. You have to admit that would be reason enough for murder," Tori said. She'd pulled yet another book off the shelf to search. "In my experience, people turn into vicious monsters when there's even just a small amount of money to be fought over. It's enough to make someone want to do something drastic."

Was my friend alluding to some personal experience? I paused from filing cards into the card catalog and used my finger to save my spot for a moment. "Is everything okay with you, Tori?"

"Just talking," she said with a laugh. "People can be terrible."

"That's the truth," Flossie mumbled. "Anyhow, I saw Charlie had the sign up for his shop. The Deckle Edge, very clever name for a used bookstore. When will he have his grand opening?"

"Not for at least another week. He still has to get a few more government permits. I'm helping him with the paperwork." Tori looked over at me. "Are you sure you're okay with him selling the books Mrs. Farnsworth let him take from the library?"

"Why wouldn't I be?"

"Well, he wanted me to ask you. He said you seemed pretty tense when he was here picking them out."

"He helped me carry more books to our secret library. It was a decent thing to do." Even so, I bristled at the memory of him picking through the library's books. None of the books should have left the library. "I suppose I'd rather those books went to his shop instead of the landfill."

"That's Charlie, as decent as they come," Tori said, smiling broadly.

"So unlike your regular type," Flossie teased.

"That's the truth." Tori shook her hips. "But his wicked good looks make up for all that depressingly good behavior of his."

We all laughed.

Quietly.

We were in a library, after all.

Over the next several days, I searched through every book we'd carried down to the basement vault. I searched for anything interesting: a stray piece of paper, a romantic note, or even a treasure map. There were grocery shopping lists, old receipts, and one bubblegum wrapper. None of it was worth killing over.

Upstairs, the library's doors remained closed to the public as Anne set up the equipment. She gave lessons to the rest of us on how to use the new electronics and machines like the 3D printers.

I spent my time upstairs trying to create a role for myself in the newly renovated library. My main contribution to the library that week was explaining to library patrons who banged on the front door why I couldn't let them in until the renovations were completed. Our library, up until this past week, had only ever closed its doors on major holidays and Sundays. Not even Hurricane Hugo or the big snowstorm of 1988 had caused a disruption to its operating hours. Mrs. Farnsworth had seen to that.

When I wasn't at work, I kept a healthy selection of salvaged library books in a tote bag. Wherever I went, whether to a garden club meeting or a lady's lunch, I handpicked books to bring with me. For instance, I knew Mrs. Rochester would want a book on growing camellias. Mr. Clayton loved reading about vintage cars. Lottie Hayworth devoured historical romances.

I told everyone that I was personally loaning out the books, a white lie. They all came from the secret bookroom. Whenever someone took a book, I'd write their name down along with what book they took. I'd then ask that the book be returned to me in a few weeks.

My process of bringing the library out to the reading public seemed to be working well. By the end of each meeting I attended, my tote bag was almost always empty. And the town's loyal readers were wearing the most pleasant grins. No one questioned where the books I carried came from. People on the street started to call me "the human book-mobile," which I thought was cute, until someone mentioned my new nickname to Mrs. Farnsworth.

Chapter Thirteen

Shortly before the end of the workday on Wednesday, Mrs. Farnsworth stopped beside the circulation desk and sighed. Her shoulders slumped forward a bit.

"Long day," I said, sharing her feelings of exhaustion.

"A human bookmobile, Ms. Becket?" Her lips formed a perfect moue of displeasure. Did she practice frowning in a mirror? Or did the talent for freezing others with a simple look come naturally to her?

I shrugged while pretending I wasn't shivering in my sensible flats. "Just trying to help out while the library is closed. It's amazing how many people rely on our services."

Her brows flattened. "You've not been happy here, have you?"

"About this, you mean?" I gestured to the wall of computer terminals directly behind me. "No, I'm not happy about it. Removing the books was a mistake."

Her gaze narrowed. "You haven't done anything in protest, have you?"

My cheeks suddenly flamed. I pressed my hands to them before realizing that I was drawing additional attention to my skin's own admission of guilt. "In . . . in protest? What do you mean?"

"You know what I mean." The relentless press of her stern expression made me want to crawl under the desk.

I forced myself to look her in the eye. "I'm worried about what happened . . . with Duggar. I think the library needs to install security cameras. We need to make sure our patrons feel like this is a safe space, or else they'll stop coming."

"I've had the same thought. But you didn't answer my question, Ms. Becket."

I sighed. "I did protest the library's renovations as vehemently as you did, not that it did any good. I'm not ashamed of it. I'm not going to apologize." And if she was going to accuse me of setting up a secret bookroom downstairs, she was welcome to do so. However, I would not, *absolutely not*, hand that information over to her.

"I'm not asking you to apologize," she said. "I'm asking if you—"

"Mrs. Farnsworth, do you mind if I interrupt?" Police Chief Fisher asked as he approached us. He was smiling like an underfed hound dog that had just been handed a juicy piece of meat.

Neither Mrs. Farnsworth nor I was surprised to see him. During this strange time in the library's life, Police Chief Fisher and Detective Ellerbe from the state law enforcement agency stopped by every day to ask questions. They often showed up shortly after I put on the morning coffee pot. I had started to suspect they came more for the freshly roasted beans I would buy from Tori's café than to investigate.

I hadn't seen or heard from Jace since he'd confiscated my screwdriver. I'm not sure I could have acted as cool around him as I had been acting with the police chief and Detective Ellerbe. My mind seemed to turn all mushy whenever Jace was looking at me, which irritated me to no end.

"What do you need, Jack?" Mrs. Farnsworth snapped.

"I . . . um . . ." He looked at the floor like a chastened child. "I need to have a few words with your assistant."

"I suppose we can finish this conversation tomorrow. I'll be heading home, then. Be sure the door is pulled shut tightly and the latch clicks when you leave." Mrs. Farnsworth headed for her office to fetch her purse. "Good night, then," she whispered on her way out.

The door's lock clicked behind her. She gave the door a wiggle to double-check the lock before walking toward her car.

The police chief continued to watch me with that hound-dog grin.

Never one to enjoy staring contests, I sighed. "What is it?"

"Detective Bailey showed me what he found in your house last Friday."

"Did he? The way he'd acted, you would have thought he'd discovered a bloody knife. It was a screwdriver. I imagine you'd find one in nearly every house in this town. We're handy people here in Cypress. You know that."

He chuckled. "He said it was sitting out as if it'd recently been used."

"It was. Did he also tell you that my kitchen table was broken? I was trying to fix it."

Fisher nodded and let the silence spread between us.

"If I were going to loosen bolts at the library, why in heaven's name would I bring in my own tools when the library has a full set on hand in the maintenance closet in the basement?"

His smile faded. "Do you think we're idiots?"

"Do you think *I'm* an idiot?" I countered. His neck reddened, and I immediately regretted it.

"We know all about the tools in the basement closet. Had a tech team on it the morning of Duggar's death," he said.

"Good," I replied.

"Not good." More silence. This time I didn't feel an urge to fill that silence. "There was just one tool missing. Do you want to guess which one?"

"Not really."

"The tools in that closet are the same brand and age as the one

Detective Bailey took from your house," he said, while appearing to watch me closely for my reaction.

"I'm not surprised. It's a popular brand. The former owners of my house left that screwdriver in the shed. They'd lived there since the fifties. And the fifties is the last time the library had the funds to procure things like new tools."

"The girl has a point," Detective Ellerbe said as he approached the circulation desk. He gave Fisher a nod and then moved to stand next to his colleague. "There's no way to prove the screwdriver came from the library's set."

"It didn't," I interjected.

He gave another measured nod. "Which is equally impossible to prove. What we have is an impasse. Someone who works in the library killed the town manager. The only workers present that morning were the elderly Mrs. Farnsworth, the technologically dexterous Anne Lowery, and you—someone who vehemently protested the town manager's efforts to modernize this place."

"Modernize? No, what he's done has destroyed—"

Ellerbe raised an eyebrow. My outburst was only proving why I should remain their number one suspect. I needed to tamp down my passion for the library books, as if that were even possible.

"We weren't the only ones in the library," I reminded them.

"Really?" Ellerbe slanted a glance toward Fisher.

"Really," I said in a rush. "The mayor and his son were also here."

Fisher barked a laugh. "You expect us to believe that either our upstanding mayor or his son, who'd not lived in this town for nearly a decade, had something to do with Duggar's death?"

I shrugged. "They were present that morning."

"And they were together," Ellerbe said. He took a step toward the desk where I was sitting. "Their alibis are solid."

I stood up. "What do we really know about Anne? Perhaps she killed Duggar for a reason we don't yet understand. Have you considered that the break-in at the used bookstore is connected to Duggar's murder? It happened the day after the owner took books from the library into his shop. Perhaps the killer is searching for something hidden in one of the books. Perhaps Duggar had interrupted that search."

Ellerbe breathed out slowly. "That sounds rather fanciful. In my experience, motives are never so complicated."

"Besides," Fisher said, "Duggar was found in the media section of the library. There wasn't a book in sight."

He did have a point, darn it.

"And I suppose you cleared Mrs. Farnsworth because of her age?" I asked.

"The woman is tipping toward eighty," Fisher said.

"That may be so, but she's also as strong as someone half her age and has a temper that leaves even the bravest in this community shaking in their britches."

"She is rather formidable," Ellerbe agreed.

"If she were the killing type, half our town would have met an early demise by now," Fisher rightfully pointed out.

"So that leaves me?" I asked.

"That leaves you," Ellerbe agreed. "Unless . . . ?"

"Unless someone else was in the library?" I finished for him.

"Now that's a novel idea." He tapped his temple. "Can you think of anyone?"

My heart beat just a bit faster. Did they know? Did they know about my work in the basement? Did they know about Flossie, Tori, and Charlie? No, if they did, they wouldn't play coy about it. They wouldn't be trying to trick me.

"You mean someone might have broken into the library that morning?" I asked. "It's something I'll have to think about."

Ellerbe rapped his knuckle on the desk's surface. "You do that."

Chapter Fourteen

Today's the day," Anne sang as she arrived early on Thursday morning. Her usual dour morning mood was nowhere to be found, which surprised me. The young techie was never chipper in the morning.

She looked younger than ever with her wide grin and purple-streaked hair styled in pigtails. She bounced happily on the balls of her feet. "Aren't you breathless with excitement?" she asked me.

"Now that you mentioned it, it does seem like I'm having trouble breathing," I said dryly.

"I knew you'd love it." She hugged me before rushing past the circulation desk. "Today's the day," she continued to sing over and over as she headed through the library to her desk in the computer mainframe room.

Today was the library's grand reopening. A ceremony was scheduled for ten o'clock that morning. Local reporter Betty Crawley had already stationed herself on the front steps. I wondered if Mrs. Farnsworth would let Betty come inside to cover the event despite having banned her from our hallowed halls.

A banner hung in the library's foyer that proclaimed, "Town of Cypress Celebrates the Future."

There was going to be a ribbon cutting. The mayor was scheduled to give a speech. And then Anne would take over to give the reporters and residents a tour of the new facilities. (The tour was something Duggar would have done if he'd still been alive. And the fact that Anne was now going to get her time in the spotlight was evidence of motive—at least in my mind—for killing him.)

During this period of show-and-tell, I was scheduled to work the circulation desk and direct patrons with questions to either Mrs. Farnsworth or Anne. Mrs. Farnsworth had warned that if I wanted to keep my job, I wasn't to make any kind of personal commentary about the new library.

At nine forty-five, Mrs. Farnsworth unlocked the front doors. She was dressed in her best dark red dress with lace trim at the neckline. Her hair was styled a little differently. Large looping curls sat like iron pipes on the top of her head. It was a style that was popular locally in the late 1980s. The taller the hair, the better.

Some of the older ladies still went to the salon and paid top dollar to have their hair "done up." Apparently, Mrs. Farnsworth had shelled out the money to look her best today.

"You look nice," I told her as she passed by me.

"Nice is for sissies," Mrs. Farnsworth scolded without even glancing in my direction.

"Wow, did I hear Mrs. Farnsworth dish out some snark just now?" asked Delanie Messervey. Delanie was one of Cypress's top social leaders and past president of the Friends of the Library Association. She was the first patron to pass through the doors that morning. Her vintage pink dress with tiny white polka dots flared at the waist. She wore matching pink pumps and looked like a housewife that had escaped from an advertisement in a 1950s magazine. The style was catching fire with Cypress's society women. I expected to see more vintage dresses like hers before the morning was over.

I glanced down at my outfit—a light blue sweater set and sensible gray dress trousers—and wondered how I'd look in a dress like Delanie's. Not for today. But perhaps for a date night. On a date. With a man. A man whom I'd yet to meet.

I'd picked out my sweater set, trousers, and comfortable flats so I wouldn't be encumbered by my clothing. I wasn't sure what was going to happen today, and I wanted to be prepared for anything.

Delanie glanced back at the banner hanging in the foyer and clicked her tongue. "What Duggar did to this place doesn't feel like progress. I should have worn black. I feel like I'm attending a funeral instead of a celebration."

Although she seemed to be grumbling to herself, I waved her over to the desk. I loved Delanie. If the library needed something (like new books), she'd always found a way to raise the funds. She'd fought just as hard as the rest of us to save the library's printed books. Not even her promise of increased fundraising efforts had changed Duggar's mind.

"There is going to be a grand opening of another kind, a *secret* kind, at noon. In the basement," I leaned toward her to whisper.

"Really?" She leaned closer to me. "What do you have planned? Does it involve booze?"

"No. Books. Actual hold-in-your-hands books. And it's very hush-hush." I pressed a finger to my lips.

She did the same.

After a moment, she giggled. Her eyes sparkled. "It'll be a kind of protest? I can't wait to see what you have planned. It's always the quiet ones you have to watch."

"I've not done anything too shocking," I warned.

"Honey, the more shocking the better. I'm hoping the Wi-Fi crashes in the middle of the presentation or one of those funny printers in the other room blows up."

"Gracious, that would be a disaster," I said, holding back a laugh.

"At least it wouldn't be boring. Could you imagine the look on Mayor Goodvale's face if something went wrong? He'd turn all purple. And that's such a bad color for him. Oh, my, that was a terrible thing to say. I can't believe it came out of my mouth." She laughed. The loud braying sound caught Mrs. Farnsworth's attention. The older woman shushed us.

Delanie slapped a hand over her mouth, which only made her laugh harder. She waved her other hand at me as she hurried toward the bathroom.

"That poor woman," Tori said as she wandered over to the desk. "She's so broken up over what happened to her favorite place, she's lost her mind, not that she had much of a mind to lose in the first place."

"Actually, I told her about our *other* opening. I think it made her uncontrollably giddy."

"She wasn't on our list," Tori admonished.

"There is no list." Not officially. While we hadn't compiled a list of library patrons to invite to our basement opening, Tori, Flossie, and I had discussed whom we should invite. Over the past week, we'd quietly talked with longtime library patrons, especially those who were the most vocal about the changes to the library. For everyone else— especially those who couldn't keep a secret even if their life depended on it—we planned to let them borrow books out of my tote bag, without letting them in on the bookroom.

Flossie had argued against including Delanie because of her close relationship with Mrs. Farnsworth.

"Delanie was close to tears when she came in," I explained. "How could I not invite her into our new library? I'm sure if we explain things, she'll keep quiet."

Actually, I suddenly wasn't at all sure about that. Delanie and Mrs. Farnsworth belonged to the same book club. Delanie drove Mrs. Farnsworth to church on Sundays. They often shopped together.

The back of my neck started to burn. Had I just made a huge mistake? Would my secret bookroom be exposed even before I had a chance to open it?

Tori shook her head. "You know what Benjamin Franklin said about secrets. 'Three can keep a secret, if two of them are dead.'"

"Yes, but this is a library. I didn't take those books for myself. I did it for the community." The *entire* community. "It's a risk we'll be taking every time we invite someone downstairs to browse the shelves."

"But Delanie?" Tori said with a look of distaste.

"What do you have against her?" I asked.

She glanced over at Delanie. The older woman had returned from the bathroom, her makeup as fresh as ever. She was hugging Mrs. Farnsworth. "Nothing. What could I possibly have against her? She's a paragon. Well, I guess I should check out the competition. Is the library's coffee shop scheduled to open as well today?"

"Promptly after the ribbon cutting. They've hired two new employees to act as baristas."

"I know. They used to work for me. I trained them." She headed off in the direction of the new café, which used to be the children's section.

"I'm surprised to see *her* here. I would have thought this would be the last place she'd want to be. And today, of all days," Betty Crawley said as she came toward me. She, too, had picked a vintage dress for the occasion. Hers was slate gray. She'd even added a matching pillbox hat. It sat on top of her blonde pageboy hairdo. Her heels click-clacked on the terrazzo floor.

"Who?" I asked.

"Why, Miss Victoria Green, of course." She scanned the circulation desk as if searching for something.

"Tori is here to support me. Can I help you with—?"

Her eyes widened. "Right. I'd forgotten. Friends. You're Becket's girl? Trudy?"

"Trudell," I corrected.

"Of course. You and Tori have been friends since grade school, haven't you?"

It sounded like an accusation. "We are friends," I said cautiously.

"Right." She rubbed her jaw speculatively. "Well, I was just thinking the other day that it was a good thing your friend wasn't at the library during Duggar's death. She'd be the prime suspect instead of . . . oops. I mean . . ." She shrugged. "There's Delanie. I'd better go and offer her a shoulder to cry on. Maybe I can wrangle a good quote from her for the article I'm writing."

"Wait," I called to her. "Why would anyone suspect Tori of wishing the town manager dead?"

"Didn't you know? Perhaps the two of you aren't as close as people say." She feigned distress. "Oh, well, I'll tell you. Duggar had been sweet-talking a tech firm. They thought Cypress, with its easy access to Interstate 95 and reasonable land prices, would be an ideal place for their newest incubator offices. That's where a tech business works on new products and programs," she added.

"I know what an incubator business is. What does any of that have to do with Tori's supposed dislike of the town manager?" I was starting to lose my patience. Maybe if I waved my hands a little bit, Mrs. Farnsworth would notice and kick Betty out of the library again.

"There's no need to get snippy. I'm getting to that," she drawled. "The business Duggar was courting was looking mighty hard at buying some buildings downtown and renovating them. They were especially excited about the building on the corner of Main and Lake."

"That's where Perks is located." Tori owned that building.

"Ding. Ding. Give this girl a prize."

"The town manager was trying to get Tori to sell her business? That's ridiculous. Tori would never sell. Everyone knows that. She loves that place. She's put her heart and soul into renovating it."

"Oh, he knew that. I overheard him talking on the phone about it several weeks ago. He was working to get the building condemned and have the town take it using eminent domain. The paperwork was already in the pipeline when he died. But that's all been put on hold now, hasn't it? Perhaps the industry he was courting has even moved on by now. Your friend has certainly benefited from his death. Perhaps more than anyone else."

"That's ridiculous," I repeated. "Tori would never . . . could never . . ."

But as Betty walked away, her sights now set on Delanie, I couldn't help but worry.

Tori?

Why didn't she tell me about the trouble she was having with Duggar? We told each other everything. Why was this one thing such a big secret?

Oh, I hated the direction my thoughts were heading. No, it couldn't be true. Still, I couldn't stop myself from thinking it.

Did my best friend take matters into her own hands and rid herself of the threat to her coffee shop in a deadly way?

Chapter Fifteen

N̲o. No. No. Not Tori. I shook my head to chase away the crazy thoughts Betty had planted. I was still shaking my head—like a nut—when Mayor Goodvale and his son, Luke, came into the library.

"Good morning, Miss . . . um . . . er," the mayor said. He looked to his son for help. "Miss . . . ?"

Luke shrugged.

"Becket," I said without taking offense. I was used to people forgetting my name.

"Ah, Becket's girl. Y'all should be proud of the recognition the library is about to get. I heard that not one, but two national television news organizations will be on hand to cover the opening. One is here only because one of the reporters got wind of Duggar's unfortunate . . ." He cleared his throat. "And four national newspapers have sent reporters. The more coverage we get, the easier it'll be to restart our sales pitches to tech industries. Dare I say it? We're about to become the Silicon Valley of the South. Or perhaps we'll be known as the Silicon Foothills. There's enough sand in these hills to earn that name honestly." He laughed at the thought. "Perhaps it should be the Silicon Sandhills, or is that too redundant?"

South Carolina's sandhills were about fifty miles north of our town, but I figured it would be rude to correct him. Cypress was inside South Carolina's coastal plain. There was a reason the town was called Cypress. Our ground was wet enough and swampy enough to encourage the kind of cypress trees that flourished in swamps.

The mayor had latched his hands onto the lapels of his seersucker coat and had launched into what sounded like the speech he'd prepared for the opening.

Luke tugged on his arm. "Father, I think you should talk with Mrs. Farnsworth and make sure everything is ready." Unlike his father, Luke spoke quietly, and his eyes darted about.

"Yes. We should do that," the mayor said. "Keep this up, boy, and I might hire you as the new town manager."

"That's not my specialty," Luke was quick to say.

"Nonsense," the mayor countered. "You can do anything you put your mind to. All it takes is a little hard work and dedication. When I was your age, I was already manager of the feed and seed store."

"I know, Father." Luke's features relaxed. He was clearly in awe of his dad. "You have always been amazing."

The two of them were so wrapped up in their conversation that they left the desk without saying another word to me. I was used to that as well. "You're a good people person, Luke. Perhaps if you weren't so trusting, you'd not be in the—*um*—you'd still have that cushy job of yours."

The grand reopening celebration was about to begin. Town Council members started streaming through the doors along with camera operators, reporters, Police Chief Fisher, and Detective Ellerbe.

No sign of Jace Bailey. I'm not sure why, but I breathed easier knowing he wasn't around.

Without Duggar to direct everyone, spectators and reporters jockeyed for the best positions and the mayor second-guessed where Mrs. Farnsworth had told him to stand. Eventually, though, everyone settled in their places and the ribbon was cut. Mrs. Farnsworth, standing to the right of Mayor Goodvale, looked as if she had an abscessed tooth. Anne Lowery, standing to his left, bounced on the balls of her feet like an energetic child.

I remained stationed at the circulation desk, happy to be away from the crowded foyer. The mayor cleared his throat several times before beginning a long speech that eulogized Duggar while also praising the local police and promoting the town's technological advances.

"It's a load of hogwash, if you ask me," someone beside me whispered.

I turned to find Krystal Capps, the town coroner, leaning against the desk. Her pink-tinted gray hair was slightly messy. She was dressed in a pink T-shirt that was tucked into the elastic waist of her jeans.

"At least I'm visiting the library under better circumstances today. Last week—" She blew out a sharp breath. "Today isn't much better, mind you." She looked around with a wistful expression. "I grew up with this library. Every week my mother would bring me and let me pick out three books. I used to think the library limited how many books a child could check out. It wasn't until I was an adult that I discovered that it was my mother's doing. When I asked her about it, she told me that she didn't want me to be greedy. There were other children in the town who needed those books as badly as I did." She sighed. "We were all poor as dirt back then. And yet, since we were all poor, no one seemed to really mind."

"Many of us are still that poor," I whispered.

Krystal shook her head. Her pink hair did a little dance. "It's all changing. I remember when you could trade a shotgun for a lake house. Now, you have to compete with the Richie Riches who want to tear down the cottages and build mansions. You think the changes to this library are bad? Just wait and see what happens to the entire town in five years. I bet we won't even be able to afford to stay in our own homes."

Mayor Goodvale had finished his speech. He cleared his throat and then introduced his son by espousing the young man's technological brilliance. "He's been my man behind the scenes, lending his expertise to our library's and our town's transformation."

Anne, still standing on the left side of the mayor, stiffened. She suddenly looked as if she wanted to punch someone.

"Oh, dear," I whispered. "This isn't how Anne envisioned the ceremony."

"How's that?" Krystal leaned closer to me.

"Anne expected to be introduced now."

Luke stammered his way through a statement about how technological advances have helped transform our lives. Clearly, he'd not prepared for this moment in the spotlight.

Anne had.

Yet she was stuck standing mutely beside the mayor. Overlooked. Ignored.

As much as I disagreed with her methods, and despite suspecting her of putting an early end to Duggar's life, I felt for her. I knew what the sting of invisibility felt like.

The mayor interrupted his blundering son. Luke looked relieved. Mayor Goodvale grabbed hold of the lapels of his suit jacket. He cleared his throat. Paused. And then announced that he was going to take the reporters on a tour of the library's grand improvements. He'd apparently forgotten his promise to Anne that she could lead the tour of the library.

"Be sure to note in your news reports," the mayor said, "how my son was my consultant and mastermind behind this groundbreaking work. And he did it without compensation from the town. That's how much he believes in what we are doing."

Anne, clearly not able to take being left out of the opening celebration a moment longer, put her hand on the mayor's sleeve. "Sir," she said, her voice a little too forceful, "I believe I should show the press around and tell them about the changes and plans *I* made. The town manager and *I* worked closely together on making sure no library in the country will rival ours. I want to make sure everyone here understands that."

Mayor Goodvale's face turned pink around the edges, but his smile never wavered. "Yes, yes, my dear." He patted her on the head. "This little girl standing next to me is Mrs. Farnsworth's assistant librarian."

I ground my teeth. *I was Mrs. Farnsworth's assistant librarian.* Anne was the digital and emerging technologies librarian.

"She's been helping Luke set up the library and making sure all the computers are up and running correctly. While I'm busy with the press, she'll lead tours for the residents here today. I'm sure everyone is eager to hear about how the library will improve their lives."

Anne tried again to speak up for herself. Mayor Goodvale spoke over her. Clearly, she wasn't used to the slick political tactics the mayor had learned in the good-old-boy system.

Anything Anne did to assert herself now would only make her look like a disobedient child, because that was how the mayor had introduced her. As a "little girl," a child.

Again, I felt a pinch of sympathy for her.

She'd worked hard and had expected much more than a crumb of attention.

The mayor, still looking pleased with himself, hooked his arm with his son's and led the press through the library. From what I could hear as his voice boomed from the main part of the library, he wasn't providing any technical information. He was only saying over and over again how cutting-edge the library had become and how high-tech industries would be begging to locate their factories in the town.

I had to give Anne credit. Instead of stomping off in a snit, she led the residents on a different route through the library, giving them the presentation she'd prepared for the press.

Both groups disappeared from view. Their voices gradually faded away.

"Well, that didn't disappoint," Krystal said with a laugh. "I'm glad I made time to come watch the show. Although I had suspected you to be the one to make the scene."

"Me? I would never—"

"No. I suppose not." She tapped her chin. "You're too crafty for that, aren't you?"

I didn't know how to reply to that. So I didn't. Instead, I asked her if she had any new information about either Duggar's murder or the break-in at Charlie's store. She feigned ignorance. But there was a twinkle in her eye that said otherwise. The police department was tiny. I'd heard from more than one source that there were very few secrets kept within those walls.

Despite my efforts to get Krystal to dish some dirt, she remained tight-lipped. Eventually our conversation turned to happenings around town.

Over an hour later, the crowd of reporters returned to the foyer. They were still paying court to the mayor. He lapped up the attention with the excitement of a child on Christmas morning. Luke must have given up trying to pretend he knew what was going on. He was nowhere in sight. Mrs. Farnsworth came out of her office. She frowned at the mayor, who was still talking much too loudly for a library setting. She then noticed the touring public, who were wandering around looking at things without Anne as their guide. Her frown deepened. She marched off toward the back of the library.

And that was that. I glanced at my watch. I hadn't seen Tori in a while. Where had she gone? In a little less than an hour, I would take my lunch break so Flossie, Tori, and I could direct an opening of our own.

In a way, it was ironic how the upstairs library's grand reopening occurred pretty much how Duggar would have planned it: sharing the credit for his work with only one person—the mayor. Anne may have wanted to be seen as the genius behind the library's revolution, but that was never going to happen.

"It's as if Duggar's murder didn't accomplish anything," I mused.

"Not so loud," Krystal warned. Her perfectly plucked eyebrows shot up. "The walls have ears."

My gaze followed hers, and I spotted Jace dressed in jeans, a gray Oxford shirt, and a blue blazer. He leaned against the wall not ten feet away.

When had he come in?

His arms were crossed over his chest. He looked undeniably grim as he watched me.

"Walls indeed," I grumbled.

He straightened and then started to cross the room toward us.

I wracked my brain to come up with something snarky to say to him, something like, "Still investigating the murder? I have a hammer in my shed that might interest you."

Yes, that. That's what I should say to him.

I stood. Drew a long breath. Opened my mouth to say exactly that when—

Someone screamed.

"Stay here," Jace ordered. With his hand moving toward the inside of his blazer where a gun was most likely holstered, he took off running toward the screamer. Krystal and I exchanged looks of horror before we both took off running after him.

Chapter Sixteen

⸺ ∘ ⸺

Fueled by a burst of adrenaline, I surged ahead of Krystal, who was starting to breathe heavily. I rounded a corner and found Delanie standing at the doorway to one of the recording studios. Her hands trembled as she held them beside her cheeks. And she was screaming. She looked like one of the hysterical girls in those old videos featuring The Beatles coming to the United States for the first time.

Jace moved her aside. He had his gun drawn as he cautiously entered the small room.

I peeked through the doorway and spotted Luke Goodvale. He was sprawled on his back on the ground, his arms spread wide. Blood oozed from a gash in his forehead and matted in his blond hair. The skin around his eyes was already starting to swell.

"Was he in a fight?" I asked Delanie, who was still screaming.

I grabbed her arms, turned her away from the doorway, and forced her to look at me. She blinked. "Shhh . . . It's going to okay," I soothed. "What happened?"

"He-he-he—" she stuttered.

Krystal knocked into me as she ran—huffing and puffing—into the room. She immediately dropped to Luke's side and pressed a finger to the pulse point on his neck. "Get the mayor," she ordered. "And call EMS. He's alive."

As she spoke, Luke groaned.

"He's going to be okay," I told Delanie.

She nodded tearfully. "He-he-he—" she stammered again.

A crowd was forming behind us. I glanced around, searching for Tori. Why hadn't she come running? I could use her help with Delanie. Tori had always been much better than me at dealing with hysterical people. I hadn't seen my friend since she went to check out the café. Where had she disappeared to?

Police Chief Fisher swore as he pushed his way through to the front. "Stay back," he ordered.

"He-he-he—" Delanie stuttered in response.

I didn't move. I had a feeling that if I let go of Delanie, she'd collapse. She'd started swaying.

"Breathe," I commanded.

I wondered where Detective Ellerbe had gone.

Jace emerged from the room. He'd holstered his gun. "I'm going to do a quick sweep of the library," he told Fisher. He barely glanced in my direction before pushing into the crowd.

"Everyone needs to back up," Mrs. Farnsworth said in that firm, whispery voice of hers. The crowd parted as if they were the Red Sea and she was Moses. She walked over to where I was still holding Delanie upright. She flicked a look into the studio room before focusing on her friend.

"You've had a shock," she said to Delanie. "Come with me. Sit in the quiet of my office. I'll buy you a coffee. Apparently, instead of lending books, my library now sells coffee."

"He-he-he—" Delanie stammered, while nodding.

"Can you find out what she's trying to say?" I asked Mrs. Farnsworth. "She keeps repeating the same thing. It might be evidence."

"I'm sure the police will question her when they're ready," Mrs. Farnsworth answered, rebuking me. "You need to do your job and get this place under control." She straightened her already starched spine. "Quietly," she added.

"Yes, ma'am." I tried to disperse the crowd, but most of them seemed determined to stay and watch. And more were coming, including a camera crew from one of the national news organizations and Betty Crawley, who was carrying a camera with a long telephoto lens attachment. The last thing the library needed was video or photos of the mayor's son, bloodied and battered, playing on endless loops on news shows. It would be a disaster for the town's plan to attract high-paying jobs. No industry would want to move to a town where people were attacked at the library.

I quickly pulled the door to the recording studio closed, and then I held up my hands. "There's nothing to see here. A member of the community has collapsed. But everything is being taken care of. Medical personnel have been called and are on their way."

"Didn't I see the coroner go in that room?" an older woman asked.

"Yes, you did. She has a medical degree. She's taking care of the man who collapsed."

"Who is it?" Betty yelled.

"Shh," came my automatic reply. "This is a library. Please, let's all respect this institution and respect the privacy of the man who is ill. If he wants to talk to the press, he can do so when he is able. Ah, here is the mayor. Please, let him come through. I'm sure he'll want to personally make sure everything here is under control."

"Yes, thank you, Miss . . . um . . ."

"Becket," I supplied.

"Becket's girl. Right." He lowered his voice. "What's going on? Why was I pulled away from my press conference?"

"Because of this." I opened the door just wide enough for the mayor to slip through. I followed him inside the room. "Someone hurt your son."

Krystal was still crouched beside Luke. The police chief had squatted down on the other side of the young man. They had helped him into a sitting position and were keeping him propped up by holding on to his arms. Krystal had pressed a cloth handkerchief against the deep gash on Luke's head. It was already soaked through.

"Do you remember what happened?" Chief Fisher was asking.

Luke moved as if he were drunk. He glanced over at his father and paled. "No. It happened so . . . came at me from behind . . . I . . . I didn't see who." It sounded as if someone had stuffed cotton into his mouth.

Mayor Goodvale sighed. "Is he going to be okay?"

"He's pretty banged up," Krystal said. "Have the ER doctor order an MRI to make sure there's no internal bleeding. But honestly, I've seen worse damage from bar fights down at the Lakeside Tap." She smiled kindly at Luke. "He'll heal up just fine."

"Are you sure you didn't see—?" Fisher asked again.

"Didn't you hear my boy? He said whoever attacked him came at him from behind." It had clearly upset the mayor to see his son injured. "Stop badgering him. Where is that ambulance? You did call one? Or do I need to do everything around here?"

"It should be pulling into the parking lot just about now." Fisher stood up. "I will need to talk to your boy some more. When he's feeling better. If you'll excuse me, I'd like to find my detective and see if he's found any witnesses."

As he left, a pair of EMTs rushed into the room with a stretcher. I pushed the door closed behind them and kept out of the way in the cramped space. Krystal spoke quietly to the EMTs, who swiftly took charge. The mayor insisted they transport Luke to the Medical University in Charleston, which was nearly two hours away.

While all this was happening, I quietly wondered how someone who was attacked from behind would end up with a blossoming black eye and a deep cut on his forehead.

Simple answer: he wouldn't.

Luke was lying. But why? And how was his attack related to Duggar's murder?

Was it related?

I needed to find out what Delanie had seen that had upset her so severely. And I needed to find out who would do something like this in the first place.

Chapter Seventeen

Noon arrived too quickly. My nerves were still sparking. Someone had beat up the mayor's son? In the library? I still couldn't believe it.

The library had been my sanctuary, my refuge. The old building was as sacred as a church. Its books were like angels. But the town had taken away the books. Did the loss of its guardians trigger the end of the library's sanctuary status?

If people didn't feel safe here, they'd stop coming. If no one used the library, the town would cut its funding, close it down. The historic building would become yet another vacant space in a town already overrun with vacant spaces.

Hopefully, the secret bookroom would be enough of a lure to keep people coming and keep the library healthy and vital. If not, I'd have to think of something else to do. I would not let this place die. *I could not.*

"What are you thinking about?" Jace asked as he walked up to the circulation desk. He'd been interviewing everyone who'd been in the building at the time of Luke's attack. "The look on your face is pretty scary."

I told him the truth, that I was worried about the library. "We have to keep this building a safe place. I'm not going to let someone ruin my library."

"Your library?" His brows shot up.

"You know what I mean."

"I'm afraid I do," he said, giving me a look that made me doubt he'd ever understand.

I didn't mean it was my library and mine alone. The library belonged to me and him and to everyone in this town. But I didn't feel like arguing. "Did anyone see Luke's attack, or at least see something suspicious? Certainly, someone saw *something*."

"You know I can't talk about that." He sighed. "But no. No one seems to have the slightest clue about what is going on."

"Not even Delanie? She was so upset. Didn't she see who did that to Luke?"

"I interviewed her. Fisher talked with her. Even Mrs. Farnsworth tried to get her to remember any small detail that perhaps she's repressed. And . . . nothing. She claims she just happened to peek into the room and found Luke like that."

"Did you find out what she was trying to say to me?" I couldn't forget how she'd kept sputtering, "He-he-he—"

"She says she was trying to tell you that Luke needed help. She was afraid he was dead."

"The poor woman. It must have been quite a shock. At least Luke is going to be okay. He is, isn't he?"

"I don't know. I hope so."

"You don't think this attack is related to Duggar's murder? It isn't, is it?" I asked.

"I don't see how it could be." But he frowned as he considered it. "Did you—?"

"Drat!" I noticed the time on the wall clock. It was already a few minutes past noon, which meant I was late for the library's second grand reopening of the day. "I've got to take my lunch break." I jumped up from my chair. I needed to get downstairs.

No press hordes.

No crowds.

Only a handful of people whom we'd personally invited.

I tried to act casual as I speed-walked toward the stairs leading down to the basement. Jace followed. Of course he followed. It was turning into that kind of day.

"It seems like you're in a hurry," he said.

"If I don't eat on a regular schedule, I sprout horns and turn into an absolute monster. No one wants that."

"You, hangry? That's hard to picture. But I'm starting to think you have all sorts of hidden depths underneath your plain, mild-mannered librarian's assistant facade."

"Assistant librarian," I corrected. "And you're wrong. What you see is who I am."

"Hmmm . . . Maybe I should join you for lunch," he said, sounding perfectly happy to be a thorn in my side. "You could tell me about—"

"My mother tells me that I should have my lawyer with me for any formal police interviews."

"You have a lawyer?" He stumbled over his feet.

I'd reached the stairs. I couldn't let him follow me down to the basement, not with readers waiting beside the vault's doors, eager to see the secret bookroom. All morning, I'd directed the most dedicated book-reading, secret-keeping library patrons to sneak down the back stairs when they had finished the upstairs tour.

"Look." I tried not to sound panicked, but everything that was happening in my library made me feel out of control. "You know I didn't see anything this morning. You were standing by the circulation desk watching me and listening in on my conversation with the coroner while someone was beating on Luke's face. So, please, let me have a moment to myself. I don't want to think about murder, or how you believe I had something to do with Duggar's death because I own a hex-head screwdriver, and I certainly don't want to think about how my library is no longer a safe place."

He opened his mouth. Closed it. His shoulders dropped. "I was going to ask you about Dewey."

"You were?"

He pulled a small rubber squeak toy shaped like a fish out of his pocket. "I saw this and thought he might like it."

"Oh, thank you." I stuffed the fish into my pocket. It squeaked. "And he's . . . um . . . good. Putting on weight. I need to go." I hurried down the steps marked "Employees Only" and said a prayer of thanks when he didn't follow me.

Downstairs, a small crowd had gathered around the vault's thick double doors. Flossie was already inside. She and Charlie had spent the morning tackling last-minute tasks to make sure everything was ready. Delanie noticed me first. She gave me a wide smile. Hubert Crawford, the president of Cypress's museum board, thrust two thumbs up. He nudged Lottie Hayworth, who held up one of the historical romances that I had already lent her. "This is wonderful, dear. I've finished this one and am ready to check out another," she whispered.

Tori spotted me. "There you are. I was worried something had happened." She wrapped her hand around my arm and pulled me to the front of the group.

"Where have you been?" I whispered to her.

"Around." Her right hand was wrapped in a makeshift bandage.

"What happened?" For the first time in our friendship, I wasn't sure I wanted to know.

"Nothing." She hastily hid her hand behind her back. "We can talk later. Right now, you have a library to open."

Charlie gave me an encouraging nod. I cleared my throat before saying, "I'm not one for making speeches. But since today is an extremely important day for this town, I'm going to make an exception. As you know, I have devoted my life to our library. I've done so because I firmly believe in the power of books and how essential they are to our lives. While I understand the reason behind the changes that are taking place upstairs, I do not agree with the outcome. Removing physical books from a library is like removing a beating heart from a man. The heart is the driving force that keeps our bodies alive."

I suddenly thought of Duggar and Luke. Duggar was the driving force at the heart of the town's redevelopment efforts. Mayor Goodvale had hinted that Luke would take over that role. Did Tori see Luke as a threat to her coffee shop?

"I . . . um . . ." I'd forgotten what I was saying.

The police would never suspect her of murder. They had no way of knowing she was at the library the morning Duggar was killed.

"Um . . ." What was I going to do?

I looked out at the familiar faces of my book-loving friends. They were here because I'd rebelled against Duggar's grand plans. I'd acted so out of character that I still could hardly believe it myself. Had Tori also done something drastic to save her coffee shop?

"To quote someone who has had to fight for access to books and education from a very young age, Malala Yousafzai. She said, 'Let us remember: One book, one pen, one child, and one teacher can change the world.' And with that, let us open these doors and change our corner of the world."

There was a smattering of quiet applause as Tori pushed the double doors open.

The familiar smell of mildew, dust, and paper—scents that had been erased from the library upstairs—flavored the air in the secret bookroom. It was as comforting as the aroma of chocolate chip cookies baking in my grandmother Mimsy's oven.

Dewey stood at the threshold. His tail held high, he greeted everyone who came into our secret bookroom with a soft meow.

During the past week, we had added several of the shelving units that the city workers had carried down to the basement for storage. The walls were covered with books and there were four additional aisles of books. We had a popular fiction section, a children's section, and a large nonfiction section. I'd even created a local documents area in the far-right corner.

My fellow booklovers cooed happily when they entered the room. They pulled books from the shelves, piling them in their arms.

"The collection isn't as extensive as what we once had," Ashley Morgan, one of our younger patrons, mused. "But it is something. A start."

"A blessing. I'm so happy you took matters into your own hands," Gary Larsen, the lawyer my mother had hired to represent me, whispered. He was holding a tower of books that looked as if it might topple over at any minute. I showed him to the desk where he could check them out.

We still didn't have a computer. Flossie manned the desk. She pulled a card from a pocket in the front flap, wrote down who checked out the book on the line, and then slipped a stamped "return by" book slip into the pocket. The public lapped up the nostalgic feeling.

"It's like stepping back in time," Hubert Crawford remarked. "I cannot thank you enough for what you've done."

I thanked him for his support. We planned to be open whenever possible. I'd sneak down to work the stacks when I could, and Flossie had volunteered to work in the secret bookroom whenever she was at the library to write. And if no one was available to staff the desk, the patrons could check themselves out on an honor system. Setting up the bookroom this way seemed safe enough. In all the years that I'd worked at the library, I'd never seen Mrs. Farnsworth come down into the basement. If something needed to be done down here, she'd always send me to complete the task. Anne viewed the basement as a place where only the maintenance staff ventured. And the small maintenance staff supported what I'd been doing down here. Three of them were here today checking out books.

"Please, remember, we're a rogue library," Flossie cautioned each patron at the desk. "If discovered, the town will likely make us close down. You are welcome to invite your neighbors, but only if you trust they can keep a secret. You know whom you can tell. They're the same ones who'll take a recipe to the grave before sharing it."

As we neared the end of the hour, the bookroom had mostly cleared out. A few residents were still wandering up and down our short stacks, collecting books to take home or browsing the reference section area.

"Charlie told me what happened up there." Flossie pointed to the ceiling. "Why would anyone want to hurt the mayor's boy? He only moved home a few weeks ago. Kind of soon to be stirring up that much trouble."

"How did he hear about Luke's attack?" I asked. Charlie was across the room, flipping through the pages of an old yellowed volume of Sherlock Holmes mysteries. "I thought he was helping you all morning."

"He left for about an hour after taking a phone call. Said he wanted to look around upstairs."

"I didn't see him upstairs."

"That doesn't surprise me." She leaned forward over the desk. "I think he was lying. I think he went to deal with whatever that phone call was about."

"You don't think the call involved Tori?" I couldn't stop thinking about her bandaged hand and how she'd tried to hide it.

"Honey"—she shook her head—"I don't know what's going on."

"What are you talking about? It looks serious," Tori asked.

"Luke," I answered.

"You," Flossie said at the same time.

"Me and Luke?" Tori shuddered. "That boy is too young for me. And too skinny."

"You do know someone attacked him?" I demanded.

"Yeah, I heard. Everyone's heard." She rolled her eyes toward the ceiling.

"Where did you go this morning? What happened to your hand?" I pressed.

"This?" She eased her bandaged hand out from behind her back. "It's nothing."

"If it's nothing, there's no reason you can't tell us what happened to it." I hated feeling distrustful. Tori was my best friend.

"I—" She sucked in a sharp breath. "Wait. You just said you were talking about me and Luke? You don't think that I hit him?" She shook her bandaged fist at me. "Why would I want to hit that scrawny little guy?"

"I don't know. Perhaps because the town is trying to sell your shop to a tech company?" I crossed my arms over my chest and tried to pretend my feelings weren't hurt.

She snorted. "Yeah, I'm angry about that. Duggar had no right to call Perks a blight. And anyhow, I know how to punch a guy without hurting my hand. I—" She shook her bandaged hand at me again. "Wait a minute. Where did you hear about Duggar's plans for Perks?"

"Certainly not from you." I half turned away from her.

"Who told you?" Tori pressed.

"Betty told me."

"That pointy-nosed tea spiller? She might call herself a reporter, but she's nothing more than a big-mouthed gossipmonger. She'd do well to keep her mouth shut about my business, if she knows what's good for her."

"Shhh . . . ," Flossie admonished, waving her hands like twin stop signs. "Now is not the time to go slinging threats around, not unless you're looking to park your butt in a jail cell."

Tori closed her eyes and huffed.

"Why didn't you tell us you were having trouble?" I asked, pitching my voice low.

"You really have to ask? It's because you had enough to worry about with the changes to the library, Tru. The trouble at my shop was nothing I couldn't handle on my own."

I put my hand on her shoulder. I started to tell her that she didn't need to do these things on her own, that I was there to help her. Always.

"Y'all can sing Kumbayah later," Flossie said. "Now hug and make up. There are more serious matters we need to discuss. Like, who in blazes is that guy?"

"Who?" I looked around and only saw friendly faces.

Flossie shrugged. "Funny. There was a guy standing right there staring at us. But he's—poof—vanished."

"Seeing ghosts again?" Tori nudged Flossie's shoulder. "Instead of wondering about our quiet patrons, I think we need to talk about Luke Goodvale getting beat up. Who would do something like that? And why?"

"Anne has a motive," I said.

Tori sighed long and loud. "Tru, you certainly have a chip on your shoulder when it comes to that girl. Sure, Luke is a scrawny guy, but I can't picture petite Anne beating on our mayor's boy."

"Why not?" I fisted my hands on my hips. "Women are just as capable as men."

"Often more capable," Tori agreed. "But—"

"But nothing." It was easier to suspect Anne of wrongdoing than to wonder about why my best friend continued to change the subject instead of telling me what had happened to her hand. "Anne had expected to get full credit for what she's done to our library. But, instead, Mayor Goodvale showered all of his praise on his son's head. He didn't even mention her name. Not once. You should have seen her. She looked angry enough to beat someone senseless."

"If that's the case, then why didn't Luke identify his attacker?" Tori asked.

"Did you see anything?" Flossie asked Tori before I could.

She started to say something but stopped herself. Her delicate brows creased as she frowned. "No. But the library was crowded. There were people at the opening I'd never seen before. And I know pretty much everyone in town. Don't forget how Number One was on the town council and was a professional politician. He taught me the value of staying connected with the community."

Her first ex-husband currently held a seat in the U.S. House of Representatives. While Tori had enjoyed his political aspirations and playing hostess at countless parties and fundraising events, she had not approved of his willingness to jump in bed with anyone who might advance his career, which was what had ultimately led to the end of their marriage.

"You think an outsider attacked Luke?" I asked.

Tori shrugged.

I wasn't convinced. I explained to them how Luke had told the police that he was attacked from behind even though all of his injuries were on his face. "Why would he do that? I'll tell you why: because he's scared. Anne is a killer, and she's downright scary when she's angry."

"I agree with you about one thing," Flossie said. "It does sound like he's too scared to talk. But let me give you an alternative reason for his fear. He saw Duggar's killer that day at the library. And the killer—who might not be Anne—is trying to silence him."

"No, no, no," I protested. "That sounds more like a plot from a thriller than real life. Besides, he couldn't have seen anything that morning. He was with his father at the time of Duggar's murder."

"What are the three of you whispering about over here?" Charlie asked. His eyes twinkled with mischief. "Something good, I imagine."

"We're talking about how good you look in your suit," Tori lied. She wrapped her arm around his. She nearly wrapped her entire body around him. "Did you have it specially made for your body?"

"As a matter of fact, I did. I was in Hong Kong two years ago." While he told an amusing story about how he'd accidentally ordered a three-piece custom suit when trying to ask for directions to his hotel, I watched a stout man with huge arms and thinning black hair walk through the children's section. Was that the stranger Flossie had seen? He headed toward the back corner where the local records were shelved.

"Best mistake I've ever made," Charlie concluded. He ran his hands down the side seams of the suit jacket. "Fits better than any of my Burberry suits."

"Excuse me." I skirted around both Tori and Flossie. Tori was giggling like a smitten schoolgirl while Flossie was trading stories with Charlie, telling him about the time she and her husband had lived in Hong Kong.

I followed the stranger and found him in the back corner of the room flipping through our only copy of the local phone book. "May I help you?"

He turned toward me, sneered, and returned to flipping through the phone book. His back was slightly hunched, but instead of implying weakness, the hunch made his wide shoulders appear even wider.

He wasn't someone I'd ever seen at the library. And he had the kind of face one remembered. After dark. In nightmares.

Who could have invited him, a stranger, to our bookroom? I suppose he could have been someone's relative or friend who had tagged along for the opening.

"Are you new in town? Perhaps I can help you find whatever it is you're looking for."

This time he didn't even look in my direction. He grunted and then ripped a page right out of the phone book.

"Hey!" I couldn't believe what I'd just seen. He hadn't even ripped the page out cleanly. The jagged edges taunted me. "You . . . you can't do that."

He dropped the phone book on the floor and took a step toward me.

I suppose I should have felt afraid. But seeing the phone book on the ground with its cover bent and then seeing him crumple the torn page before stuffing it into his jeans pocket ignited a rage inside me. "Sir, if you can't treat our collection with care, you will need to leave. Immediately."

His lip curled as if amused. "No one tells me——"

Someone behind me cleared his throat. The man froze. His gaze shifted past my shoulder.

"Was leaving anyhow," he grumbled as he lumbered like an enormous raccoon down the aisle.

I whirled around to see who had frightened that horrible man and found Charlie with a strange smile on his face.

"Do you know him?" I demanded.

"Know him?" Charlie crossed his arms over his chest.

"Who is he? He ruined the library's phone book. What kind of monster does that?"

He sighed. "He shouldn't be here," he said and started to walk away.

"But who is he?" I followed him. Clearly, he knew the man. "What is he doing down here, in the library's secret bookroom? How did he find out about this place? I need to——"

He grabbed my arm with a startling jolt. "Don't pursue this, Tru. Don't ask about Grandle. Don't even think about him. When it comes to guys like that, a ruined phone book is the least of your concerns. If you see him again, walk the other way. Do you understand me?"

No, I didn't. I didn't understand any of this. But his grip had tightened, and quite honestly, he was scaring me. So I nodded.

"Good." His hands dropped to his side. "I need to get back to my shop." He turned and left me standing there feeling too stunned to run after him. I had to wonder, yet again, what was happening to our peaceful small town.

It seemed as if it was just yesterday when you knew the people around you. You knew their parents and their grandparents too. You didn't have to lock your doors. Now, there were robberies and murders and vicious attacks. If this was progress, I didn't want any part of it.

Chapter Eighteen

———•———

After the library had closed for the day, I went down to the bookroom to collect Dewey and turn off the lights. I'd told Mrs. Farnsworth that I'd leave through the basement's back door. Ever since I'd started sneaking Dewey into work with me, I'd been leaving through the back exit. At first, Mrs. Farnsworth had acted suspicious. Now, it was simply odd behavior from her otherwise efficient assistant librarian.

When my kitty saw me, he gave a happy meow and jumped into a travel carrier that looked like an oversized tote bag. I'd taken him to the town's vet the Saturday after finding him. She'd confirmed that Dewey was indeed a male cat. She deemed him a healthy one-year-old tabby, although quite underweight.

He head-butted my hand. I scratched behind his ears, earning a loud purr. He butted his head against my hand again.

"Let's get you home, little guy. We can play more there. Plus, there's a can of stinky fish waiting for you."

When I started to zip the carrier closed, Dewey bit my hand. Hard.

"Ouch!" I hugged my hand to my chest. "What did you do that

for?" He didn't answer. Of course he didn't. He was a cat. He didn't even look sorry as he jumped out of the carrier. "Where are you going?"

I checked my hand. It stung, but his sharp teeth hadn't broken the skin. That little troublemaker! I jumped up and chased after him.

He was making a dash for the vault's thick double doors. I hadn't pushed them all the way closed. Though they'd been left open only a sliver, it was enough for a skinny cat to shimmy through. I tossed open the doors and made it into the basement's hallway in time to watch him scamper up the stairs.

"Dewey!" I whisper-yelled. I'm not sure why I bothered. He didn't stop.

Had Mrs. Farnsworth left yet?

Had Anne?

He'd behaved so well all week. What was Dewey doing? Why had he bitten me?

I took the steps two at a time and quickly reached the main library. The space still felt foreign and cold without the rows of shelving filled with books. I wondered if I would ever get used to the changes.

Without the shelves, Dewey had fewer places to hide. Or so I thought. He scurried toward a row of computers and disappeared in the shadow of the tables.

Hitching his carrier's strap higher on my shoulder, I hurried after him. *"Dewey,"* I whispered and clicked my tongue. *"Dewey! Come back here."*

Again, because he was a cat, he ignored me.

All I could do was hope I could catch him before he got himself into trouble. He emerged from under the tables and ran toward the media room, where Duggar had been killed. Like a well-trained minion, I followed. I watched, somewhat transfixed, as he sniffed the exact shelf that had toppled over onto Duggar. He then scratched at the base of the shelf.

This was my opening. I lunged forward to catch him. But my little

scamp saw me coming and skittered away, his nails clicking on the terrazzo floor. As he rounded a corner, heading directly toward Anne's
office, I noticed he had a ripped piece of paper hanging out of his
mouth.

Where did he get that?

I crouched down next to where he'd been scratching and found
nothing. With a sigh, I continued my pursuit of my errant cat. I didn't
have to go far. He'd stopped in front of Anne's open office door. The
lights inside were still on. Her machines were still humming.

I was about to make another mad dash to try to catch Dewey when
I heard Anne's voice. She sounded upset.

"Nothing is working out how I'd planned. Nothing," she sobbed.
"I don't know what to do."

I froze. Who was Anne talking to?

"Eavesdropping?" someone whispered in my ear.

I jumped. Once I'd prised myself off the ceiling, I whirled around to
find Jace standing directly behind me, a puzzled grin on his face. I put
my finger to my lips and then pointed to the open door. Dewey's ears
flicked front and back as he peered inside Anne's office.

"What—?" Jace started to ask.

He cut the question short when we both heard Anne say with an
exasperated sigh, "What happened to the mayor's son was an accident."
There was a pause. "Yes, I was angry!" she shouted. "It won't affect—"

She fell silent again.

Much to my chagrin, Dewey sauntered into Anne's office as if he
owned the place.

I stifled a yelp and started to go after my cat. Jace put a hand on my
shoulder.

"Wait," he mouthed.

"Nooo," Anne cried, her voice growing louder. I walked a few paces
to my left until Mrs. Farnsworth's office came into view. Her door was

partially open, but the lights inside had been turned off. She must have left for the day.

Good. If she spotted Dewey, she'd tear me to pieces, and I mean pieces that were smaller than what came out of the paper shredder she kept in her office.

"You told me that if I came to this little section of nowhere and did what I've done, you could get me nationwide front-page coverage. Why did the mayor ignore me? I thought you told me that you had every-thing under control, Auntie. That you would take care of getting me the recognition I deserve. But he handed it all over to that idiot son of his who can't even hold his own in a fight."

"Who is she talking to?" I mouthed.

Jace shrugged.

Dewey sauntered back out of Anne's office. He batted at the scrap piece of paper he'd been carrying in his mouth. He hit the paper back and forth, back and forth.

"I can't talk about this right now. I'm too upset. I don't know what I might do," she shouted.

A moment later, Anne stomped out of her office. She nearly stepped on poor Dewey. He hissed and ran over to me. Her startled gaze flicked from the cat to Jace and finally to me.

"What are *you* doing here?" she demanded.

"Chasing after my cat." I picked up Dewey. At the same time, Jace bent down and picked up the piece of paper Dewey had been using as a play toy. He stuffed it into his pocket without even looking at it. "I've been bringing him to work with me. I can't leave him home alone. He needs to eat three times a day. And if I leave a large amount of food in the bowl, he'll gobble it all down at once and throw it back up. As you can see, he's terribly underweight." All of which was one hundred percent true.

I carefully lowered Dewey into his carrier.

"You should hire someone to come and feed him in your own

home," Anne snapped. "You can't let him run around here. There's too much electronic equipment. He might damage something. If I see him here again, I'm going to have to tell Mrs. Farnsworth."

I pushed down the kneejerk anger that flared whenever she spoke to me. She was upset. Understandably so.

Had her anger flared like this earlier today? Did her anger make her violent? I already suspected her of killing Duggar to clear the way for her to take center stage. Had we just overheard her confessing to her aunt that she'd attacked Luke? Was this the proof I'd been hoping to find?

I drew a steadying breath before asking, "Are you okay?"

"Why would you care? You've tried to stop me from doing my job from the moment I've arrived."

Well, she was right about that.

"If you don't mind, Ms. Lowery, I'd like to talk with you about what happened here today," Jace said, slanting me a look I wasn't sure how to interpret.

Anne backed away from Jace. "I already told you what I know."

"Just a few follow-up questions."

Anne backed even farther away from him.

"Please, Ms. Lowery." He gestured toward a nearby seating area. "Just a few questions to help us catch whoever is responsible for the troubles that have plagued this library."

Anne gave a sharp nod. "I . . . I suppose I could spare a few minutes."

Jace gestured for Anne to precede him. I started to follow along. After all, I wanted to hear what she had to say. Would she break down and confess to attacking Luke? If she did, that would be a relief. I could stop wondering about Tori and her bandaged hand. And Charlie. I could stop wondering why he'd gone upstairs when he should have stayed in the basement helping Flossie.

We were nearly to the seating area when Jace turned toward me. "Don't you need to get home and feed Dewey his dinner?"

I refused to take the hint. "He should be fine for a few minutes."

"Tru"—he smiled that devastating smile that had the power to melt my knees—"go home."

I reluctantly left. Jace was finally taking my suspicions about Anne seriously. He would do the right thing. He would ask the right questions. I didn't, however, leave the building. There was a question that still needed to be answered.

Who was Anne's aunt?

Anne had told me that she used to spend summers at the lake with her aunt in Cypress. I'd taken that to mean that her aunt wasn't a resident of the town but had owned one of the seasonal cottages on the lake. Most lakefront homes were only used in the summer.

Yet from what I'd overheard from Anne's side of the phone conversation, it sounded as if her aunt was a powerful member of Cypress society instead of some nameless summer resident. Well, if that was the case, I knew exactly where to go to find the name of Anne's local auntie. I headed straight toward the library's South Carolina Room, where the local documents were stored.

I'd reached the door when I remembered how the renovations had changed everything.

The South Carolina Room was now a "teen hangout" space.

I spun on my heel and then raced back downstairs to our secret basement bookroom. There, in the far right corner, it was easy to find the papers I'd saved from the landfill. In less than ten minutes, I sat back in the wooden chair.

The name on the paper in front of me wasn't the name I'd expected to find. But there it was, in black-and-white. I bit my lower lip. She'd promised to help Anne? But I'd thought she was helping *me*.

Chapter Nineteen

———◦———

Delanie Messervey was Anne's aunt? If that was true— and, according to the papers I'd found, it was—why had Delanie pretended to be upset over the changes to the library? After all, Anne had told me herself that her aunt was the one who'd supported her move into town. She had encouraged it.

Why had I stupidly invited Delanie to the secret bookroom? I knew she was close friends with Mrs. Farnsworth. That should have been reason enough to keep my mouth shut around her. And now this?

I was still berating myself for being too trusting by the time I pulled into my driveway that evening. I groaned as I fed Dewey. I cursed under my breath as I changed into a pair of comfortable shorts and an old T-shirt. My stomach twisted as I glanced into my fridge. I quickly shut it again. I felt too upset to eat, which meant I was pretty upset. I rarely missed a meal.

Sitting on the living room floor playing with Dewey took my mind off, well, everything. Like a dog, my little kitty played fetch with the new toy fish Jace had bought for him. I'd squeak it and then throw it. He'd proudly carry it back to me and nudge my hand until I threw it again. The way he'd pounce and roll made him look like a furry ninja in training.

After a while, even his antics couldn't keep my mind from the library's reopening and the attack on Luke. Without really paying attention to my kitty, I tossed the toy fish. Dewey didn't return it. Instead, he jumped up onto his favorite chair—an old recliner my father had given me. The skinny kitty started to thoroughly clean the fish. Even across the room, I could hear the scrape, scrape, scrape of his rough pink tongue.

I pushed myself up from the rug and brushed at the cat hair clinging to my shorts.

Enough sitting around and moping. I needed to talk to Delanie. I needed to confront her.

But not alone.

I texted both Tori and Flossie and asked them to meet me at Perks in a half hour. I then texted Delanie and asked her to meet me there an hour after that. When she didn't reply right away, I told her that I needed to talk with her about undoing the changes Anne had made to the library. I figured that would get her attention.

It did.

She agreed to meet me.

For a Thursday night, Perks was crowded. Heck, I didn't remember ever seeing the place this crowded, not even during a Monday morning coffee rush.

"What's going on?" I asked Tori after air-kissing her cheeks. "Why's everyone here?"

"Sunshine Diner had a pipe burst about an hour ago and had to close its doors. And there's also him." She nodded toward the barista bar, where the crowd was the thickest. Even the police chief was there, eating a croissant.

"Who?" I craned my neck one way and then the other. I couldn't see who had captured everyone's attention.

"Luke," she said. "He checked himself out of the hospital. He said he needed a strong cup of Joe to fix his headache, not a hospital bed."

"Really?"

Tori grinned. "He's good for business."

"Who is?" Flossie asked as she rolled up beside us. Tori and I both air-kissed her cheeks before answering. Flossie whistled. "Where's the mayor?"

Tori shrugged. "Not here. He never comes here."

"Has Luke said anything about what happened to him?" Flossie asked. "He'll have to say something eventually." Luke had stepped into view. He was carrying one of Tori's extra-large cups. He had a slab of gauze taped to his forehead, and one eye was completely swollen closed. "It's not like his 'I was attacked from behind' story is going to hold up with him walking around looking like that. He's a mess."

"That's the truth," Tori said. "He doesn't look like the triumphant hero returning from a battle. He simply looks scrawny and beat up. I'm surprised he's showing his face in public at all."

I squinted as I watched him. Unlike at the library, where he'd been clearly uncomfortable and unprepared to play the role of technological wizard that his father had expected of him, here he worked the room with the same political effortlessness as his father. His smiles came easily. He joked with everyone around him as if they were all old friends. But there was something off about how he was acting. I didn't simply mean how he was superficial, like his father. No, there was something else, something I didn't realize I was noticing until he glanced over at the door for the fifth time.

He was watching for someone. He hadn't come to Perks to socialize or to convince the locals that he hadn't been seriously injured. It looked like he was here to meet someone.

"We should question him," Flossie said.

"Yes," Tori agreed. "I bet if I turn on my charm, I could get him to tell me what really happened in that little room. I'll sashay my hips like this"—she demonstrated—"and he'll tell me who hit him."

"It was Anne," I said.

"Not that again." Tori rolled her eyes as she looked up at the pressed tin ceiling.

"Honey, you've got to look beyond your feelings about that girl," Flossie said, gently. "You're hindering our investigation."

"I'm serious. This isn't about Anne calling me a dinosaur or making snide comments about how my job is irrelevant. I overheard her talking with Delanie on the phone. She practically confessed to attacking Luke. Jace was there. He heard her too." I drew a long breath. "Delanie is helping Anne."

"Have you lost your mind? You're accusing our Delanie of helping take apart the library? That can't be true." Flossie wheeled her chair toward me. "Delanie is a defender of the library. She's worked as hard as the rest of us to save those books."

Tori snorted.

"What?" Flossie demanded. "The Friends of the Library Association has raised more money in the past couple of years under Delanie's presidency than it has in the history of the organization."

Tori snorted again.

"Go on, say what you're thinking instead of hissing and spitting like an angry cat," Flossie demanded.

"All I'm saying is that she's not the paragon everyone thinks she is. And one day the truth will come out."

"I think that day is today," I said, still stinging over the realization that Delanie had been helping the enemy all along. "I invited her to meet us here. I hope you don't mind. I could use the support when I confront her."

"Why would we mind?" Flossie asked. "That's what friends do. Besides, I look forward to giving Delanie the chance to explain herself. I'm sure when her side of the story comes out, we'll all be friends again."

"I don't know about that. I'm glad to be here to help you pull her down from that high horse she rides around on, Tru," Tori said with a sly smile.

"That's not going to happen," Flossie said. "The both of you will see for yourselves that Delanie is honest and modest. She's not someone who rides around on a high horse."

We moved toward a table that had just opened up. Luke was still working the room like a pro. I considered sending Tori over there to work her wiles on him, but I needed her. Luke could wait. He was still watching that door the way Dewey watched that toy mouse of his. Just then the door swung open, and once again Luke's gaze flew over to the entrance. This time, though, he stopped mid-sentence and stared.

The man at the door was tall, slender, and devastatingly handsome. Nearly as handsome as the irritatingly good-looking Detective Bailey.

"Charlie's here," Tori cooed. Why would Luke be watching the door for Charlie? "Excuse me for a moment." She hurried over toward Charlie.

Cypress's new bookseller wasn't looking in our direction. He scanned the room until he spotted Luke. The two men nodded at each other.

Luke's smile grew wider but tighter. He turned back to the man he'd been talking to. He laughed. Everything seemed to go back to normal for him. But he kept looking over his shoulder in Charlie's direction. Tori brushed a kiss on Charlie's cheek before wrapping her arm around his. She pulled him to the front of the line at the barista counter. And all the while, Luke kept watch. All the while, the mayor's son's smile grew tighter.

What was going on here? Was Luke jealous of Tori and Charlie?

"Did you know Luke before he moved away?" I asked Tori when she returned to our table. She carried a tray with three mugs of coffee and (bless her) three chocolate croissants.

"Not really. He must have still been in elementary school when we were in high school. Remember, I married Number One right out of high school."

She had. Number One was twenty years older than she was. In some towns, their marriage might have caused a scandal. Here in Cypress, where jobs were scarce and nearly everyone was poor, most folks congratulated Tori for hitching her wagon to such a fancy horse to ride out of town on.

"Do you think Luke had a crush on you?" Flossie asked. "That boy has been watching you ever since Charlie stepped foot in Perks." She sniffed the coffee before setting it aside. "Still not selling Coke?"

"What? My coffee isn't good enough for you? Fine." Tori rolled her eyes. "I'll put some soda in the fridge just for you."

"Good." Flossie said. "Now, about Luke."

"It's not me that boy has a crush on." Tori nodded over toward Luke. "He's watching Charlie."

Tori had a point. Cypress's newcomer was sipping the coffee Tori had gotten him while chatting happily with Police Chief Fisher. Luke had now moved as far away from the pair as the coffee shop would allow. But he kept looking over at Charlie.

"How would the two of them even know each other?" Flossie asked. "Luke hasn't lived here for decades. And Charlie just moved here—"

"From Las Vegas," I finished for her. "Tori, didn't you tell me that Charlie said he was from Las Vegas?"

"Yeah. He was some kind of security expert or something sexy like that. Whenever I ask him about it, he changes the subject back to his love of books. It's the only thing I don't like about him. I mean, nothing is sexier than a bodyguard. Do you think he protected some big-name star?"

"I don't know. Maybe," I said. "But that's not the point. Listen, Charlie moved here from Las Vegas and so did Luke. Mayor Goodvale was talking about it. Well, he didn't say Las Vegas, but he did say Nevada." My words came faster as pieces started to fall into place. "Charlie told us that he heard about Cypress and its affordable real estate. That's why he picked our town to open his bookstore. Who in Nevada would even know Cypress existed? One person: Luke Goodvale."

"I don't get it." Tori crossed her arms over her chest. She no longer looked happy. "What are you saying?"

"I don't know exactly." I wished I did, but I didn't. "There is something about the connection between Charlie and Luke, something we need to pay attention to."

"I think I know what you're getting at." Flossie tapped her chin. "We've been thinking that our darling Charlie has no connection to Cypress and so we've kept him off our suspect list. But what if—?"

"What if nothing!" Tori exploded. "I'm not going to let you weave some badly plotted fiction regarding my boo, Flossie. You're just jealous that I'm young and pretty and that I'm able to attract a man like him." She grabbed her coffee with such force, the hot liquid sloshed over the rim. With an angry huff, she stalked off toward Charlie.

"She didn't mean that," I said. "Ever since her last divorce, she's been even more sensitive about having someone question her choices when it comes to men."

"That's because her choices are always all wrong for her. Except . . ." Flossie tapped her chin again. "I like Charlie. I hate to think he might be guilty of committing a crime. And Tori is wrong. If I were to come up with a plot for what's happening here in Cypress, it would be tight and clever and the best dang plot any of y'all would have ever seen, because that's the kind of writer I am."

"I do wish you'd let me read one of your books," I said.

"Don't worry. You've read them," Flossie said, preening. "Everyone has. But that doesn't do a blasted thing to help solve our problem with Luke and Charlie or our problem with Delanie and Anne. Speaking of which, there's Delanie now."

The woman I had long considered the library's best friend stood just inside the doorway of Perks. Her hands were clasped in front of her chest. She licked her ruby red lips as she scanned the room. When she spotted us, her mouth curled into a warm smile. She waved.

I waved back but didn't have enough emotional energy to even fake a smile.

Delanie had arrived exactly on time. And the three of us hadn't even gotten around to discussing how we planned to confront her. We needed to tread carefully around Delanie. If we upset her, she could easily retaliate by tattling to Mrs. Farnsworth about how I'd broken all the rules and opened a secret bookroom right under the rule-loving woman's nose.

That would be a disaster.

But we were out of time. Delanie was here. And we didn't have a plan.

"Don't worry, honey." Flossie patted my hand. "We've got this."

Chapter Twenty

———•———

Delanie refused my offer to buy her a coffee. "If I drank caffeine at this time of night, I could forget about sleeping for the next week. As it is, I've been having trouble enough with sleeping lately."

"You have?" Flossie steepled her slender fingers in front of her lips. "And why is that?"

The question seemed to startle Delanie. Her hands trembled as she retrieved a lacy handkerchief from inside her bag. She didn't do anything with the little scrap of cloth other than let her nervous fingers play with it. "There's been too much drama in this town. Cypress was founded as a gentle farming community. Then they built the lake. Still, everyone expected to be able to live a quiet life, a life only occasionally interrupted by tourists. And now"—she waved the frilly handkerchief in the air—"it feels like soon I won't even recognize this place. The library's renovation is only the first step. If Marvin can actually get a few tech industries to open shop in our town, we will find ourselves losing everything that makes Cypress special."

Flossie looked at me and nodded encouragingly.

"We agree." I reached across the table and rested my hand over her fidgeting fingers. "We're worried about preserving the town's character as much as anyone. You know that. That's why I did what I did for the library."

"I know. I know." She shook her head in dismay. "We fought side by side trying to change Duggar's mind about stripping the library of its books. You told him and told him how valuable those books were to the town. I told him too."

I waited a beat before revealing the real reason we wanted to talk to Delanie. "I know that Anne Lowery is your niece. I overheard her talking on the phone with you this afternoon. I heard her say how you'd promised to help her."

Delanie blinked. That was her only reaction. Actually, she blinked twice. And then she sat back and smiled. "Why wouldn't I agree to help her? She's my favorite. Don't tell anyone you heard me say this, but the other children my brother spawned are brainless twits. You know I have no children of my own. It's a decision I don't regret, but sometimes I wish Anne were mine. And I do love having her living nearby instead of all the way across the country. So yes, I made sure she met with Duggar when he traveled to Silicon Valley to promote our town. I made sure she transitioned smoothly into her new position. And I've been working my butt off helping her get the recognition for the hard work she's been doing, not that I've been successful. The good-old-boy club is as strong as ever in this blasted place."

"You helped her?" I squeaked. "She's destroying the library, and you've been helping her?"

"No, dear. She's been doing her job. She's bringing new technologies to the library, which isn't a bad thing." She shook out her frilly handkerchief and then spread it neatly on the table. "It was Duggar who insisted the books had to go. It was Duggar who wouldn't let go of his vision of a modern bookless library, despite how many times we told him what a mistake he was making. Anne had nothing to do with those decisions."

"Are you telling us that you were honestly trying to help both Tru and Anne?" Flossie asked.

Delanie nodded. She finger-pressed away an imaginary crease in her handkerchief. Her eyes were wide and innocent. "Why would I not? I've dedicated my life to the library. Well, perhaps not my entire life, but the past couple of years have been all about promoting the library, keeping it relevant, and filling it with as many current books as possible. I'm still shocked that Duggar insisted we get rid of the printed books."

"Anne loves the idea of a bookless library as much as Duggar had," I pointed out.

"Of course she does. She's young and fond of those electronic toys she plays with. But she's not the one we're talking about. It's Duggar who was the ultimate decision maker when it came to the library's future. We told him and told him that the books were worth more than money and certainly worth much more than an electronic file on a screen. Not that the stubborn fool needed educating. He's been collecting rare books for decades now. He knew better than the rest of us how many of those books were worth something."

"Wait. What?" I said.

"That hypocrite," Flossie cried at the same time.

Delanie nodded. "The collecting bug bit him when he was in high school. I remember he'd bought an old Hawthorne book at a garage sale. The local newspaper wrote a story about it. The book he'd found was a children's book Hawthorne had penned. He said he'd purchased it for a grand sum of fifty cents. Turned out the book was worth more than a thousand dollars. That's why the newspaper was interested. There was a picture of him holding the old book. He had it wrapped in linen and was holding it gingerly as if the tome were made of spun glass instead of paper. He refused to sell it. To him the book was priceless.

Over the years, he'd occasionally show me a new book he'd acquired. He'd tell me stories about how hard (and dirty) he sometimes had to fight to win an especially rare book. The book-collecting business, apparently, is particularly cutthroat."

"Are you sure you're talking about Duggar Hargrove?" Flossie demanded. "The town manager? The man who carried a tablet around with him everywhere just in case he wanted to jot down a note to himself because he refused to waste his time with a piece of scrap paper?"

"He may have loved those old books of his, but he also believed investing in technology was the only way forward for our town," Delanie said. She picked up her lacy handkerchief and pressed it to her lips for a moment. "Gracious, we all heard him pontificate on that topic enough times to have memorized that silly speech of his."

"Duggar collected rare books?" I had a hard time believing it. If the town manager had loved old books, why would he tear apart the library? Why would he send books that were actually worth money to a landfill? Why would he ignore everyone telling him that those books were worth *more* than money to our residents?

Delanie clicked her tongue. "I suppose Duggar was so blinded by his vision for building the town of the future that he couldn't see past it. If that's all you wanted to talk to me about, I'll say goodnight. I have an early appointment in the morning and a woman my age can use all the beauty sleep she can get. Surely you understand that, Flossie."

"I don't understand anything you're saying," Flossie said tartly.

I didn't understand it either. No matter how hard I tried, I couldn't get my head around the idea that Duggar collected old books. How could a fellow bibliophile betray an entire town like that? What could turn a bibliophile into a biblioclast—a destroyer of books? Didn't he care that he was robbing future generations of the joy of opening up a favorite book and surrounding themselves with the sweet scent of leather and paper?

"I didn't miss any of the juicy stuff, did I?" Tori asked. She walked up just as Delanie rose from her chair.

Anne's aunt stuffed her lacy handkerchief back into her purse. "Excuse me. I was just leaving."

"Not because of me, I hope." Tori sounded a little too happy.

"Excuse me? Have I done something to upset you?" Delanie asked.

"What's going on here?" I asked.

"Nothing," Tori said with a wide, somewhat malicious, smile.

"That nothing sounds like a heaping amount of somethings," Flossie said. "Y'all better sit and explain why there's all this bad blood between the two of you."

"Perhaps another time. I do have to get going." Delanie tried again to slide past Tori.

"Please," I said. "We need to all be working together if we're going to have any hope of figuring out what's going on with this town."

"You mean with the changes to the library?" Delanie asked.

"No, Tru means with Duggar's death and the attack on Luke." Tori's giddy tone sharpened. "She means how you pretended to be her friend while stabbing her in the back."

"Stabbing Tru? Child, you must be madder than everyone thinks, which is really saying something. I already explained to Tru that I have always been a supporter of the library."

"Really? You tell us that, and yet I personally heard you brag to Mayor Goodvale how Anne was going to whip our shabby library into shape. You told him how she was the best thing that had ever happened to the library. You told him that you wholeheartedly supported what Duggar was trying to do with the library, since everyone working there was as moldy as the books on the shelves."

"You told the mayor that?" I asked Delanie. That hurt.

"Delanie tells everyone what she thinks they want to hear, don't you?" Tori said to her.

Delanie opened and closed her mouth several times before finally saying, "I wanted to help Anne. Things can be difficult when moving into a town as set in its ways as ours is. That's not a crime."

"No. But dripping poison in your niece's ear and convincing her to kill Duggar in order to smooth the way for her might be a crime. Tell her, Tru. Tell her how you believe Anne is responsible not only for Duggar's death but also for sending Luke to the hospital."

Delanie turned and gaped at me.

"I—" My entire face felt as if it had caught fire.

"Anne would never hurt anyone," Delanie declared. She lowered her voice. "I thought y'all were my friends."

"I thought you were *my* friend," I countered. "Until this evening, I didn't know Anne was related to you. I didn't know you were supporting her. She's never mentioned you. And it's not like she's been staying silent. She's been telling the police every chance she gets that I'm the one who killed Duggar. Did you know that?"

Delanie looked away from me. "She might have expressed concerns about—"

"That niece of yours has been on a one-woman campaign against our Tru," Flossie said. "It makes one wonder why she's so set on making sure the authorities think Tru looks guilty. The more Tru looks into the matter, the more she's realizes that out of everyone who was in the library at the time of the murder, it's Anne who has the biggest motive."

I bit the inside of my cheek. The more I thought about the murder, the more Tori's motive seemed to outshine everyone else's. Duggar's death had actually stopped the town from closing down her coffee shop. Plus, we hadn't ever considered Charlie. Did he have a motive for wanting Duggar out of the way? Had he also benefited from the town manager's death?

"Isn't that why you were so upset when you found Luke all beat up and unconscious, in the library today?" Tori demanded. "You were worried your precious niece had taken her anger at being overlooked out on the town's newest golden boy, the mayor's son."

"I . . . I . . . I would never think . . ." Delanie's face blazed red.

"But you did," Tori insisted. "You hate that you did. That's why you called her at the library, isn't it? You needed to hear her deny that she hurt Luke. Do you believe her? She sounded angry, didn't she? So perhaps, just perhaps that worried voice in your head is now wondering whether your sweet Anne is ambitious enough to have also killed Duggar. We all know how he had been planning all along to take credit for Anne's work."

It was my turn to gape at my friends. From the first moment I'd mentioned Anne and my theory that she was a murderess, they'd teased me. To see them standing up for me and my suspicions made me feel all warm and gushy inside.

"I have to admit that finding Luke hurt like that did send me into a panic," Delanie said quietly. She pulled the frilly handkerchief from her purse again. "But Anne has sworn to me that she didn't have anything to do with the attack. And I believe her." She twisted the handkerchief into a knot between her trembling hands before crying, "I have to."

After a few minutes, Delanie excused herself and quietly left the café. On the other side of the room, Charlie and Luke were standing right next to each other. Charlie had a frothy cappuccino cupped in his hands, while Luke sipped an iced coffee through a straw. While they weren't looking at each other, both men were taking turns speaking.

That seemed . . . suspicious.

Tori would howl when I asked her, but I needed her to find out what Charlie and Luke were talking about while pretending they weren't talking to each other. I had a sinking feeling that I was going to have to tell both Jace and Fisher how Charlie was in the library the day Duggar died. Which meant I'd have to tell them why I'd let a near-stranger into the library that morning. Which *also* meant I'd have to tell them about the unauthorized library tucked away in the basement.

I sank back into my chair and took a long sip of my rich Colombian coffee. Delanie hadn't said anything to prove Anne's innocence. So maybe I didn't have to go running off to the police yet. After all, believing Anne guilty of murder made my life so much simpler.

Chapter Twenty-One

———o———

Tori swatted my arm. "Oh! Oh! Don't look now. Your nemesis just walked in."

"My nemesis?" Despite her warning, I turned and looked. Who wouldn't have?

Detective Jace Bailey stood a few feet inside the entrance of Perks, his hands on his hips, his gaze scanning the room as if searching for someone. He nodded in my direction before continuing his visual exploration.

"What in blue blazes happened between the two of you?" Flossie asked. "Your cheeks turn as ripe as cherries every time you see him."

"Ancient history," I grumbled as I sank down a bit lower in my chair.

He was nothing more than a bad memory. He wasn't the kind of guy I'd want to actually date.

"He led Tru on," Tori said quietly. "In high school. She thought he was interested in her romantically when all he was doing was stealing from her. He wasn't even interested in getting tutored in English. He stole the essay Tru had written for their senior English class and turned it in as his own. He took her only copy on the day it was due."

The entire time Tori was speaking, I was hissing for her to stop. Tori was the only person in the world who knew the full story. I'd met Jace in the hallway. We'd been spending loads of time together. He needed to pass senior English. If he failed, he would lose his football scholarship to the University of Alabama. I promised to help him with his essay and make sure he could ace the last couple of tests. But when he was with me, he didn't seem all that interested in studying. He spent the time we had together telling jokes and flirting and even (I cringed to remember) kissing me a little too.

It had all felt like one of those after-school specials, where the nerdy girl ends up with the football hero. If it happened on TV, why couldn't it happen in real life? That's what I'd told myself because I was a naive idiot.

After a couple of weeks of tutoring sessions that felt more like romantic dates, I convinced myself we were actually "a couple."

"Hey, Jace," I had sung as he passed by in the hallway at school. I leaned nonchalantly against my locker. Being the uncoordinated teen that I was, my attempt to look cool failed miserably. My legs ended up slipping out from under me. I landed on my hands and knees.

All of the kids in the hallway had started to laugh.

"Isn't that the girl who wrote your essay?" Sissy Philips had asked as I helped myself back to my feet. My books and notebooks were scattered all across the hallway. "Or do all the ugly girls in the school fall down and worship at your feet?"

"All girls worship at my feet, not just the ugly ones," he'd said and had looked me up and down as if he'd never seen me before.

"Jace, what is she saying? I didn't write an essay for you."

"I guess it wasn't her." Sissy had wrapped her arms around him as if she owned him. They started down the hall. The witch made a point of stepping on my notebooks as she passed. "She doesn't look smart enough to write much more than her name."

Jace had glanced back at me. I had tears in my eyes and my heart felt as crumpled as my papers, but he didn't say a word in my defense.

"He was the world's biggest jerk when we were in high school," I told Flossie, while remembering the cold panic I'd felt when I'd realized my essay wasn't in my backpack. Jace had stolen it.

"The jerk not only broke my girl's heart but almost ruined her chances of getting into college. She had to beg our teacher for an extension and worked all night, frantically researching and writing a brand-new essay. Though it was as good as the first one—because that's how Tru worked—Mrs. Scoggins only gave her half credit for it because it was a day late. Jace had been worried about his scholarship. Tru had been worried about keeping her scholarship as well—a full ride to the University of South Carolina. Not that Jace cared," Tori explained.

"That's rough." Flossie sneered in his direction. "Jeez, he's heading this way. Do you want me to spit on him?"

"Please, no." I wanted to crawl under the table. "He's nothing to me. Really."

"You poor, poor dear." Flossie rubbed my arm. "Keep telling yourself that, kid."

A moment later, Jace slid into a seat next to me. He had two cups of coffee. He put one on the table in front of me. "I noticed yours was empty."

Flossie looked at me, her perfectly plucked eyebrows shooting up to her hairline.

"Um . . . thanks," I said.

Tori kicked my leg. I wasn't sure what she wanted me to do or say differently. But since she'd kicked me rather hard, I reached down and cried, "Ow!"

"Are you okay?" Jace asked.

"Sorry, leg cramp." I smiled despite my discomfort. "Did Anne explain what she was talking about on the phone? Do you think she took her upset over being dismissed during the press conference out on Luke?"

"You know I can't discuss the details of an active investigation," he said before taking a long sip of his coffee.

"Come on. Don't give us that," Tori cooed. "I heard that you came back to Cypress with something to prove. Do you want to tell us about that?" Her eyes glittered with mischief. "What wicked thing did you do in the Big Apple that got you kicked out?"

"I don't know what you're talking about," Jace said. He finished his cup of steaming hot coffee in one gulp.

"Let's get back to talking about Anne." After seeing Charlie with Luke, I needed to reassure myself that Anne was indeed our lead suspect. "You've never suspected her of any wrongdoing, isn't that right?"

"That's not precisely true, but she is new to—" he started to say.

"Did you know her aunt, the aunt she was talking to on the phone just a few hours ago, is Delanie Messervey?" Had Anne tried to make me look guilty of attacking Luke in the same way she'd tried to make me look guilty of killing Duggar? If she had, the joke was on her. I had an alibi this time, and he was sitting right next to me.

Jace leaned back in his chair and eyed me. "Delanie is Anne's aunt, is that so?" He lifted his cup to his lips to take a sip before realizing it was empty. He gave his head a rueful shake and set the cup back down. "Oh, before I forget"—he reached into his pocket—"I saw this at the pharmacy and thought about Dewey." He pulled out a feather that had been dyed purple and had a string attached to it. A piece of paper also fell out of his pocket. It fluttered to the floor.

"What's that?" I pointed to the paper he'd dropped.

"This?" He waved the purple feather in front of my nose. I frowned at the gift, not sure I wanted it. "You hang it from a door handle. Dewey will think he's chasing a bird and bat at it." His smile flattened when I didn't immediately take the feather. He placed it on the table in front of me and said softly, "It'll make Dewey happy."

"That is kind of you." I shoved the feather into my purse. I didn't like him being nice to me. It made me feel all itchy. I'd fallen for his nice act once before. Fallen far too hard. He was using me that time. Was he using me now? Was he using me to clean up his tarnished reputation?

Did he still think I killed Duggar? Was he pretending to be my friend in hopes that I'd slip up and prove my own guilt?

Well, I'd learned my lesson from him. I knew I needed to keep my guard up around men like Jace. I snorted. *Handsome men.* They couldn't be trusted.

"What?" he asked. "Y'all are looking at me like I said something wrong."

"It wasn't anything you've said," Flossie answered with a glower.

"I think it's sweet," Tori said, and yet she'd crossed her arms over her chest in a gesture of defense. "It's sweet that you're bringing our Tru kitty toys and all, but—"

"Don't mind them," I interrupted. "They're worried about everything that's been going on."

"Well, I'm glad they're worried. You should be too." He pushed his chair back from the table and stood. "There is a killer on the loose."

"Kind of hard to forget. That's pretty much all anyone is talking about lately," I said while Tori and Flossie both nodded in agreement.

"Still . . ." He rubbed the back of his neck. "Anne said something about you that troubled me."

I knew it! It was like being in high school all over again. Girls talking behind each other's backs. It was awful.

Unlike in high school, though, I managed to keep my cool. "Anne said something? Why am I not surprised? Oh, right. It's because she's been talking behind my back to the police ever since the murder." My voice remained as cool as ice.

"She sounded concerned," he said.

I just bet she was. I bet she was extremely concerned about keeping the police from looking too hard at her motives.

"She told me that you've been asking questions about Duggar's murder. Loads of questions, Tru. She made it sound like you're playing amateur detective. And I suspect that where one of you is playing, all three of you are."

Flossie pursed her lips.

Tori smiled.

And I worked like the devil to keep my expression blank.

Jace snorted in frustration. He leaned toward me. "The three of you do understand that someone killed our town manager. Poking around and trying to find that person is akin to sticking your hand in a haystack in search of a rattlesnake."

We continued our wall of silence.

"You know, rattlesnakes? Rattlesnakes are deadly," he said.

More silence.

"Come on, Tru, just tell me you'll stick to doing whatever it is you do at the library now." He pointed to Flossie. "And you stick to writing your novels." He pointed to Tori. "And you stick to brewing coffee."

"All rightie, Detective." Tori gave a mock salute. "We hear you loud and clear."

"Good." He looked back at me. His stern expression softened. "Will you be at the library tomorrow?"

"All day," I said. "Should I have my lawyer meet me there?"

"No, just your cat." With a nod to Flossie and Tori, he walked away, heading straight for the exit.

"He's right, you know," Flossie said as we watched him exit the building. "What we're doing is dangerous."

I scooped up the paper that had dropped out of his pocket. "Do you want to stop?"

"Of course not," she answered quickly. "I haven't had this much fun since my late husband Truman passed through heaven's shining golden gates."

I started to put the scrap of paper with the rest of the trash, but something stopped me. Likely some sort of sentimental feeling I should have been squashing. With a huff, I dropped the scrap of paper into my purse. As much as I hated to admit it, I was looking forward to seeing Jace again in the morning.

"How about you, Tori?" I asked. "Do you want to stop?"

"Are you kidding me? If there is anything I've learned in all my marriages, it's that a woman should never let a man talk her out of doing anything."

Chapter Twenty-Two

The next morning, I arrived at the library to find Anne standing outside on the front steps. She looked unhappy.

"What's going on?" I asked her.

"Mrs. Farnsworth isn't here. She's always here."

That was the truth. You could set your clock by Mrs. Farnsworth's punctuality. She arrived at the library at eight-thirty on the dot. It was nearly nine and there was no sign of her.

"I told her just a few days ago that she needed to give me a set of keys," Anne said. "I have work to do."

"But she's never late," I said with a frown.

"She is today."

"Yeah, she is." And that worried me. As I walked away, I pulled my cell phone from my pocket and dialed the police department. I explained to the dispatch operator, Janie Curry (who also happened to be my next-door neighbor), that Mrs. Farnsworth wasn't at the library.

"Honey"—Janie snapped the gum she was chewing—"that is worrying. I'll send an officer by her house. I hope the poor dear didn't take a tumble in the bathroom. That's what happens to too many of our older folks. They trip over the bathroom rug or slip in the shower and that's the end of them." She snapped her gum again. "Oh, my lamb, I hope that's not what happened here. Can't imagine the town without Mrs. Farnsworth."

"I can't either," I admitted. "Janie, could you please do me a favor and call my cell phone as soon as you hear something? We're locked out of the library until she arrives."

"Can do, sweetie," she drawled. "Hanging up now."

While Anne paced the library's grand front steps, I headed across the street to the Sunshine Diner for a morning snack and coffee. The mayor spent several hours every morning there, "getting face time with his constituents." I could use this opportunity to question him about whether he remembered anything new that he'd seen or heard on the day Duggar was killed. I also wanted to ask him about Luke's relationship with Charlie.

The diner was packed with residents, but oddly the mayor wasn't there. "Haven't seen him," an overworked server reported as she rushed by to deliver a plate of eggs and bacon to one of the tables.

"I heard he's dealing with some kind of crisis at town hall," Gwynne Hansy added. She was sitting at a nearby table. I knew the older woman—a shameless gossip—loved gardening and I just happened to have a gardening encyclopedia written by English gardener Monty Don in my tote bag.

I thanked her for the information by handing her the book and telling her to get it back to me in a couple of weeks.

She was thrilled. So thrilled, in fact, that she leaned toward me and whispered, "Heard there's going to be an arrest for Duggar's murder today."

"Really?" I whispered back. "Do you know who?"

"Honey, if I knew that, I'd be telling everyone," she said and then thanked me again for the book, which she was now hugging to her chest. She told me how much she missed the old library. I was tempted to tell her about the secret bookroom, but if that information ever fell into the hands of a gossip like Gwynne, the entire town would know about it before the day's end.

I declined her offer to join her at the table. While talking to the mayor had seemed like a good idea, there was another source nearby who could tell me what was going on between Luke and Charlie and why they were acting so oddly last night.

A better source than the mayor, since I doubted he would want to talk to me (or anyone) about his son's troubles. He didn't even want the public to know that Luke was the one who had been beaten up at the library. I could only imagine how much it'd upset Mayor Goodvale when he learned how Luke had showed up at Perks last night looking as if he'd lost a fistfight.

I stepped outside and glanced down the street toward Tori's coffee shop. A new shingle was hanging from the wooden canopy on a building near the library. "The Deckle Edge" had been painted on the sign in fancy looping white letters. The term "deckle edge" refers to a rough-cut edge of paper in a book, which leaves the edges of the pages of the bound book uneven. It was a popular process used in book production during the late nineteenth century. Some of the books in the secret bookroom—and even a few of the newer books—have that rough-cut deckle-edge look. What a perfect name for an antiquarian bookstore.

Naturally, Charlie would know all about deckle edges. He was, apparently, an expert on old books. So was Duggar.

Worry twisted in the pit of my stomach. We never should have left Charlie out of our investigation. Don't get me wrong. I loved and trusted Tori. Generally, she could read people better than I read books. But when it came to the men in her life, it was as if all her instincts shut down. We should have never taken her word that he was a good guy (even if he seemed like one).

The bookshop's large display window—the one the thief had

smashed—had been replaced with a double-paned window that looked thick enough to repel any future break-in attempts. Several old books were displayed quite artistically in the window.

A "Closed" sign hung on the shop's front door, but the lights were on. I knocked.

For a few minutes nothing happened. I was about to give up and head down the street to Perks when I heard Charlie call out, "We're closed."

"It's Tru," I called back.

"Just a minute." It took a full minute for him to get to the door and for the old brass lock to click.

The door swung open. Charlie glared at me, making him look more dangerous than ever. Immediately regretting my impulsive decision to talk with him alone, I took a step backward. "This doesn't look like a good time," I said.

He growled, actually growled. He sounded like a wild animal. "When is it ever a good time in this money pit?"

That's when I noticed his dark blue button-up shirt sleeves were rolled up to his elbows and his forearms were dripping wet.

"Plumbing trouble?" I asked.

"The worst. When I came down this morning, there was water all over the floor. Thank goodness I have all the boxes of books set up on tables. Could have lost tens of thousands of dollars in inventory." He started to run his fingers through his hair but stopped himself at the last moment. He glared at his wet hand in disgust. "And the only plumber I managed to reach on the phone can't get here until tonight to just look at it, so I'm trying to fix it"—he sucked in a sharp breath—"myself."

"Have you turned off the water to the building?" I asked. That was pretty much the extent of my plumbing knowledge. There were, however, several books in the secret bookroom on the topic. Not that I could get to them with Mrs. Farnsworth missing and the library locked up.

Well, I could pick the back door lock again, but I didn't think that would be wise to do in broad daylight.

"Yeah, the water's turned off. If I hadn't done that right away, there'd be a flood gushing out this door and rushing down the street by now." Before I could make my apologies for bothering him and leave, he opened the door wider and stepped aside. "Despite the mess this morning, I'm glad to see you. There's something I think we need to talk about." When I hesitated, he added, "It's about the murder."

"Mrs. Farnsworth didn't come in this morning. I've alerted the police. They're looking for her."

He swore quietly. "In that case, you'd better come inside."

"The police department knows where I am and will try to call me any minute with an update," I warned him.

"Good." He sounded like he meant it. He gestured for me to precede him into his store.

"I've been worried that something might happen to one of you." He swore again. "I shouldn't have kept quiet. I've been arguing with myself all morning about whether I should have said something yesterday after Luke got hurt." He tried to drag his rusty, wet hand through his hair again, but stopped himself at the last moment.

"Is this about that man I saw in the secret bookroom? What was his name? Grundle?"

"Grandle," he corrected. "And no, forget that you met him." He sucked in a quick breath. "I'll never forgive myself if someone gets hurt."

"Someone like Mrs. Farnsworth?" I asked, starting to panic.

"Or yourself." He stepped around a puddle on the concrete floor.

"Me?" I asked. While the flooding had subsided, I could clearly see a waterline about a foot high on the wooden shelves that were being built along the walls. As Charlie had mentioned, there were boxes of books set up on folding tables all over the shop. "Why would anyone be interested in hurting me?"

"Hmmm . . ." He picked up a roll of paper towels that was sitting out on the shop's ancient checkout counter and used several pieces to wipe off his hands.

"What? What aren't you telling me?"

"You, Mrs. Farnsworth, and Anne Lowery—the three of you—were all at the library at the time of the murder. One or all of you might have seen something you shouldn't have. That makes you a danger."

"To the killer?"

He frowned for a moment before nodding.

My heart started beating faster. "What . . . what do you need to tell me?"

He crossed to the other side of the room, rummaged through a box of books, and hurried back. He handed me a copy of *The Maltese Falcon* by Dashiell Hammett.

I ran my finger over its spine. It didn't have Cypress's color-coded library label, but it was nearly identical to the book he'd been admiring in the secret bookroom. "Why are you giving me this? Did you take it from the library?"

"No! I'd never steal from you." After a tense moment he huffed. "I promised not to tell anyone about"—he paused—"about something that probably has nothing to do with the murder. I *hope* it has nothing to do with the murder. But it might. And the uncertainty is eating at me."

"Just tell me what's going on."

"I would if I could, but I'm a man of my word. However, me providing you with a clue isn't breaking that promise. I hope it isn't. And that's what I've done." He tapped the book's cover. "I've handed you a clue."

I frowned at the hardcover classic mystery novel. "A clue?"

He smiled and nodded.

"Do you mean this actual book or the plot of the book?"

He tilted his head to one side. "What do you think?"

"I think this isn't helpful."

"Isn't it?" He sounded surprised. "I should think my clue would explain everything to a knowledgeable librarian like you."

"We're talking about a murder, and you think you're helping by handing out riddles?" I waved the old book at him. "Just tell me what you know."

"Sorry, Tru, I made a promise. It's a promise I regret. But a promise is a promise. And in the end, it might have nothing to do with the town manager's demise. I sincerely hope it doesn't. But if it does, I'll break my word and go straight to the police."

Still frowning at the old book, I started to leave. But then I remembered the reason I was there in the first place. "I noticed that you and Luke were talking at Perks last night. The two of you were friends when you were both living in Vegas, right?"

"Not friends," he said, shaking his head. "I knew him from the casinos. We talked a few times about Cypress. He's the one who gave me the idea to open a shop here since the real estate prices were so low."

"Lucky for us," I said. "Our town hasn't had a bookstore, used or otherwise, for decades. Do you know anything about Luke's former job? Did he work at a casino?"

"Work there? No. He went to the casinos to play sometimes. But he was mostly there because that's where the moneylenders liked to do business. That boy couldn't control his, er, habit. It got him into"—he paused as if searching for the right word—"trouble."

"Trouble? He's in debt?"

Charlie nodded. "More debt than he can handle. He didn't get laid off from his job. He quit and ran back to Daddy. He ran back home to escape some less-than-friendly moneylenders."

"You mean Grandle? Oh, my goodness, are you suggesting that scary guy who destroyed the library's phone book attacked Luke?"

Charlie shrugged. "I wouldn't be surprised."

"Tori told me you worked in security in Las Vegas. Did you work for a casino?"

"Something like that."

"Something like what?" For someone who acted as if he wanted to be helpful, Charlie was frustratingly short on information. "What did you do there?"

"I don't want to bore you with details."

"Oh, I'm rarely bored," I said, but I could tell he wasn't ready to talk about his past life in Vegas. "What were you and Luke talking about last night?"

Charlie huffed before admitting, "Grandle."

"Let me get this straight. Luke gambled his way into debt, and now he's hoping his daddy will get him out of trouble?"

"He wasn't a serious gambler," Charlie said. "Online shopping is what did him in."

"Online shopping? Are you serious?"

Charlie snorted. "Serious as that thug who beat up Luke."

"What did he buy?" I asked.

"What didn't he buy? Apparently, he'd click on every ad that popped up on his screen. Electronics. Clothes. Gadgets. Stuffed dogs with flat, squishy faces. The ugliest angel figurines. Tons of those. Never seen so many in my life. Luke told me last night that his dad had sold it all, but he didn't earn back even a fraction of what Luke owes Grandle."

"Why doesn't the mayor take out a loan and make the problem go away?" That seemed like the easiest solution.

"I don't know," Charlie said. "I imagine that it's because he can't. Guys like Grandle don't travel across the country for small sums of money."

I held up the book he'd given me as a clue. "And you think this business with Grandle and Luke is somehow linked to Duggar's death? Is that the thing you can't talk about?"

He opened the door, a clear invitation for me to leave his store. "You'll have to excuse me. I have a pipe to fix."

I started to leave. But then something struck me. "You don't think Grandle somehow got inside the library and killed Duggar, do you?"

"No. If I did, I'd go to the police right now." He tried to close the door.

But I had more questions. "Then why are we worried that something might have happened to Mrs. Farnsworth? Did she see Grandle doing something shifty at the library's grand reopening? Did she confront him? Do you think he did something to Mrs. Farnsworth to keep her quiet?"

"Honestly, Tru? I don't know. I hope not."

I crushed the copy of *The Maltese Falcon* to my chest while fumbling with my phone. I needed to warn the police to keep an eye out for murderous loan sharks. I needed to warn them that Grandle might have done something to Mrs. Farnsworth.

Just as I'd started to dial the number, my phone rang. "You'll never believe what's happening over here," Janie Curry, the police department dispatcher, whispered when I answered. "Mrs. Farnsworth is *here*. Giving testimony. Not like testimony in church, mind you, but close."

"Testimony?"

"She's saying she remembered something about the day Duggar shuffled off his mortal coil. I don't have all the details, but it has both the police chief and the mayor excited. Reminds me of a bunch of wasps flying out of a nest someone just bumped, the way they're running around."

"Thank goodness." I breathed a deep sigh of relief. Mrs. Farnsworth was safe.

"Thank goodness? I don't know what there is to be thankful about. Mrs. Farnsworth isn't acting normal. She came in fluttering her hands everywhere. And that ain't like her. I've lived in this lake town long enough to know when I'm smelling fish. Oh, look, that fellow from the state just ran into Fisher's office. Oops, I've gotta go. There's a call coming in on the other line." Janie hung up.

I stood on the sidewalk staring at my phone while I replayed the conversation in my mind.

Mrs. Farnsworth had remembered something about what she saw on the day of the murder? Something she hadn't thought to mention earlier? That didn't seem likely. Her mind was a finely honed machine. She noticed everything. She remembered everything. It wouldn't take her a week to recall a key piece of information. And she certainly wouldn't rush over to the police station to deliver that information without making sure the library opened on time.

Janie was right. Everything about this morning held the foul odor of rotten fish.

I was still standing in the middle of the sidewalk trying to figure out what was *really* going on when Flossie wheeled toward me as if trying to win the Indy 500.

"There you are!" she shouted. "You need to get to the library. Detective Bailey is searching for you."

"He is?" I asked. "Why?"

"Well, it's not to steal an English essay. Come on. Come on." She maneuvered her wheelchair around and started back the way she'd come. I raced after her.

Chapter Twenty-Three

———○———

Jace looked awful. Well, let me amend that. He looked awful
for someone as handsome as him. Compared to the rest of humanity, I
suppose he appeared pretty normal. His hair was disheveled, and not
artfully disheveled the way he usually wore it. His clothes, which looked
like they were the exact same black T-shirt and jeans he'd worn to Perks
last night, were rumpled and grubby with dirt. And dark smudges underlined his soulful blue eyes.

By the time Flossie and I reached him, he was unlocking the library's front door.

"Mrs. Farnsworth gave you her key?" I squeaked.

"She insisted the library open on time. And Fisher isn't done taking
her statement," he explained. "She was going to walk out on him until
I promised to supervise you and Anne. She has threatened to flay the
three of us alive if anything goes wrong, by the way," he added, paling
a bit.

"What can go wrong?" Anne asked. Apparently, she'd been pacing
in front of the entrance the entire time that I'd been off in search of

answers. She pushed Jace aside so she could get into the library. "The system I set up practically runs itself."

I grabbed Jace's arm before he could follow her. "What's really going on?"

He looked at Flossie, who was beside me with her arms crossed, and then at me again. "You know I can't—"

"I know Mrs. Farnsworth didn't suddenly remember some important piece of information. That's not how her mind works."

His jaw tightened. "Yeah, I know." He sounded angry about it. "And it sounds as if you already know as much as I do. Who inside the police department is feeding you information?"

"I called and reported Mrs. Farnsworth missing. That's how I discovered she was there."

"What in blue blazes is happening?" Flossie demanded as she rolled up the handicapped ramp to the front door.

"Lots of things I can't talk about. Please, just come inside and help get the library open so none of us ends up suffering Mrs. Farnsworth's wrath."

We did as he asked because, quite frankly, we were all honestly terrified of Mrs. Farnsworth. Flossie set up her computer in the library's new café area, where one of the baristas, who had come in behind us, was busy preparing for the morning.

I stashed my purse and oversized tote bag in a lockable drawer at the circulation desk and started my morning routine.

"Where's Dewey?" Jace whispered.

"At home," I whispered back. "I was concerned that Anne would make trouble for me if I brought him this morning."

"Good thinking. Hey, wait. I thought y'all had disposed of all the printed books," Jace said. Was it my imagination, or did he sound suspicious?

"That's what the mayor ordered," I replied, hoping I didn't sound guilty.

"Then what are you doing with that?" He pointed to the copy of *The Maltese Falcon* Charlie had given me that I was still holding.

"Oh, that? It's a gift from a friend of the library." I dropped it into the drawer with the rest of my stuff.

While he frowned as if he didn't believe me, I went to get the first step in my morning routine started, which was to brew the staff coffee. Jace followed me into a small storage closet that had been converted into a cramped employee break room. The room was barely large enough to hold two people, much less two people and two folding tables, a coffee maker, and a small refrigerator that hummed loudly.

"You agree that Mrs. Farnsworth wouldn't miraculously realize she witnessed something important on the day of the murder?" he asked after a long span of silence between us.

"Even if she had, she wouldn't go to the police station before opening the library." She was a stickler for routine.

He nodded.

"Not to change the subject, but there was a man in the library yesterday, a stranger." I figured someone needed to warn the police about Grandle. Charlie had already said he wouldn't. Luke and the mayor were too ashamed to talk about Luke's troubles. That meant the burden fell on me.

"Lots of strangers came to the town for the library's reopening ceremony." Jace sounded tired. I added an extra scoop of coffee to the coffee maker's filter. "I was told that Duggar had sent invitations to half the residents in the state."

"This man I'm talking about isn't from around here. Not this state either." The coffee maker started to gurgle. "He . . ." I couldn't tell Jace about how he'd ripped out a page from the phone book, since the library wasn't supposed to have phone books anymore. "He intimidated me."

"Intimidated?" He crossed his arms over his chest. "I'm sure plenty of people—"

"No, I'm not some library mouse jumping at shadows. After the . . .

um . . . incident, Charlie told me to avoid this man. He told me that if I ever see him again, that I need to walk in the other direction. He told me his name was Grandle. He's a loan shark from Las Vegas."

"Charlie?" Jace raised a brow.

"Not Charlie, Grandle. Grandle is the loan shark."

"And Charlie is the new guy in town who is opening a used bookstore?" Jace asked.

"Yes, Charlie Newcastle. You met him the other day. He was helping me carry books. I mean, I was helping him carry books to his car." I hated lying. It was too hard to keep the stories straight in my mind. "He's moved here from Las Vegas. Luke had been living in Las Vegas too."

"It's a big city."

"Yes, I know that. But Charlie and Luke knew each other. Charlie also told me how Luke had gotten himself into some kind of financial trouble. Big financial trouble. He believes this thug, this Grandle, is in town to collect."

"Really?" That piece of information seemed to catch Jace's interest. "Sounds like I need to talk with Charlie."

"That might be prudent. It's easy to connect the dots. Charlie warned me to avoid Grandle. Charlie and Luke are both from Las Vegas. Luke is running from moneylenders. Grandle, who probably is also from Vegas, would logically be the man who attacked Luke."

"I thought you believed Anne is the source of all the library's recent troubles," Jace reminded me.

"I do. I mean, I think I do." Didn't I? "This new information complicates matters, doesn't it?"

"It might." He nodded toward the coffee pot. The machine was still gurgling. "I could sorely use all of that right now."

"Give it another minute. It'll taste better if you let it brew to the end."

We stood in silence with only the murmur of the coffee maker. He pulled his notebook from his pocket and started to take some notes. Finally, he looked up and asked me to describe Grandle. He wrote down everything I told him. "If you happen to see him again, I want you to call me, okay?"

I agreed, and he handed me his card.

"With this new information Mrs. Farnsworth is giving to Chief Fisher, are—?" My voice cracked. I cleared my throat. "Are y'all ready to make an arrest?"

"Yeah," he said angrily. "And what you're telling me is only strengthening our case against him."

"You don't mean Luke?" I asked stupidly. Who else could he have been talking about? "Are you sure? That doesn't make sense. Duggar was like an uncle to Luke."

Without even thinking about it, I pulled out my phone with the thought of texting Charlie. Why did he give me a copy of *The Maltese Falcon*? Yes, the book ended with a betrayal. But was that really the clue he was trying to give me? I could think of at least a dozen books better suited for delivering such a message.

Jace put his hand over mine to keep me from typing. "You can't go telling everyone what I just told you."

"That's not what I'm doing." Not precisely. "I need to text someone about that book I had. Honest." When he didn't release my hand right away, I said, "What? You don't trust me?"

"Not particularly."

"Fair enough." I didn't trust him either.

My distrust didn't stop my hand from feeling tingly from his touch or for time to feel as if it had stopped dead in its tracks when his gaze met mine.

He abruptly turned away. "I'm the biggest idiot alive."

"What do you mean?"

"I shouldn't have said anything about Luke. It's just that I haven't had any sleep and I think the police chief is wrong. And I shouldn't have said that either."

"I'm not a gossip. And you already know I kind of agree with you.

I don't think Luke could have done this." The coffee maker behind me had fallen silent.

"Because of Anne?" he asked. "You still think she killed Duggar?"

I shrugged.

He tapped his fingers on the top of the humming refrigerator. "Luke had returned to Cypress with the hopes of making a fresh start."

"Just like you're trying to do? My mom told me about the mistake you made in New York."

He spun back around. "What exactly did you hear?"

"Oh, you know . . . this and that." I hoped if he thought I already knew the details about the scandal he'd left behind in New York that he'd let his guard down and talk about it. My ploy didn't work. He just frowned. "I'm not one to judge. And, please, don't look so surprised that I know what happened. I learned my investigative skills from the best." When he raised his brows in question, I explained, "Nancy Drew. Don't worry, now. I'm not going around gossiping about you."

He grunted as if he wasn't sure he believed me. This lack of trust between us was getting in the way of my investigation.

"Look, I'm simply saying I understand how you might relate to what Luke is going through. He may have run from crushing debts, but that didn't stop his past from following him here. And because of that past, he's being accused of a new—and much worse—crime. It must be difficult to not put yourself in his place. You might even start to wonder if something like that could happen to you."

"We're not talking about me or my past." His tone convinced me that I shouldn't push him to change his mind about sharing.

"Fine. Let's talk about Luke, then."

"I don't see the point. The evidence—which I can't talk about—is pretty damning against him. And getting more damning by the minute, apparently." Although he still sounded upset, his tension had seemed to ease when I shifted the conversation off him and back to the investigation.

"Okay, so Luke was in debt up to his eyeballs and was looking to escape to a better place where he could be in control of his life again. When those troubles followed him to Cypress, he felt trapped. He ended up doing something drastic."

"Maybe." Jace curled his fingers into a fist. "Only, I can't believe he'd kill a man he loved for money. Something about that explanation, well, it . . . it just doesn't sit right."

"Over money? I don't understand." Duggar had money? Did Jace mean the town manager's book collection? "Is Luke inheriting Duggar's assets?"

"Sorry. I shouldn't have said that either. Open investigation and all. But things will come out soon, won't they? I guess it wouldn't hurt to tell you that no, this isn't about an inheritance. Duggar's kin will split his belongings. However, there was something found at the crime scene, a document that has suggested a motive."

"A document?" I thought about the tiny scrap of paper Dewey had been batting around. The same one that Jace had picked up and then later dropped. I'd tucked it in my purse. I needed to look at it. I held up my hand. "I know. I know. You can't discuss it. That's fine." I rushed out of the room. "Help yourself to the coffee. It's done brewing by now."

After glancing over my shoulder to make sure he wasn't following, I went straight to the circulation desk and dug around in my purse until I located the scrap of paper. I put it on the desk and smoothed out the wrinkles.

On the crinkled paper there was a name, "Keene," and then "Est. Value $5,000."

Luke needed money. Loads of it. And fast.

"Of course." I pressed a finger to my lips.

The police had found a document at the crime scene. Dewey had found this fragment in the same place. I would bet anything that this was a piece of that document.

But, surely, the tiny snippet from a larger document couldn't mean what I thought it meant. Could it?

Duggar had argued that the books going to the landfill were old and moldy and not worth anything. How could he—a book collector—not have realized that some of the books could be worth *five thousand dollars*?

He must have known! Was this part of a document he had in his possession when he was killed? Or was this from documents the killer—*Luke?*—had dropped at the time of the murder?

If Luke was planning to sell the library books, I supposed he would have had to wait until they were carted off to the landfill before he could take them. That way, he wouldn't be stealing (or selling) library property.

Did Duggar find out his plans to sell the books and decide he wanted the money to go to the town or into his own pockets instead? Did Luke, out of desperation, kill Duggar to stop the town manager from interfering? Luke needed to repay his debts. That brutal beating proved how dangerous the moneylender was. If Charlie was right about Grandle being Luke's attacker, that would be proof.

Luke killed Duggar. I repeated the thought in my mind several times, letting the idea settle there. With the murder investigation closed, I wouldn't have to worry about the police discovering my secret bookroom. I might even finally be able to get a full night's sleep. That would be a blessing.

I should be heaving sighs of relief like a romantic heroine who'd survived a narrow escape from the villain just about now.

So why didn't I feel happy? Why wasn't my chest heaving—not even once—with relief? Why did one unwelcome thought keep forcing its way into my mind? I needed to talk to someone.

Jace emerged from the cramped employee lounge holding a mug of coffee. (No, not him. I needed to talk with someone else. Someone I trusted.) He took a sip before sending me a quizzical look. I slid the scrap of evidence off the desk and crammed it into my pocket. It wasn't something Jace needed, since the police already had the rest of the document.

I needed to talk to my friends. I texted Tori: Can you come to the library ASAP?

She texted back almost immediately: B there in 10.

"Have you heard the news?" Betty Crawley practically sang as she swept into the library, her large camera hanging around her neck.

"What news?" I asked.

She glanced over at the employees' closet and spotted Jace coming toward us.

"Didn't your detective friend tell you? Or isn't he in the loop?" She stepped closer to me and whispered, her words coming at a rush. "I heard he messed up big time in New York. He got romantically involved with a criminal. His daddy pulled a bunch of strings to convince Fisher to hire him after he was forced to leave New York."

Jace came to stand next to the desk.

"Stop with the games and just say what you've come here to say," I said to Betty.

"Fisher made an arrest just now. Luke Goodvale killed Duggar. We're all trying to figure out why."

Jace scowled.

Thanks to those darn nagging doubts that wouldn't leave me alone, I reacted to the news with a scowl too. Betty lifted her camera and clicked several shots.

"That look on your face is perfect," she crowed.

"I didn't—" I started to protest.

But she talked over me. "A mixture of shock and relief. Couldn't have staged it better myself. I bet the article I'm going to write will be picked up by the AP wire. Could go national. Perhaps I'll even get a job offer from a major newspaper out of it. This could be my ticket out of this nowhere town and out of covering ladies' lunches all the time."

"I don't want my picture in the—" I started to protest again.

"Toodles!" she sang over her shoulder as she scurried out the door.

"I hope she does get a job offer from another newspaper, one far, far away from here," I muttered.

"That would suit everyone all around," Jace agreed. "So . . ." He took another sip of his coffee. "Is the library open to Mrs. Farnsworth's exacting standards?"

With all the changes to the library, I honestly wasn't sure what those new standards would be. Did we test all the computers each morning? Did we test the 3D printers? I glanced around. "Sure," I said with a shrug.

"Then I probably should go." He didn't leave.

"Dewey is fine. I'll run by the house and feed him during my lunch break."

He nodded. And he still didn't leave.

"Is there something I can help you with?" I asked.

His gaze searched mine for a while before saying, "Fisher is making a mistake."

"No, don't say that." But Jace was right. This was all wrong. Luke had an alibi. He had been with his father. But what if the mayor had lied? What if Mrs. Farnsworth had known he was lying? No, I didn't want to think about those things. "I want life in Cypress to go back to normal. I want to put this entire ugly business of murder at the library behind us." I spoke emphatically, hoping my words would help quiet my own naysaying thoughts.

"We all want life in Cypress to go back to normal, but it won't. Not if there still is a killer roaming around." He drew a slow breath. "Be careful, Tru."

Chapter Twenty-Four

If not Luke, then *who killed Duggar?*

As soon as I had a moment alone, I picked up the copy of *The Maltese Falcon* Charlie had given me. This was supposed to be a clue?

It'd been years since I'd read the mystery novel. It wasn't one of my favorites. It didn't bring me the same joy of discovery as my Nancy Drew books. But I still remembered many of the book's details. The Maltese falcon was a jewel-encrusted golden statue. It had been made as a gift to the king of Spain but was stolen by pirates and passed from owner to owner until the start of the novel.

Was that why Charlie had given me this book? Did he want me to guess that printed books were the treasure? Was Luke planning to take old books from the library to give to Charlie to sell? Was that the clue Charlie wanted me to tease from the plot? Or was he hinting at something else?

I sat there puzzling over the book for a few minutes before asking Anne to cover the circulation desk for me.

In the café area, Flossie was tapping away on her computer. Her bright green tie-dyed silk tunic flowed like trees waving in a breeze as she typed. Her fingers kept flying over the keyboard even after I sat down next to her. She didn't look up until I cleared my throat.

She yelped. "Honey, don't sneak up on a body like that!" She slammed her purple laptop closed.

"There's been a development," I said. "Tori is on her way." I told her about Luke's arrest and then retrieved the paper Dewey had found in the media room from my purse.

By that time Tori had arrived, and I had to start the explanation all over again.

Both Tori and Flossie frowned over the crinkled paper I'd placed in front of them.

"You think this is from a formal estimate worked up by an antique bookstore?" Flossie asked. "A store like Charlie's?"

"It could be his shop or another one. There are plenty of them in Charleston, and look at this. It says 'Keene.' As in Carolyn Keene. As in one of the Nancy Drew books I'd thought I was saving from the land-fill," I said.

Flossie studied the tiny piece of paper some more. "Those books you put into the secret bookroom, they're first editions?"

"Some of them. That's one of the many things that makes the Nancy Drew books so special. Those early editions are different from the later ones that have been rewritten and reworked over the years." The copies the Cypress library had in its collection contained the words originally written by Mildred Wirt Benson. They are the actual books that launched a series that inspired scores of successful women.

"This valuation doesn't seem too far out of line for a popular first edition book," Flossie said.

"Not at all," Tori agreed. She showed us her phone's screen with the results of an Internet search she'd completed on the value of first editions of *The Secret of the Old Clock*, the very first Nancy Drew book.

Her search results matched the price given on the paper Dewey had found.

"I wonder . . . have we found the plot of our mystery?" Flossie asked. "You think Duggar discovered Luke's plans to sell the library's books and confronted him? Is that why Luke killed him?"

"It does wrap things up nicely, I suppose," I said slowly.

"Not really." Flossie tapped her chin. "Oh my, I need to pluck. Now, what was I going to say? Don't tell me. Oh, right. It was this: Why wait for the books to be carried off to the landfill? They might get damaged during transport. Wouldn't it be easier if Luke simply checked out the books, sold them, and then claimed to have lost them?"

"No, that wouldn't work. If he stole the books and then sold them on the open market with his name as the owner, we'd know he'd taken them. The Town of Cypress, by right, would be entitled to any money made from the sale of stolen books."

"But if he took them from the dump, he'd own them," Tori finished.

"Exactly," I said. Talking it through actually made me feel better. Yes, this did sound right. Luke was planning to steal the books. He got caught and, in a fit of panic, killed Duggar.

"But . . ." Flossie frowned.

"What's the problem?" Tori asked. "Why the hesitation? The police have their man. They must have evidence against him. They wouldn't have pressed charges otherwise."

"But . . ." Flossie said again.

"Jace doesn't believe they've arrested the right man," I said.

"Maybe Jace doesn't know everything," Tori was quick to say. "It sounds like Mrs. Farnsworth provided a piece of evidence that might be the key to making sense of everything else the police have collected."

"Maybe . . ." I shook my head. I wanted the case to be solved, didn't I? Even if I wasn't the one to solve it, I was ready for all of this to be over. Wasn't I?

"You're still stuck on the idea that Anne is guilty." Tori poked me in the arm.

"Maybe I am." Anne's ambitions did give her a powerful motive. Plus, she did have the opportunity.

And then there was Tori. Was that relief I saw on her face? Was she relieved the police had arrested someone that wasn't her? Or perhaps she was simply glad to know the killer had been caught.

Oh, this entire thing was giving me a headache.

"What do you think we should do?" I asked my friends.

"Celebrate," Tori said with a cheer. "It's over."

Flossie didn't look nearly as convinced. "But Duggar was the book collector."

"So?" Tori said. "If Luke and Duggar were as close as everyone is saying, Luke would have learned about the value of books from Duggar."

Duggar knew the value of old books. *He knew.*

Flossie leaned across the table to put her hand on mine. "Take some time. Think about what's bothering you. Once you've done that, we can figure out what, if anything, we need to do."

"There is something else," I said, thinking of the book Charlie had given me. The most obvious clue in the book was the Maltese falcon itself. Was there a hidden treasure in the library right under our noses? Were the books the treasure Charlie was trying to alert us to, or was it something else?

Or perhaps—and this was the thought that suddenly stilled my tongue in my mouth—perhaps Charlie had given me the book for another reason. The femme fatale—the deadly woman. Brigid O'Shaughnessy, beautiful and an accomplished liar, played the role of the femme fatale in *The Maltese Falcon.* It was the role that made the book's plot famous.

Charlie had emphasized how he'd made a promise to keep a secret, a secret he was worried could prove to be a motive in Duggar's murder. I'd assumed the secret involved Luke, because we were all thinking about Luke and how he'd been attacked in the library. But Charlie had never mentioned Luke in connection with this grand secret of his. All he'd said was that he hoped his secret wasn't connected to Duggar's murder.

If Luke and Charlie weren't friends—as Charlie had claimed—why would Charlie care if Luke was involved in killing Duggar or not? This secret felt personal for Charlie.

Too personal, perhaps.

Tori and Charlie's relationship had become quite personal over the last week.

"What is it? Stop with the suspense, and spit it out already," Tori complained in her usual brash manner, a part of her personality I'd always loved. That was my Tori—never holding back what was on her mind.

Except lately.

Over the years we'd shared everything. Our troubles and our triumphs. But recently, she'd shut me out. Was it because she had done something truly awful? Was she the femme fatale Charlie was warning me about?

If I confronted Tori with this wild hunch and I was wrong, I could damage our friendship. Tori meant too much to me to risk that.

"Um . . . it's Charlie," I stammered while scrambling for something to tell them. "Tori, he's having trouble getting a plumber to come to his shop, and a pipe broke last night. The place flooded. Maybe you can give him a few names?"

"Why didn't you tell me this right away?" She jumped up. "I've given Taylor Plumbing enough business with Perks over the years to put his son through college. He'll do anything for me. If we're done here, I'd better go. I'll tell Charlie that you sent me." She then muttered to herself as she hurried away, "Men and their egos. Can't imagine why he didn't call me in the first place."

I could think of a reason why Charlie didn't call her. And I hated myself for thinking it.

Why couldn't he have given me a Nancy Drew mystery as a clue instead of *The Maltese Falcon*? I understood Nancy Drew books. They were as straightforward as . . . as . . . well . . . as a trusted friend. A friend who'd never consider murder a means to solving a problem.

Perhaps Luke did kill Duggar after all.

Chapter Twenty-Five

Being wrong had never felt this good.

Luke was guilty.

Case.

Closed.

That afternoon, while Flossie watched over the secret bookroom, I used my lunch hour to rush home and feed Dewey. As I munched on forbidden fried cheese with horseradish dipping sauce that I'd picked up from the local fast-food joint, the Grind, Dewey carried over the toy mouse Jace had bought for him and dropped it at my feet. We played fetch with the mouse. Dewey ran so hard and so often, bringing back the mouse each time I tossed it, he actually started to pant.

"You fetch like a dog, and pant like a dog. Are you sure you don't have canine roots?" I asked him.

He gave me a squint-eyed look that suggested he didn't find my sense of humor funny.

"Okay. Okay. You're all cat. Perhaps we should take a break. Besides, I need to get back to the library."

Dewey looked over at his carrier and meowed.

"Sorry, little guy. Maybe tomorrow you can come with me. I need to make sure Anne isn't searching around for you."

I was putting my leftover fried cheese into the fridge when someone knocked. With a trilling purring sound, Dewey ran to the front door. I closed the fridge and followed.

"Anne said you had gone to lunch, and I remembered you'd said I could find you here," Jace said, after I'd opened the door. He smiled down at Dewey.

"We just saw each other at the library." That was why I kept the screen door closed between us.

Dewey yeowed and scratched at the door.

"He's got a healthy set of lungs on him," Jace said, peering through the screen as he tried to get a better view of my kitty. "I saw you posted 'Found' signs around town."

My heart pinched at the thought that I might have to give up my little kitty. I'd only had Dewey for a little over a week. It amazed me how attached I'd grown to him. He filled my house with his happy purrs, making it feel like a home. Cat or not, he was already part of my family.

"I should have posted the notices sooner. I hate to think someone out there is missing him."

Jace nodded sadly, which made me feel uncommonly defensive.

"It's the right thing to do." Were the posted notices the reason for his visit? "You . . . you're not here because someone is missing their cat, are you?"

He held up his hands. "No. No. No." He smiled down at Dewey again. "I imagine it'll be hard to give him up if someone comes forward. He's a special little guy."

As if agreeing, Dewey batted at the screen door again, which was odd. He never batted at the screen, not even when he'd chatter at the birds frolicking in the trees in the front yard.

"Stop that," I said, worried his sharp claws would put a hole in the mesh.

"Are you going to invite me in?" Jace asked.

"I don't think so." Dewey batted at the screen door even more vigorously. I gently nudged him away from the door.

"I want to talk about the investigation," Jace said.

"You said it yourself. There isn't an investigation. Not anymore."

"Tru, please." He closed his eyes as he drew a slow breath. "I know we're not friends, but you are the only one in this town who seems to agree with me that Fisher has arrested the wrong man."

I propped my hands on my hips. "I don't know, Jace. The more I think about it, the more sense Luke's arrest makes. It doesn't take a detective to see that Luke was in trouble. People make mistakes all the time. And sometimes those mistakes lead to even bigger ones."

"You know Luke didn't kill anyone. He's an easy scapegoat. I don't have a clear picture of what might have happened in the library that morning. But I have a feeling that you do."

"You think I'm withholding evidence from the police? That's a serious charge, you know. I think I need to contact my lawyer." I started to close the door.

Dewey had other ideas. He gave the screen door a hard push with his tiny paw and managed to wedge it open wide enough that he could squeeze his skinny body through. I tried to stop him, but my little scamp moved too fast for me.

With a muttered oath, I tossed open the screen door and ran after him.

Not that I needed to run. Instead of dashing away, Dewey went no farther than that pushy detective. He rubbed lazy circles around his jeans-clad legs.

Jace crouched down to pet my naughty cat. "I still can't get over those unusual markings. It sure looks like he has a skull on his head."

"If you say so," I grumbled. "What do you want me to say to you, Detective?"

He sighed. "I don't know, Tru. The truth?"

He picked up Dewey and cradled him in his arms as he straightened. His blue eyes searched mine for a moment. "Perhaps coming here was a mistake." He tried to hand Dewey over to me, but my confounding cat dug his claws into Jace's black T-shirt and held on tight.

I don't know why, but Dewey's affection for Jace made me feel cranky. "If Fisher didn't think there was enough evidence against Luke for Duggar's murder, he wouldn't have arrested him. This is the mayor's own son we're talking about. The chief of police likes his job. Don't you think he would make doubly sure he was right before acting against the man who signs his paycheck?"

"Tru," Jace said quietly, "you're hiding something about the town manager's murder. Please, tell me what you know."

I hesitated a moment before shaking my head. "Give me Dewey. I need to get back to the library. My lunch break ended about ten minutes ago."

One by one he pried Dewey's nails from his T-shirt and handed my kitty over. "We don't have to be enemies, Tru."

"We don't?" As much as I wanted to think I'd grown past all my old high school hurts, I had to admit I hadn't. "I think, maybe, we do."

"I'm sorry to hear that. Fisher might think this investigation is over," he said as he walked away, "but it's not. Not for me. Not until the murderer has been caught. You're hiding something, Tru, and I promise you I'm going to find out what it is you're too afraid to tell me."

When I returned to the library, I found Mrs. Farnsworth sitting at the circulation desk.

"Are you okay?" I asked her.

"You're late," she growled as she pushed the chair back from the desk. "Your lunch break ended sixteen minutes ago."

"I know. I'm sorry." I gathered all my courage and asked her what everyone in town had to be wondering. "Is it true that you remembered seeing something on the morning of the murder? Did you see Luke do something suspicious? Is that why Fisher arrested him?"

She stood, her posture as straight as a flagpole. "I don't suffer gossip, Ms. Becket. You should know that better than anyone." Despite her scolding manner, her lips quivered. Her hands trembled.

"What happened down at the police station?" I asked, feeling suddenly alarmed.

"Nothing. Tell anyone who comes in here talking about Duggar's demise or today's arrest that I don't allow gossip in my library. Tell them they'll either have to keep their tongues locked behind their teeth or they'll have to leave."

Was she serious? The library had always been a hub for gossip in Cypress. People came not only to pick out a new book to read, but also to pick up the latest news about their neighbors. Besides which, telling someone not to talk about what had to be the most explosive thing to have happened in the town's recent memory would be akin to trying to put out a forest fire with a cup of water. It wasn't going to happen. The mayor's son had been arrested for murdering the town manager, for heaven's sake. It'd be unnatural if that didn't set tongues wagging.

"You concentrate on doing your job. I'll be in my office." Mrs. Farnsworth issued the order with a stern look. She headed straight for her private space and closed the door behind her with a slam so loud that it would have had her "shushing" if anyone else had dared close a door like that in *her* library.

About a half hour later, Mayor Goodvale came in. "Good afternoon, Miss, er . . ." He looked over to his right, where his son usually stood. His shoulders dropped about an inch. "Miss . . . I'm sorry."

"Becket, sir," I said kindly.

"Right, Becket's girl."

"I heard what happened," I said. "I'm in a state of shock. If there's anything I can do. It's so hard to believe."

He looked momentarily confused. His brows creased as he studied me. "About my boy, you mean? Yes, yes. He didn't harm anyone. The situation will be cleared up in no time. I promise you that." His wide politician smile returned. "Now, is Mrs. Farnsworth around? I need to have a word with her."

"She's in her office, but—" I started to tell him that I didn't think she wanted to be disturbed. But he wasn't listening.

He entered her office without bothering to knock. Several minutes later he reemerged, his grin even brighter than before. He nodded in my direction before heading out the door. I watched as he crossed the road and went directly to the Sunrise Diner.

Mrs. Farnsworth's door remained ominously closed for the rest of the day.

Chapter Twenty-Six

W hat a busy day!" Flossie exclaimed with a happy sigh when I went to check on her a few minutes before closing time the next day. It was Saturday. She'd spent the day volunteering in the secret book-room. "I must have checked out close to a hundred books." She tapped the nearly full library card box sitting on the old desk.

"I hate to say it, but I think we'll need to computerize the system. Technology does make some tasks easier." I grabbed my oversized tote bag and started to fill it with books I thought my more gossipy readers might enjoy. I planned to make several stops on the way home to personally loan out books.

"Technology can be a real time-saver, but sometimes it's not nearly as fun," Flossie said with a smile. "Let's hold out a little longer and see if we can get used to doing it by hand."

"It's a system I've never actually used. When I was a child, I remember having to use the book slips. I think. But by the time I took the job here at the library, the process was automated."

"Computers do have their uses," Flossie agreed. "They've put even the most obscure information at our fingertips. Just this morning, I looked up when a certain kind of pistol was first used in the UK. Not ten seconds later, I had my answer."

"Are you working on a historical thriller?" I asked her.

"Now, wouldn't that be telling?" she said with a laugh.

"I don't know why you won't tell anyone what books you write."

"And ruin my image of International Woman of Mystery? Never!" She wheeled around the battered old desk and moved toward me. "Everyone is gone. I assume you've been thinking about Duggar's death and Luke's involvement ever since we talked yesterday. I want you to tell me what's bothering you about his arrest."

"Bothering me?" I tried to act surprised.

"Honey, that smile you're wearing right now looks as brittle as a beauty queen's bleached hair."

"That's mean," I said, though I still chuckled. I ran my hand over the spines of a few of the books on the shelves. "Something isn't right. Don't get me wrong. I want to believe this matter is over. Yet Mayor Goodvale came in after lunch yesterday to talk to Mrs. Farnsworth. The man didn't seem the least bit upset over his son's arrest for murder. His son is sitting in a jail cell, and the mayor is grinning like he's just won another election."

"Marvin is a politician through and through. He's good at hiding his emotions when it suits his purposes."

"No one is that good." I paused at my favorite Nancy Drew mystery, *The Hidden Staircase*, and pulled it from the shelf.

Flossie frowned. "The mayor is acting fishy? What are you going to do about it?"

"What can I do?" I opened the book to my favorite passage, where Nancy discovers the secret staircase. "In this book it's vividly clear who the villains are from the first chapter. Why can't real life be so easy?"

"Honey, if life were easy, we'd all be bored out of our minds. What you need to do is focus on what you do know and let others in your life help you figure out the rest."

I considered telling Flossie about the copy of *The Maltese Falcon* Charlie had given me, and how it had fed the doubts I'd already had about Tori and her odd behavior. But just as quickly as the idea had entered my mind, I dismissed it. Speaking about it aloud felt like the worst kind of betrayal. I couldn't do that to Tori.

After returning *The Hidden Staircase* to its shelf, I found the library's copy of *The Maltese Falcon*. It looked identical to Charlie's "clue." They had to be the same edition. I pulled it from the shelf and opened it up to the cover page to see if it said it was a first edition. Perhaps Charlie had given me this particular printing of *The Maltese Falcon* because of how much these books were worth and not because he thought I should be wary of our town's femme fatale.

I wasn't sure why I hadn't checked this right away. The stress of Mrs. Farnsworth going missing and then word of Luke's arrest must have distracted me. Well, at least I was looking into it now.

Books that are first editions will often state it on the copyright page. But sometimes even that's misleading. A book might say "first edition," but to a collector it isn't a true first edition. It might be an anniversary "first" edition, for instance. From my limited research on the topic last night, I'd learned that the books that are worth the most to book collectors are the ones that are the first printed appearance of that particular work.

Nothing on the copyright page indicated that this particular book was a first anything. Like the copy Charlie had given me, the library's copy had a gray cloth cover. No title on the front, only a dark green image of a falcon. The title appeared on the spine along with the author's name and publisher.

The date on both books' cover pages read 1930. Supposedly, older books listed their printing date on the cover page. If the date on the copyright page didn't match the date on the cover page, that would mean it wasn't a first edition.

The first copyright date on the copyright page was 1929. The date on the cover page was 1930. Not a first edition. It wasn't a book that would be worth a small fortune.

I slid the library's copy into my tote bag. It was the kind of mystery novel my father enjoyed. I knew from organizing his extensive home library for his birthday last year that he didn't have a copy of the book. He'd probably enjoy rereading it. And he might be able to give me some new insights on the book's many meanings.

"Everything feels wrong," I said as I patted my tote bag. "The books shouldn't be in the basement. Mrs. Farnsworth shouldn't feel like she needs to hide in her office. And the library should be the safest place in town, not the most dangerous." I quickly turned away from Flossie. "Let's get these books shelved." I grabbed a pile from the stack of returned books.

Luke was in jail and the police chief, who was a respected man, was saying the case was closed. I shouldn't still be thinking about Charlie's clue or worrying about Tori and whether she'd done something horrible. She hadn't. Luke had.

Still, no matter how hard I tried, I couldn't stop my thoughts from traveling back over the investigation. My mind raced through the many Nancy Drew mysteries I'd read and reread over the years. I couldn't remember even one instance in which Nancy had ever suspected either Bess or George of wrongdoing. I wish I could remember something like that from one of those books. Then, perhaps, I'd know what to do now.

Chapter Twenty-Seven

The next day was Sunday, the one day the library remained closed in Cypress. I'd looked forward to sleeping in. But I had a cat now. After I spent yet another sleepless night tossing and turning and worrying about Mrs. Farnsworth and what the mayor might have said to her on Friday, Dewey batted at my nose until I dragged my bedraggled self out of bed at first light.

Dewey trilled—a mix between a purr and a meow—as he trotted directly under my feet while I stumbled toward the kitchen. He trilled even more loudly at the sight of food in his dish. And while he ate, he purred like a high-performance race car.

I poured myself a bowl of cereal. I stared at the food in my bowl as I sat, slightly slumped, at the table. From my purse, I retrieved the torn paper Dewey had discovered in the media room. I wondered if I should give it to Jace. Unsure what to do with it, I set it aside. I then found in my purse the copy of *The Maltese Falcon* Charlie had given me and the small blue notebook that I'd jotted notes into when this investigation had still felt like a new and exciting game.

On the notebook's first page I'd written the names of everyone who was in the library at the time of Duggar's murder. Flossie and I topped the list. But we had both been in the basement when I heard that ominous thud of the shelf being pushed over onto Duggar. Next on the list was the mayor and his son, Luke. I'd drawn lines through both their names, since the mayor and Luke had provided each other with alibis. Had Mrs. Farnsworth somehow blown a hole in Luke's alibi? She must have.

Had the mayor lied about being with Luke to protect his son? Did he suspect his son of murder? And had he visited Mrs. Farnsworth yesterday to put pressure on her to recant whatever she'd told Fisher? Was that why he didn't seem at all worried about his son's arrest?

I put a star next to Luke's name and wrote "likely killer."

Next on the list were Anne Lowery and Mrs. Farnsworth. Neither of them had an alibi (that I knew of) and both of them had their own reasons for wanting to kill Duggar.

I put a question mark beside both their names.

Finally, at the bottom of the list were Tori and Charlie. Charlie had connections to Luke, but other than that, I couldn't come up with a good reason why he would kill Cypress's town manager. Sure, Charlie might have planned to sell the books Luke was going to steal, but I couldn't imagine a middleman becoming so invested in a book sale that he'd resort to murder. And Duggar's death certainly hadn't helped Charlie in any way that I could find.

Only Tori, out of everyone on the list, had actually benefited from Duggar's untimely death. Though it hurt me to do so, I had no choice but to ink a question mark next to her name. And add a star.

"This is getting me nowhere." I pushed the notebook away.

I needed to clear the noise from my mind. Perhaps then I could look at this problem from a fresh perspective. After scratching Dewey behind the ears, I headed out to the backyard shed where I kept my mountain bike.

The humid heat already seared as it did on any given August day. To ward off the dangers of overheating, I wore a light-colored tank top. I filled an insulated water bottle with ice-cold water. The water bottle with its book-themed pattern had been a gift from Tori on my last birthday. I took it nearly everywhere with me.

I then sorted through the library books in my tote bag and tucked several into a small saddlebag attached to my bike, including both the library copy of *The Maltese Falcon* and the copy Charlie had given me. The plan was to hand out books, talk to my neighbors about their thoughts on Duggar's murder, talk to my father about the two copies of *The Maltese Falcon,* and use my bike ride to clear my mind. Once my gear was ready, I tightened the bike helmet on my head, clicked its strap closed, and set out on my ride.

Although I lived in town, the streets in Cypress were not much different than the rural roads one would find in the middle of acres of farmland. The asphalt was pitted. The edge of the road often dropped abruptly off onto low, grassy shoulders. As long as a rider understood the situation and kept a keen eye out for cars and trucks, the ride wasn't exactly treacherous.

Lake Street, which bisected Main Street, was the main artery that led from the center of town toward the cottages and mansions lining Lake Marion. After making several stops along the way, I turned onto Lake Street. The street ended at a public fishing pier and boat landing.

Turn right onto West Marion Drive, and the road passed by a fish camp, three shacks, and two mobile homes before coming up to the mayor's lake house. It was a generously sized log cabin built by the mayor and his brothers nearly twenty years ago. Past that, the road continued up a steep hill and into a neighborhood of new and expensive lake houses.

Turn left from Lake Street onto East Marion Drive, and the lake spread out like a deep blue void between occasional copses of cypress. The land here was lower, swampier. The asphalt road was even more crumbly and pitted from seasonal flooding. About a quarter mile down the road was my dad's lake house, a battered old shack built in the 1950s.

The sun was high over the lake by the time my dad's sagging, unpainted shack came into view. I parked my bike next to his front porch, stepped over the rotted steps, and knocked loudly on his door.

"He's not home," a voice from next door shouted.

"Gone fishing?" I called back to Marianne Carsdale, a widowed schoolteacher who'd lived in her tidy little white house for as long as I could remember. She leaned heavily on her cane.

"He should be churching. That's where I'm headin'." She straightened her peach-colored flowered hat. "But he took that old boat of his out onto the water instead. Won't see him again until tonight."

"That lake is my dad's church," I said.

She scoffed at that and then quoted several lines of scripture. "Why ain't you at that church of yours?" she demanded. "Mama Eddy won't like sittin' alone."

"My mama never sits alone, even at church." But she was right. Mama would come looking for me later today. Every Sunday she expected me to sit on her left in the third pew from the front. "After the past couple of weeks I've had, I needed some exercise and fresh air to clear out my head."

"Clear out your head?" She snorted a short laugh. "With all this pollen in the air? More like fill it up with congestion." She hobbled down her steps toward her ancient Oldsmobile, which was the size of a yacht.

"Wait, Miss Marianne. I have something you might like to borrow." I pulled a book about growing roses out of my bag and held it up for her to see. "Dad said you've been complaining about mites."

"Lovey, those spider mites are eating my plants all up." She looked at the ragged bushes growing around her front porch and shook her head.

"Chapter five offers some remedies for that." I jogged over and handed her the book.

She tilted her head and looked at me askance. "I'd heard you'd been acting like a one-woman human library lately."

"Does that bother you?" I asked with a smile.

She pressed her lips together and frowned as she considered my question. "I'd be ungrateful if I complained about someone carrying out a public service without expecting anything in return. You ain't expecting anything, are you?"

"Not a thing." I pantomimed drawing an X over my heart. "Just give that book back to me when you're done with it, and I'll make sure it gets to someone else who might need it."

I started back toward my bike. Before I could take a step, Marianne grabbed hold of my arm. "Watch yourself, now," she said. Her voice had deepened. "Not everyone around here thinks what you're doing is right. I've heard whispers that someone is downright furious about your book-lending practices."

"Really?" That surprised me. "Who?"

She shook her head. "Didn't catch a name. But as I said to your daddy the other day, 'That girl has got to take care if she doesn't want to end up all battered and bruised like that Luke boy.'" She tsked. "Still can't believe that boy would kill a man. But there's some rotten doings going around. And it seems to be stirring up all sorts of violence."

I thanked her and promised I'd be careful.

As I pedaled down the road, her warning troubled me. Someone in Cypress was furious? That was the word Marianne had used, and she wasn't one to overstate a matter. Someone was furious that I'd been lending out books? That didn't make a lick of sense. And Marianne was worried that same person might try and hurt me? That made even less sense.

I had promised her I'd watch my back, and I planned to. But that wasn't going to stop me from keeping the secret library going.

Nothing in this world could do that.

• • •

I pedaled faster and faster. With each revolution of the bike chain, my indignation grew. How dare someone take offense at my efforts to help this town? Duggar should have never taken away the printed books. If there was anyone to be furious at, it was the dead town manager. Not me.

Speak of the devil . . .

I rounded a bend in the road and Duggar's midcentury-modern house came into view. The town manager's house, which sat across the street from the lake, was bathed in the shadows of the towering cypress trees surrounding it. But there was a light shining inside one of the rooms. And the front door sat open.

I pulled my bike to the side of the road and took a long sip from my water bottle. Duggar had lived alone, but his parents and grandparents and aunts and uncles and assortment of cousins all lived in Cypress. Any one of them could be at his house sorting through his things. There was no reason for a chill to be tiptoeing up my spine, especially when the daytime temperature was steadily rising into the mid-nineties.

The tingling at the back of my neck reminded me of Marianne's warnings to tread with care. Perhaps I should keep my head down and continue on my ride past his house.

Oh, who was I kidding? I had no plans of leaving, spine tingling or not. If I'd learned anything from those Nancy Drew mysteries, it was that any intrepid sleuth would see an open door as an invitation to investigate.

I parked my bike and was about to march up to the house when a movement at the door caught my attention. A tall, slender man emerged from the house carrying two boxes, one stacked on the other. At first his face was in shadow.

He was probably one of Duggar's relatives. I raised my hand in greeting. Maybe he could give me more information about Duggar's obsession with old books.

I'd barely called a halting "Hello!" when the man turned down the driveway. He walked toward a sleek black sports sedan, providing me with a clear view of his face.

That man wasn't a cousin. Or an uncle. Or anyone from Cypress.

The man carrying those boxes was—

"*Charlie?*" I called.

Chapter Twenty-Eight

What was Charlie doing carrying boxes out of Duggar's home? I don't think he heard me call out his name over the sputtering, coughing engine of a dusty white sedan that pulled into the driveway.

Grandle, the squat loan shark who'd destroyed library property, jumped out and jogged toward Charlie. He grabbed one of the boxes. Charlie didn't protest.

What in the world was Charlie doing with *him*?

The two of them spoke in low tones as they loaded the boxes into the luxury car's open trunk. As they headed back toward the house, Charlie glanced in my direction.

He stopped.

"What?" the other man grunted. He turned toward me as well.

They both frowned.

Had I caught them doing something they shouldn't be doing? Were they robbing Duggar's house? Was this the motive I'd been searching for? Did Charlie need Duggar out of the way so he could get his hands on Duggar's expensive collection of books? Delanie had said book collectors could be ruthless.

Was Charlie furious that I'd been running an underground lending library because that meant I'd taken the books he'd wanted to sell—books that Luke was going to steal for him—and kept them in the secret bookroom? Marianne had warned me to be careful.

And here I was, blithely walking into . . . into . . . who knew what!

Grandle reached out his muscular arm and pointed at me. My heart jumped up into my throat.

"Hey!" he shouted and took a step toward me.

I ran back to my bike and jumped on it.

"Hey!" Charlie pointed and shouted too.

Great Caesar's ghost! They were coming after me!

I pedaled as fast and as hard as possible away from the house. Too afraid to look back to see if they were following in their cars, I made turns onto unfamiliar dirt roads. A car's engine roared behind me. Like, directly behind me. Was that the roar of that dusty sedan? My breath came in short spurts as I realized a bike couldn't outrun a car. I made an abrupt turn down a bumpy path that wove through a thick forest of trees. The trail was too narrow for a car to follow. Even so, I didn't stop pedaling.

What was Charlie doing at Duggar's house? Why was Grandle there helping him? And why were they chasing me?

I needed to warn Tori. She was not going to like hearing this. Why did my BFF always pick the wrong man? Perhaps there simply weren't any *right* men available in Cypress. It wasn't as if I'd found any. Ever.

There's Jace, my mind whispered.

"He's the worst," I said aloud.

Not even a second later, my bike's front wheel hit a tree root. The bike flipped back end over front. And I went flying.

I hit the ground headfirst. Thank goodness I was wearing my helmet.

I stayed where I'd landed, facedown on the hard-packed trail, breathing carefully. Testing this arm and that leg, making sure I hadn't broken anything important. I felt a twinge of pain in my left wrist. But it was no more than a twinge. Good.

Still, I didn't dare move. A leaf tickled my nose. Something scampered in the trees above my head. An osprey cried in the distance. My ears felt slightly stretched as I continued to listen.

Grandle could be lumbering down the narrow trail right now, searching for me.

I listened a moment longer. Hearing nothing but nature, I pushed up onto my knees. I listened a bit more. Still nothing.

My lungs finally started working again. I drew in a deep breath and then another. Feeling stronger, I pushed up to my feet. My legs felt strong. After brushing off my skinned knees, I picked up my bike. The front wheel wobbled and then fell off.

"That's not good." I took my cell phone from my pocket. After saying a quick prayer of forgiveness for cursing technology these past several weeks, I started to call the first person who came to mind—Tori. Not only did she need to know about Charlie, but she had always been the go-to friend I called whenever I needed, well, anything.

The phone rang once. I quickly canceled the call.

No, I couldn't call her. I couldn't drag her into this. I didn't even understand what *this* was. All I knew was that I thought a dangerous man had followed me. He could still be out there on the road, waiting for me to ride back out. I couldn't ask Tori—or any of my friends—to come pick me up. Not when doing so might be leading them directly into the arms of a—

Was Grandle a killer?

Had he somehow slipped into the library and killed Duggar? No. Not slipped in. Had Charlie invited a killer into the library? It would have been easy enough for him to let Grandle through the back door when we were all packing up the books and carrying them to the basement.

So no, I couldn't call Tori. Not yet. Doing so might get her killed.

I needed to call someone skilled in handling a potentially deadly situation.

My fingers stumbled over the numbers on the screen as I dialed the number he'd given me. The same number I'd glanced at before tossing his card into the bottom of my purse. Somehow, those digits had imprinted themselves on my brain. I'd worry about the reason my mind had held on to those numbers later. Right now, I was grateful to know them.

"Detective Bailey," he answered practically after the first ring.

"*Jace*," I whispered.

"Tru, hey, what's going on?" He chuckled lightly. Did he think my whispery voice sounded sexy? "Is Dewey enjoying lazing around with you on this hot Sunday?"

"What?" His question shouldn't have surprised me. He'd had a soft spot for my cat from the first moment he met him. "No, I'm not home. You were right. I'm in danger." I hoped that didn't sound like a come-on. I didn't want to give him the wrong impression. I was still upset with him for what he'd done in high school, wasn't I? "Grandle, the loan shark, is chasing me. I think. I escaped into the woods but crashed my bike. And . . . and I'm afraid to go back to the road, because he might be waiting there."

"Wait. You crashed? Motorbike or bicycle?" His tone immediately changed. He sounded all business. "Are you injured? Do you need EMS? Where are you?"

"I'm okay. Just bruised. My bicycle will need work." I told him about my winding escape down several dirt roads. "To be honest, I don't know where I am."

"That's okay. I can get a lock on your location through your cell phone. Are you in a safe location? I mean, are you away from the trail?"

"Um . . ." As I moved off the trail, through a thick clump of bushes, and down a hill, I asked, "You can trace my location through my cell phone? That seems awfully . . . stalkerish."

"Not me personally. The police department."

"Oh. That makes sense."

"Keep your phone turned on." After a pause he said, "You didn't answer my first question. Are you in a safe place?"

"I'm working on it. But—ouch!—I just stepped into a blackberry bush." The thorns dug into my bare legs. "Oh, that smarts."

"Try to find a less prickly hiding place. Stay on the line. I'm going to put you on hold and call the station."

I backed out of the bush and landed in a tall (and thankfully soft) clump of grass. This was much better.

"Tru? Are you still there?"

"I'm here."

"Good. You had me worried for a moment when you didn't answer me. I'm putting you on hold now."

"Okay," I whispered.

It felt as if I were squatting forever in that grass. Mosquitoes buzzed around my head and gnats nipped at my ankles.

"Tru? Are you still there?" he asked a hundred years later. Or maybe it was simply a hundred mosquito bites later.

"Haven't moved," I said.

"Good. Hold tight. I'm on my way. I'm going to hang up now. Put your phone on silent. I don't want your phone ringing or beeping. It might give away your hiding place if someone is out there looking for you." I hadn't thought of that.

"Will do." I disconnected the call and then turned off the sound on my phone.

After a while most of the mosquitoes and gnats flew away in search of fresh prey. White fluffy clouds floated in a brilliant blue sky overhead. Two playful fox squirrels chased each other up and down a nearby tree. A soft wind tried its best to cool the humid August air. It was really a lovely Sunday, a perfect day to be out in nature. Too bad I couldn't enjoy it.

I'd been sitting there, staring at the sky and listening for dangerous squatty men when I noticed the steady crunch of twigs and leaves growing louder.

I hunkered down, pressing myself flat in the grass. Would that scary thug spot my broken bike and follow my trail to this ridiculously exposed patch of grass? Should I stay? Should I run?

All I knew was that I didn't want to die out here in the middle of nowhere, especially not before I found out what was going on.

Chapter Twenty-Nine

———◦———

Tru!" Jace's voice seemed to echo through the forest.

Two weeks ago, anyone suggesting I'd ever be happy to hear the detective's voice would be a stinking liar. Today, the sound of his voice made me downright giddy. I jumped up and waved my arms. "Over here!"

Jace hurried over with two uniformed officers following cautiously behind him.

"Did you see the car that was following me? Was it parked at the road?" I asked.

He plucked a stick from my bike helmet. "It's all pretty deserted out here."

"Usually is," one of the officers said. "Ain't nothing out this way but soybeans and corn."

"And trees," I added. The thick canopy of trees had felt so disorienting.

Jace took my arm and helped me step around the blackberry brambles. "Let's get you and your bike out of here. You can give a statement about what happened back at the station."

He nodded to one of the officers. "Do you mind carrying her bike?"

The officer grunted. "Pardon me, ma'am, but if you were being pursued, why in sugar-honeyed-iced-tea didn't you ride toward town instead of out toward the boondocks where there's no one to help you? Makes no sense to me."

"I—" Why didn't I head back toward town? Or back toward my dad's house? "Actually, I didn't think about where I was headed. I just went. No one has ever chased me before." And apparently my Nancy Drew skills weren't as sharply honed as I'd hoped they'd be.

"Officer Franks teaches a self-defense course at the community center," Jace explained. "I think you should take it."

"I'd say you should, ma'am," Officer Franks said with a nod. "With all the mistakes you've made, you're lucky to still be alive."

"Well, that is, if anyone was actually chasing the girl," the other officer grumbled.

"You think I made this up?" I demanded. "You think these scraped knees were just for show?"

He looked me up and down and shrugged.

"Easy now." Jace guided me toward the trail. "I'll get your story when we get back to the station. Do you think you need to get medical attention first? You told me on the phone you weren't hurt. But you look—"

"I'm okay. I just want to get this over with and get back home."

Officer Franks picked up my broken bike. That's when I noticed that the water bottle Tori had given me was missing from its carrier.

"Did you happen to see an aquamarine bottle on your way in?" I explained how it was an insulated bottle with a book-themed pattern. I hated to lose it.

I started to poke around in nearby bushes searching for it. But there was no sign of the bottle.

"Tori gave me that bottle. I loved it." I looked forlornly at the empty carrier on my bike.

"I'm sorry, Tru." Jace put his arm around me. "We can keep an eye out as we follow the trail back to the road."

Even though I'd sworn I wasn't injured, I limped back to the road as sharp pains shot up from my right ankle.

Jace let me ride in his car—a new green Jeep—which I was grateful for. Otherwise, I would have had to ride in the back of the marked police car like a criminal.

"This all started at Duggar's house. Something odd is going on there," I told Jace. "I think it was being robbed."

But when we approached Duggar's house, I saw right away the driveway was empty.

"The front door was wide open," I said. "Charlie came out with boxes."

"You mean the new guy opening a used bookstore?" Jace turned toward me.

"I'm beginning to wonder about him."

"You think he was robbing the home of a dead man? In broad daylight? On a Sunday?"

"When everyone is supposed to be in church," I pointed out. "Anyhow, he wasn't alone. Grandle was with him. You know, the scary-looking guy from Vegas I already told you about?"

Jace frowned. "You think they were robbing the house and then chased you when you just happened to see them?" He glanced up and down the road. "Sunday or not, the roads circling the lake can be quite busy on the weekends, especially on a nice day like this. Anyone could have driven by and seen them. Would they have chased any random person, or do you think they would only chase you?"

"They were—" I started to argue that their behavior was suspicious. But Jace had a point. The two men weren't acting sneaky. They'd been taking their time, acting as if they had every right to be there. But still, it was suspicious that Charlie would be there with Grandle. He didn't have anything good to say about the loan shark.

"After you told me about the connection between this bookseller and Luke, I talked with our newcomer. He seems fine. He gave me as much information about Grandle as he was able."

"He's got plenty of charm. I'll give him that. Mrs. Farnsworth is half in love with Charlie. And Tori is in love with him."

"Add the mayor to his fan club. He vouched for Mr. Newcastle," Jace said. "He sees him and others like him as a vital part of his grand plan to bring new life to our downtown."

"I am excited about the bookstore. Truly, I am. And he does seem knowledgeable, but I do wonder if he isn't . . ." I hesitated, unsure how much to tell Jace.

"Yes?" Jace asked.

"What were Charlie and Grandle doing at Duggar's house? Why would they be together? What was in those boxes? I don't know. I do know, however, that they shouted at me, and I'm pretty sure Grandle chased me in his car."

"I'll talk to Charlie again," Jace said with a sigh. "I'll ask him about his connection with Grandle again."

"But . . . ?" I definitely heard an unsaid "but" in that sentence.

He put the Jeep into gear and pulled away from Duggar's house. "But you have to admit that you're not giving me much to work with here. Why would Grandle, a man you don't even know, chase after you?"

Why indeed?

I sat back and turned the bicycle helmet in my lap over and over. "When I asked Charlie about what job he had in Las Vegas, he evaded the question. Tori said he did the same with her. Have you heard anything about Charlie's background?" I asked.

"Charlie mentioned he was recently retired from law enforcement." We were halfway to the police station. He paused to turn a corner. "He was vague with details."

"Huh." Law enforcement? That didn't make sense. "But he's rich.

And well traveled. And well read. That doesn't sound like a retired cop to me."

"I take offense at that last jab," Jace grumbled.

"What? You mean about being well read? Why?"

"Cops aren't vapid meatheads, you know. We have to think in creative ways in order to solve crimes."

"Sure, I'll give you that. Police officers aren't without brains. But I'm talking about books. You rarely opened a book in high school," I pointed out.

"After messing up my leg in college and losing my spot on the football team, I found time to start reading."

"Really?"

"Really, but we're not talking about me."

"We're talking about Charlie and his obvious wealth. You don't get that from law enforcement. Not unless—"

"You're not going to suggest that he was on the take." Jace groaned at the thought.

"He was in Vegas." That had to mean something.

Jace sighed. "I'm sure not everyone from Vegas is crooked."

"Not everyone. Just one rich ex-cop." Had Charlie given me the copy of *The Maltese Falcon* because he wanted me to think a femme fatale was behind Duggar's murder? Perhaps he wanted to drive a wedge between Tori and me. Perhaps he was worried that if we combined what we knew about him, we'd figure out that he was a clever master criminal pretending to be a charming, suave booklover.

"Okay. I see I'm not going to convince you," Jace said as he turned another corner. "And maybe I *shouldn't* convince you that Charlie is a good guy. I don't know him. Let's just wait until we get to the station to talk about what happened today."

We spent the rest of the ride into town in an awkward silence. Blessedly, it was a short drive.

Cypress's police station wasn't much to look at. It was located three blocks north of Cypress's marble-clad town hall. The rather grand town hall had been constructed at the same time as the library, in the early 1900s. The police department, on the other hand, was built in the late 1960s when money in town had already become scarce. The one-story, flat-roofed brick building had very few windows. And the windows it did have were the tall, narrow kind that let very little light into a building. The eaves were rotting. The trim desperately needed painting. Before today, I'd never been inside the police station. Never had a reason.

As I'd expected, the inside was even less impressive than the outside. Water stains created interesting mosaics of brown and yellow on the sagging drop ceiling. In the reception area, yellowed wallpaper with a fake wood pattern was peeling at the edges and seams. The floor was made of old asbestos tiles. Some were loose here and there. Some were missing altogether.

I glanced back over my shoulder at the officer who'd insinuated that I'd made up being chased. I felt compassion for him. The library had just received an impressive renovation, and it was a beautiful building to begin with. This place was simply awful.

An officer I didn't recognize sat at a tall, pressed wood–paneled desk. He nodded at the four of us as we entered but didn't say anything.

"Would you like something? Coffee?" Jace asked as we headed through a locked door marked "Staff."

"I'm fine. Let's just get this over with," I said.

He led the way down a narrow hallway and then opened a door to a small conference room.

"Good heavens, Tru, what happened? You look an absolute mess," the coroner, Krystal Capps, squealed as she stepped out of another room down the hall.

I explained—very briefly—what had happened.

She wagged her finger at the detective. "You can't let our girl bleed all over the place. You should have taken her to the urgent care center. At the very least, she might need a tetanus shot."

"I asked her more than once if she wanted medical care," Jace argued.

"I just want to go home and get into a bath." That was the honest truth.

Krystal clucked her tongue. "Let me grab a first aid kit and patch up her knees. I'll take a look at that wrist while I'm at it. It looks swollen. Honey, don't you dare protest. Joey, who does maintenance around here, will thank you when he doesn't have to mop up a puddle of blood off the floor."

She was exaggerating, of course. I wasn't bleeding that badly. Perhaps a few rivulets of blood had oozed down my leg and stained my already muddy socks, but that was a far cry from bleeding out all over the floor.

She helped clean up my knees, slapped some oversized bandages on them, and then told me to get my wrist, ankle, and the bump on my head checked out by the local urgent care center. Cypress's rural hospital had closed its doors nearly a decade earlier. She stood up and looked me over from head to toe before declaring that I was healthy enough to give a statement.

The conference room had molded plastic orange chairs that had been old-fashioned when I was a child. The one I took had a crack down the back that had been patched with duct tape.

Jace sat across from me. He fussed with a tape recorder and his notebook for a while before asking me to tell him, from the beginning, what had happened.

I described every detail about my wild bike ride and crash. He took notes and asked probing questions. He leaned forward, his eyes filled with compassion. It seemed as if he was taking it all very seriously. That is, until he closed his notebook and sat back in the orange plastic chair. His chair squeaked.

He broke eye contact and frowned.

"What?" I asked. "What's wrong?"

"You never looked behind you?" He sounded disappointed. "You never saw the car that you thought was chasing you? Not even once? Not even out the corner of your eye?"

I hadn't. "I was too worried about getting away. I'd read in a book once how coaches tell track stars that if you start to look behind you, you've already lost."

Unfortunately, I could see by the tense expression on Jace's face that by *not* looking behind me I'd lost all credibility. "You don't believe me," I said.

"I believe you believe it happened like you said it did," he said kindly.

That didn't make me feel better. I bit the inside of my cheek. Not that I was going to cry or anything. Tears were the farthest thing from my mind. Something was going on that I didn't understand, something potentially dangerous. And the police seemed unwilling to listen to me, which made me feel angry enough to scream.

But screaming would make me appear unstable. Besides, librarians didn't scream.

I closed my eyes and drew a couple of deep breaths, while desperately clinging to my inner Nancy Drew. Stopping the troubles happening in my beloved small town was my main focus. I needed to find Duggar's killer. I needed to figure out why someone would attack Luke in the middle of the library. And I needed to find out what Charlie was up to.

Jace could ignore me or think I was hysterical. I didn't care. Well, I *shouldn't* care.

Right.

I opened my eyes. "You told me my life could be in danger," I reminded him. "You told me you didn't think Luke killed anyone."

He reached over and turned off the tape recorder. "We've already had this conversation."

"Not really. Remember Dewey was playing with that piece of paper in the media room? The one you picked up and put in your pocket?"

Jace's hard expression softened. "He is a scamp."

"When you joined us at Perks that night, you dropped the paper. I thought it was trash. But when I looked at it, I found something interesting on it. It looked as if it'd been torn from a formal price quote for books. From what you told me Friday morning, I suppose the police have the rest of the price quote sheet."

He raised his brows. "Were you planning to hand over this . . . this evidence?"

"Of course." Eventually.

"You saw me on Friday. We talked about it then."

"I hadn't looked at Dewey's treasure that carefully yet."

Someone knocked at the conference room door. Jace pressed his lips together before calling out, "Yeah?"

The door opened. Officer Franks poked his head into the room. "Dude, Fisher wants a word with you. Pronto."

"Tell him I'll be right there."

"Oh . . . kay . . ." Franks said slowly. He gave me a hard look before leaving.

"That guy doesn't like me," I said.

"He thought you killed Duggar," Jace said with a shrug. "Before Luke's arrest, half the police force thought you pushed over the shelf. Some still think you stink of guilt."

That was a chilling bit of information I didn't need to know.

I straightened my spine. "Look, I know you said Chief Fisher considers the case closed. You have your man. I'm glad. But what I saw today—"

"We have someone in custody for the murder." He sat back and crossed his arms over his chest. "That takes the heat off you. Why not enjoy it?"

"You told me yourself that you were afraid I might be in danger. Not just me, but everyone who was at the library that morning, because the killer is still at large."

"I did. But what I want to know is why you've suddenly changed your mind. Why do you suddenly think I might be right? Is it because you think your girlfriend's new beau is robbing the dead?"

"No." I crinkled my brows. "Not exactly. Friday afternoon, Mayor Goodvale came into the library looking to talk with Mrs. Farnsworth. When I offered him my sympathies about his son, he told me that Luke would be released in a matter of days." I pointed to the door. "When that happens, all those cops out there that you say think I'm guilty will shine their spotlight of suspicion right back on me."

Jace eased forward again. "Wait. What exactly did the mayor tell you?"

"That his son wasn't guilty. He didn't act at all worried that Luke had been arrested for Duggar's murder."

Jace chewed on that tidbit of information before saying, "That doesn't make sense."

"Well, after talking to me, the mayor spent quite some time with Mrs. Farnsworth. Perhaps in a day or two she'll recant whatever it was she had miraculously remembered. Fisher's closed case might find itself flung wide open again."

"Hmm . . ." That news seemed to trouble Jace.

"Why does that worry you? It's what you wanted, isn't it? You told me yourself you didn't believe Luke was guilty."

"And you reminded me what a lousy detective I was," he shot back without even blinking.

"I didn't say you were incompetent. So why don't we talk for a minute about the investigation and why we both think the mayor is, for once, right? His son is innocent."

"Here's another idea." Jace stood up. "Why don't *you* tell me that big secret you're keeping from me?" He tapped the scarred wooden tabletop. "Think about it. I'll be back as soon as I'm done with Fisher."

After Jace had left, Officer Franks stepped into the room. He leaned against the door with his arms over his wide chest and glared. I tried to make conversation, but he refused to participate.

"You need to stay away from him," he grumbled after several tense minutes of silence.

"From whom?" I asked.

"From Detective Bailey. He's a skilled investigator with a big heart to boot. Too big. We're lucky to have him back in Cypress. It'd be a crying shame if he was forced to resign over something stupid he does with someone like you."

"Someone like me?"

"A femme fatale. Yeah, don't look surprised. I read mysteries, just like you do. You act like a damsel in distress, which feeds right into our boy's hero tendencies, but you and I both know you don't need saving."

"I never said I—"

He stabbed his finger at me. "He doesn't need your kind of trouble."

"I've never been considered anyone's trouble before. I don't know if I should be flattered or insulted."

"Why should you be insulted?" Jace asked as he returned to the conference room, banging the door on Officer Franks's back as he opened it. "What's going on here, Franks?"

"Just chatting with the suspect while we waited for your return," Franks said.

"She's not a suspect." Jace looked over at me and then raised his brows as if to say, "See, I tried to warn you."

"Ri-ight," Franks drawled as he left. "Not a suspect."

"Is everything okay?" I asked.

"I was about to ask you the same thing," Jace said. "He wasn't harassing you, was he?"

"He was acting like a protective big brother. Seemed to think I was out to ruin your career."

Jace's cheeks colored at that. "Sorry about that."

"He made it sound like his reasons for worrying about your future here go back to why you had to leave New York. You got involved with someone you shouldn't have."

Jace swung the door wide open. "Let me drive you home."

I didn't move. "Aren't you going to explain what's going on?"

"No. I'm going to take you home."

Chapter Thirty

We need to talk.

The text from Charlie came in just as I climbed into Jace's Jeep. Then a few seconds later, my phone chimed again.

I have something of yours.

I squinted at the screen. Was that some kind of threat?
"Is everything okay?" Jace asked.
"I don't know. Um . . ." Another text made my phone chime.

Can we meet at my shop?

I texted back. No.
For one, I didn't trust Charlie, not after seeing him with Grandle at Duggar's house. And I hadn't read all those mystery novels without learning a few things about self-preservation.

Still, that didn't stop me from wondering what Charlie could have of mine that he could use as leverage against me. Obviously, he could tell people about the secret bookroom, but that's not what his text had said. I swallowed hard as I realized what (or rather who) he might mean.

Tori.

I texted my friend right away. Where are you?

She texted back, Perks. Shorthanded today. Why?

I breathed a sigh of relief before replying, Wanted to make sure you were safe. Text me before you leave?

She sent two emojis: a woman shrugging her shoulders and a thumbs-up sign.

With that settled, I slid my phone back into my pocket. Not that the texts with Tori had stopped me from worrying.

"Do you want to talk about it?" Jace asked.

"No." Not with him. Not yet. I still needed to protect the secret bookroom. I was already concerned that I'd said too much to him about Charlie. If he wanted to, Charlie could easily expose me and the secret bookroom.

But then again, I could ruin things for him by telling the police that he was at the library when Duggar was killed.

"If you change your mind . . ." Jace said as he turned into the parking lot of Cypress's urgent care facility.

This unexpected turn jolted me out of my thoughts. "I thought you were taking me home."

"I will after you get a doctor to check out why you're limping—"

"I'm not limping!" I argued.

"Okay, you hobbled—slower than my great-grandmother, by the way—every step to my Jeep. And I want you to get that swollen wrist of yours looked at too."

Two hours later Jace's Jeep pulled to a stop in front of my small bungalow. The doctor at the urgent care facility had wrapped both my wrist and ankle. The x-rays she'd taken had found no breaks, only sprains, and not bad sprains at that. She ordered me to spend what was left of the day with my right ankle iced and elevated.

"Are you expecting someone?" Jace asked while I gathered up the paperwork and ice packs and prescriptions the urgent care center had handed me on the way out.

"No, why?" I looked up and saw what he saw.

My front door was wide open. The screen door was hanging off to one side as if someone had ripped it from its hinges.

"Dewey!" I cried.

I tossed aside everything and jumped out of the Jeep. I whimpered when I landed on my sprained ankle, but I didn't let a little thing like sharp, shooting pains slow me down.

"Tru! Wait!" Jace shouted.

Wait? How could he ask me to wait? I had to find Dewey.

I ran as if I were trying to take home the gold in the Olympics. My arms pumped. My lungs burned.

Thank goodness my house wasn't set too far from the street. I really wasn't in the best of shape. My bike rides around town were at the pace of leisurely strolls, not athletic training sessions.

"Dewey!" I coughed and sputtered, quite embarrassingly out of breath by the time I reached the open front door.

"Let me go in first," Jace said, not sounding even the least bit out of breath. The jerk. He nudged my wheezing, heaving body aside. "Cypress Police!" he announced.

With gun in hand, he cautiously stepped into the living room.

"Dewey?" I croaked. I rested my hands on my knees. They made a perfect prop for keeping me upright. Gee, I really needed to pedal harder during my bike rides. My muscles might be strong, but my cardio clearly needed work. "Dewey greets me at the door. He greets everyone at the door."

"Stay outside," Jace ordered.

My heart had taken residence in my throat. Whoever had broken into my house had made sure I'd notice. There was no other reason for damaging an unlocked screen door. Or for kicking in an equally unlocked front door.

I rarely locked up my house. This was Cypress, for goodness' sake.

Despite Jace's instructions, I stepped inside. "Dewey?"

The living room was a wreck. All the books had been tossed from the bookshelves. The sofa slashed. My dad's old recliner tipped over.

No sign of my little stray kitty.

The kitchen hadn't fared much better. The cabinet doors sat open. The contents of my fridge and freezer were spilled onto the floor. The tote bag I'd used to carry home the library books had been upended. The books scattered.

"No one's here," Jace said as he came in the room behind me.

"What about Dewey?" I asked.

"I didn't see him. I'm sorry. I need to call the department and report the break-in."

I hobbled out the back door and called Dewey's name several times, pausing to listen for him, and hearing nothing.

While everything in my house seemed out of placc, nothing appeared to be missing. Other than my cat.

I have something of yours, Charlie had texted.

I closed my eyes and let out a slow breath. It didn't help.

"He has my cat," I whispered on a sob.

Two strong arms reached around me and pulled me tight to a warm, comforting chest. "Please, don't cry, Tru. We'll find Dewey."

"What if . . . what if . . . ?" Dewey was an innocent in all this. A kitty with unusual markings who, like Charlie, had arrived uninvited to my book-saving mission. I should have taken better care with him. I shouldn't have left him home alone, not when I knew things surrounding Duggar's death hadn't been settled. Luke was a convenient scapegoat for the murder. His arrest had also kept him safe from Grandle. Grandle, whom Charlie seemed to be helping.

My skin felt cold. I wiggled out of Jace's embrace. I had no business enjoying the feel of his arms around my body, not with Dewey missing.

"I have to go to his shop." I found my purse on the kitchen floor. I slipped its strap onto my shoulder and started toward the door. "He'd warned me that this had happened. He wanted me to meet him, and I told him no."

Jace grabbed my arm. "Wait. What are you talking about? Who warned you?"

"Charlie. Let go of me. I have to go to him. What if he's done something to Dewey to punish me for refusing to go earlier?"

I tugged. His grip tightened. "I can't do that."

"He has Dewey!" I shouted.

"How do you know?" The louder I shouted, the calmer Jace became.

"He texted me!" I don't know why I couldn't stop shouting. It was so unlike me. Everyone knew librarians never shouted.

"Can I see?" He held out his hand. I dug my phone out of my pocket and thrust it at him. Somehow he managed to keep his grip on my arm while also flipping through the text messages on my phone.

"He doesn't mention Dewey," he said, looking up at me.

"What else could he mean?"

He handed the phone back to me. "A book?"

I gave him a look that I hoped expressed how stupid I thought he sounded.

"He is a used book dealer," Jace said quietly.

"Fine. It's a book. He has a book of mine. Let go of me. I need to get to his shop to pick up a book." When he still didn't release my arm, I added, "You don't need me here. Someone broke in. Tossed things around. The only thing missing is Dewey." I drew a ragged breath. Even so, what I said next made my voice crack. "He's just a cat."

His fingers slipped from my arm. He gave a nod. "I'll drive."

Chapter Thirty-One

Like all the shops on Main Street on a Sunday, save for the Sunshine Diner and Perks, the Deckle Edge had a "Closed" sign hanging on the door.

Jace stood by my side. He gave my hand a squeeze before I knocked.

It took a few minutes before we noticed any movement in the shop. I'd texted Charlie to let him know I was coming. I'd told him that I was anxious to retrieve what he had of mine. I'd expected him to be waiting at the door. I'd expected to find Dewey *scratching* at the door.

I hadn't expected silence.

"Do you think something happened to him?" I asked. What if he was being forced to help that phone book–ripping villain? What if my refusal to meet him at his shop had endangered his life?

"Look." Jace nodded toward the large display window. A light in the back of the shop had turned on. A heavy velvet curtain rippled before it parted.

Charlie walked slowly, stepping around tables piled with cardboard boxes. He'd changed out of the casual clothes he'd been wearing when

I saw him at Duggar's house. He must have taken a shower too. His hair was damp. He'd changed into his trademark immaculately tailored suit pants and white button-up shirt. He had rolled the shirt up to his elbows. His feet, however, were bare.

He unlocked the door and pushed it open. His brilliant smile made his dark eyes sparkle.

"Tru, I'm glad—" he started to say. His voice, deep and sexy. He must have noticed the bruising and scratches on my face. I suppose he would've had to have been blind not to notice them. He sucked in a sudden, sharp breath. "What happened to you?"

"Bike accident," I said.

"Gracious, come in. Come in," he said before I could say anything more. "Oh, and you've brought a friend. Good for you," he said, looking Jace over with a discerning eye. "Detective Bailey, right?"

"That's right," Jace said, his tone all business.

"Tori has told me about you." Charlie wagged his finger at him. "Color me even more surprised," he said as he turned to me, his eyes wide. Was he trying to give me a warning? Was it a mistake coming here with a cop on my arm? "Still, come in."

"Just give me Dewey back," I said without moving.

He feigned a look of confusion. "Dewey? I don't—"

"You texted that you have him. Give him to me."

The cheerfulness faded from Charlie's eyes. "I texted that I needed to talk with you."

"And you wrote that you had something of mine. My cat. You stole him from my house." Why was he making this so difficult?

Charlie's charming facade slipped away. He suddenly looked as dangerous as the first time I saw him. I should have taken that as a warning. But I was worried about Dewey. I would have done anything, risked anything, to get my innocent little kitty away from the likes of him. Besides, Jace was standing right next to me. What could go wrong?

"Tru . . ." Jace put a staying hand on my arm. Did he sound worried? Well, it didn't matter. Charlie had taken Dewey. I'd run through fire to rescue him.

"If you simply wanted to talk to me, you could have called. You didn't need to break into my house, destroy everything, and take my cat to get my attention. Now, give me Dewey or else I'll have you arrested." I poked Jace in the side. "Arrest him."

Charlie backed up a step. His features had hardened even more. "You cannot come here with a police officer and threaten me. I am sorry about your cat. I liked Dewey. But, Tru, you are going to have to leave."

"*Liked* Dewey?" As in past tense? I lunged at the jerk. "What did you do?"

Jace wrapped his arms around my waist and held me back. "Tru, this isn't the way." He set me on my feet. My ankle throbbed like the devil. But I didn't care.

"If you won't do anything, I will," I hissed at Jace. "Dewey deserves justice."

"Mr. Newcastle, do you mind if I take a quick look around?" Jace nudged me to stand behind him.

"Actually, I do mind." Charlie crossed his arms over his chest. "Come back when the shop is open to the public. There will be a grand opening ceremony next week."

"If you have nothing to hide, I don't see why you would mind," Jace said. "It wouldn't take but a moment."

"Do you have probable cause to suspect I had anything to do with this break-in you're talking about? Do you have probable cause to be here harassing me?"

"I'm not here in an official capacity. I'm here as Tru's friend."

Charlie scoffed at that.

Jace shrugged. "Fine. Did you or your friend, Grandle, chase Tru away from Duggar Hargrove's house this morning?"

Charlie looked momentarily taken aback by the question. His brows wrinkled as he looked over at me. "No. Of course not."

"Why did you text me?" I demanded. "What did you want to talk to me about?"

Charlie clicked his tongue angrily. "Nothing that can be said now." He stepped closer, herding us toward the door. "If you're done accusing me, go. I'm busy."

"Come on, Tru." Jace wrapped his arm protectively around me and guided me back out to the street.

The door closed behind us with a slam and a click of the lock. Charlie didn't look back at us, not even once, as he worked his way through the shop to the back again and disappeared through the velvet curtain.

"Do you think he has Dewey?" I asked.

Jace was watching the shop just as intently as I was. "I honestly don't know." He turned to me and frowned. "Let's get you home and off that ankle."

We returned to find a police car parked in front of my house. Officer Franks and his partner were standing outside talking. While we were gone, someone had fixed the front door lock and put the screen door back on its hinges. Had Jace arranged for that?

"We've processed the scene. It's just as you described it in there, a total mess," Franks said to Jace. He then gave me a grim look.

"Are you certain she's not doing this to get attention?" Franks's partner bent close to Jace's ear to whisper. Not quietly enough, though. I easily heard every word.

Jace glanced in my direction before answering, "It doesn't seem like that's the case, Pitts."

"No?" Pitts glared at me. "I suppose you wouldn't think so."

"What's that supposed to mean?" Jace demanded.

Pitts only shook his head and walked away.

"Trouble?" I asked, hoping he didn't notice how hotly my cheeks were burning, hoping he didn't guess that I knew exactly what was going on.

"Nothing for you to worry about," he said with a frown. "Let's get you off that ankle."

As he walked toward the house, a terrible thought hit me like a punch in the chest. I held my ground. "That's why you took me to the urgent care center, isn't it?"

He turned back around. "What?"

"You didn't take me to see the doctor because you were worried about my injuries. You took me there to make sure I wasn't faking."

He gave me a weird look, like he'd gotten a whiff of Aunt Sal's egg salad. The poor woman overcooked everything. "You were limping. I was worried. I did what any decent person would do. Come on. The doctor wanted you to elevate that ankle."

Although I'd already seen it, the wreck inside the house still startled me. The broken side table. The overturned chairs. The slashed cushions on the sofa. The books scattered everywhere. The sight of it made my heart clench.

"I'd never do this to my own home," I said quietly.

Jace picked up a book that had landed partially open on the hardwood floor. The pages were crumpled. The cover bent. He tried to smooth out the worst of the creases before closing the book with care. "Yes, I know you wouldn't do this. Not to your books."

He helped make the living room appear semi-livable. Once we'd finished, he went to search for the ice packs in his Jeep that the urgent care center had given me. I unpacked the few library books left in my bike's saddlebag. The last book I withdrew was Charlie's copy of *The Maltese Falcon*. My hands shook as I held it and thought of poor Dewey.

If Charlie had done something with that sweet little kitty, well, I didn't know what I'd do. I couldn't remember ever feeling this angry. Not even after Jace had stolen my essay. Not even after he'd acted as if

I was no more important to him than a gnat at a church picnic. And, surprisingly, not even after Duggar had refused to listen to reason and had insisted the library get rid of all of its printed books. And the emotion directed toward Duggar had been an awful fury burning in my chest. But as strong as the anger was that I'd felt then, it paled in comparison to the tidal wave of rage surging through me now.

Dewey was an innocent—*is* an innocent creature.

I should have listened to my mother and found him a different home. If I had, he'd be safe right now, and I wouldn't be feeling as if someone had violently ripped my heart from my chest.

Sucking in a series of deep breaths helped keep the tears at bay. My head swam from the sudden influx of oxygen. The room tilted like a carnival ride.

Unfortunately, those calming breaths did nothing to calm the storm churning in my heart.

I shouldn't have left Charlie's shop. I should have stayed there until he told me where he'd put Dewey. Even if I had to beat him over the head with one of his valuable books, I would do it. As much as I loathed hurting books, Dewey's safety was more important.

I needed to get back to the bookstore. I'd grabbed my purse and car keys when Jace opened the screen door. "Look what I found!" He sounded far too cheerful for the situation. He had an ice pack in one hand and a goofy grin on his face.

"This isn't funny. Get out of my way. I've got to—"

Dewey slunk into the living room. His tail held straight like a flagpole, he approached me with a cautious stride.

"Dewey?" I whispered as the tears all those deep breaths had been keeping at bay rushed down my cheeks. "He's okay. He's okay."

I could barely believe it.

Jace leaned his arm against my doorframe. "He walked into the yard like nothing had happened."

"Do you think Charlie got worried you might search his shop and returned Dewey?" I whispered.

"I don't know, Tru. My accompanying you to his shop might have spooked him. Or maybe he didn't have anything to do with Dewey's disappearance."

"He looks unharmed, don't you think?" Ignoring my throbbing ankle, I crouched down and held out my hand. Dewey sniffed it.

"What do you have there?" I asked my kitty. A dark blue bit of cloth was sticking out of the side of his mouth.

I had to wrestle the little beast for it, which only underscored the unharmed state of his health. He didn't want to let go of his prize.

"My goodness," I said, my lips curving into a smile.

"What is it?" Jace crouched down next to me.

"It looks like Charlie will need to replace one of those expensive suits thanks to his adventures with Dewey. I hope it was the custom-made one from Hong Kong."

One of Jace's eyebrows rose. "Hong Kong?"

I handed over the torn piece of wool. "You'll have to ask Charlie about it when you arrest him. I hope Dewey left his legs with some good scratches too."

Dewey gave a startled mewl when Jace started to laugh. "This piece of wool isn't exactly a smoking gun. Charlie could claim he ripped his pants when he visited last week and was climbing under your table to fix it."

"But—"

"I'll talk with him again. Maybe I'll even get him to show me his leg so I can see if Dewey left some scratches. But short of a confession or any witnesses, it's going to be difficult to find out who broke into your house and stole Dewey." He rubbed my skinny kitty behind his ears. "I'm just glad he's back home where he belongs."

Dewey took turns headbutting both me and Jace. He seemed to

realize there was something wrong with my ankle and was careful to only rub against my uninjured leg as I stood up.

Jace followed. "Well, I'll leave you to rest." He started for the door, but then swung abruptly back toward me. "Are you sure you don't want to tell me that secret of yours now? Hiding what you know has already caused you to hurt yourself"—he nodded toward my bandaged wrist—"and it's putting those you love in danger too." He nodded toward Dewey.

The two of us had a short staring contest before I heaved a long, defeated breath. "I have no idea what you're talking about, Detective."

"Sure you don't." His jaw tightened. "Be careful, Tru," he said before he headed out the door and back to his car. "I'll let you know if I find out anything about who broke into your home."

Chapter Thirty-Two

I spent the rest of the afternoon resting in my dad's old recliner with Dewey dozing, curled up on my chest, and an ice pack cooling my swollen ankle.

Between cooing over Dewey and plotting ways to prove Charlie's guilt, I thumbed through the copy of *The Maltese Falcon*, reading passages here and there. I'm not sure why I felt the need to obsess over the book. Had Charlie given it to me as a ruse? And what in the world was the bookseller doing at Duggar's house? Why would a man like him feel the need to rob a dead man? Was he truly that obsessed with old books? I mean, even I wouldn't steal books. And I considered myself completely obsessed with the printed word.

"Knock, knock!" Mama sang through the screen door.

"It's unlocked," I called, while remembering I hadn't thanked Jace for getting those doors fixed. I set the book on the side table but didn't bother to get up. How could I? I had a cat on my chest.

"That Bailey boy called. He said you fell off your bike." She tsked when she spotted me. "Did you land on your face?"

"My face?" I touched my cheek. Now that she'd mentioned it, both my cheek and my brow felt sore. "I suppose I've been avoiding mirrors."

"Scratches everywhere. You're going to need to wear a concealer with extra heavy-duty coverage tomorrow to work. Do you need me to bring you some?"

"Um . . ." I rarely wore makeup to work. She knew that. She'd lectured me enough times about how women needed to armor themselves with makeup. "I think I have—"

"I'll bring you some." My mother frowned as her gaze took in the clutter in the living room.

"I haven't had a chance to pick up everything, but the doctor said I need to keep my ankle elevated."

"The Bailey boy also told me about the break-in." She picked up a stack of books and slid them on one of the empty shelves without any thought of organization.

"You . . . you don't have to do that. Seriously." She was making more work for me.

As usual, she didn't give any indication she'd heard me. "That's one of your father's favorite books." She picked up the copy of *The Maltese Falcon* I'd been leafing through.

"I wanted to show it to him. That's why I was at his house when someone was tearing through my house. I wanted to see if he could tell me more about the book, but he wasn't home."

"Out fishing, huh?"

"He was," I said.

She shook her head and laughed bitterly. "That man is as predictable as the summer rain. You should have known he'd be out on the lake."

"I'm usually in church on Sunday."

"As you should have been today. You wouldn't have fallen off your bike and hurt yourself if you'd been where you were supposed to be."

"You're right."

My ready agreement seemed to trip her up. She straightened. Her perfectly coiffed hair trembled. "Um . . . well . . . of course I'm right. I'm your mother. What did you want to ask your father about this book?" She tapped the copy of *The Maltese Falcon* she was still holding. "He's read all the classic mysteries, you know. He always had one around. I once found a copy of *Murder on the Orient Express* in his sock drawer and a copy of *The Red-Headed League* tucked behind the dresser."

"Really? Why would he do that?"

"No clue. It was so irritating, like living with a squirrel. I'd find his books tucked away in the oddest places. And whenever I confronted him about one of them, he'd snatch the book I'd found out of my hands and refuse to talk about it. That's your dad, impulsive and full of secrets."

"Sounds like pretty much everyone else in this town," I muttered.

"What's that?" Mama asked without looking up from the book.

"Nothing," I said.

"Your father would talk to himself as well." She flipped to the front of the book and tapped one of the pages. "I hated that."

"Sorry. There's . . . there's just been so much going on lately."

"At least you don't have to worry about who killed that poor town manager anymore."

"I suppose," I said. "That's a relief."

"You don't sound relieved." She closed the book with a snap. "Is this one of the old library books?"

"No. The library has one just like it. But Charlie, the bookseller you met the other night, gave me this copy. Why do you ask?"

She handed the book back to me. "It's a first edition. You should consider giving it to your father. You do remember his birthday is coming up? He'd really like it."

"What?" I sat up so quickly that my foot slid off its perch and slammed down on the hardwood floor. Dewey jumped down with an irate meow. I groaned. "No, it's not a first edition. I already checked."

"Sweetie, there's a reason why I'm so hard on you girls in cotillion classes." She lifted my foot and put it back on the recliner's padded footrest. "Moving with purpose and grace isn't just for looks. It's also to save you from hurting yourself."

Once I'd settled and my ankle had stopped throbbing, I opened the book to the copyright page. Just as I'd already seen, there was no mention that it was a first printing or a first edition, just a copyright date of 1929 on the copyright page and 1930 on the cover page. Just like the copy I'd kept for the library, the book lacked the iconic yellow dust jacket that made first editions of this book so very valuable.

"What makes you think it's a first edition?" I asked.

"The copyright date is both 1929 and 1930. Isn't that when the book was first published? Anyhow, I think he once said something about how the first editions of *The Maltese Falcon* were odd like that. They had two different copyright dates."

"How would you remember that?" How would anyone remember anything like that?

She shrugged. "When he wasn't keeping secrets, your father would blab on and on about the history of his favorite books. I suppose some of it got stuck in my head." She shuddered. "Call him tonight when he gets back from fishing. He knows more about these things."

"I will," I said slowly.

I'd been so focused on the story contained within the pages of *The Maltese Falcon* that I hadn't spent enough time researching this *specific* printed book.

I needed to think.

Chapter Thirty-Three

Mama stayed for the rest of the afternoon, cleaning up the mess from the break-in and fussing over me. She fluffed the pillow under my ankle and fixed me a healthy—but tasty—vegetarian dish with yellow squash, eggplant, tomatoes, green peppers, and a creamy coconut sauce. It was so good, I started to lick the bowl.

"I can get you more," she offered with a warm smile.

"I'd love more," I said. "Thank you."

After she had refilled my bowl, she sat beside me with a surprise second helping of her own. She told me all about who was doing what in her women's club and what their daughters were all up to. We laughed. We joked. It was one of the best afternoons I'd had with her in a long time.

When we were done eating, she took the plates.

"Just put them in the sink," I called as she headed into the kitchen.

A moment later, I could hear the water running and the clank of dishes. Clearly, she was washing them. Instead of feeling annoyed,

I leaned my head back and enjoyed—just for a moment—having some-one take care of me. Dewey jumped back up on my lap and batted at my arm until I started to pet him.

"Tru! Are you decent?" Tori called a moment before the screen door swung open. Dewey gave a startled meow and dug his claws into my arm in his haste to skitter behind the chair.

"What's going on?" I said, sitting up. Why would Dewey run from my best friend?

"I come bearing gifts." She held up a greasy paper bag.

"Victoria Kaitlyn Green, tell me you didn't bring my daughter fried chicken." Mama stood at the doorway between the living room and the kitchen. She wiped her hands on the dish towel she'd wrapped around her waist like an apron. "You know our family can't eat fried food. It's like poison to our systems."

"It's not fried chicken, Mama Eddy," Tori said, her smile unshaken. "It's vegetables."

My mother scoffed. "Looks fried to me."

"It's from the Grind. They deep-fry everything, even the sweet tea." She held up a tall to-go cup that was dripping with condensation.

"Oh! Gimme! Gimme!" I reached out for the cup. The Grind made the best sweet tea in Cypress, perhaps even the world. I didn't know what they put in it. Some guessed the restaurant added fresh strawber-ries and lemons with the sugar syrup. Whatever magical ingredients they used, the tea tasted like summer.

"Manners," Mama scolded.

"What in the—" It was the first time Tori had taken a look at me. She glanced over at my mom and cleared her throat. "What happened to you, Tru?"

"Fell off my bike." I reached out for the sweet tea again. "Can I have that?"

"I'll take the bag." Mama marched off into the kitchen with the greasy bag. I winced when I heard the trash can lid slam. The loss of the fried goodies didn't stop me from enjoying the tea.

Tori flopped into the seat my mother had been using.

"Sorry about that," I said, nodding toward the kitchen.

"You mean about Mama Eddy? Everyone in Cypress knows what she's like. You should have texted me that she was here. I would have figured out a way to sneak food in here without her knowing . . . like we used to do in high school."

"My life shouldn't involve us sneaking around like we're still in high school."

"She loves you."

"She does. What was in the bag, anyhow?"

"Fried okra."

I closed my eyes and cried a little. Even though I was stuffed to my ears from two servings of my mom's vegetarian stew, my mouth watered at the mere thought of the salty, slightly slimey flavor of fried okra. The Grind fries the okra with cornmeal, which adds sweet flavor notes to the already delicious treat.

"Any luck with getting their recipe?" I asked. Ever since Tori opened Perks, she has waged a campaign to convince Jesse and Donovan, the owners of the Grind, to hand over their sweet tea recipe.

"Donovan said today that the secret to their tea is that they brew it with swamp water."

"Ewww!" I laughed so hard, I almost spit out my tea. "He didn't!"

"I'll let you two have some girl time," Mama said when she came back into the living room. She'd removed her makeshift dishtowel apron and fluffed her hair. "I put the dishes away and you can find the leftover stew in the fridge. There's enough for the two of you to make a light dinner from it. I'll drop off the makeup you'll need for that"—she waggled her fingers at my face—"later tonight."

"Thank you, Mama. I love you."

My mother raised her brows at my rare expression of the kind of gushy emotions she preferred to avoid. With an imperial sniff, she came over and brushed a kiss on my cheek. "Don't let Tori talk you into . . . into, well, into anything," she whispered in my ear.

"I heard that!" Tori said with a laugh. "And I'll have you know that it's your daughter who is leading me astray."

"We all know that isn't true," Mama said. "It wasn't true when you were in high school and it certainly isn't now. I raised my Tru to be like me. Good. Honest. She's a librarian, for goodness' sake."

"That she is," Tori agreed with a smirk.

"What?" Mama demanded, her gaze narrowing. "What is going on here?"

"Tori is teasing," I said. "Aren't you, Tori?"

My friend shrugged. It didn't look convincing, but my mom seemed to let it go. At least for now.

"Goodbye, Mama." I gave her a tight hug. "Thank you for the meal and the company. Both were truly wonderful."

Which wasn't the most surprising part of her visit. My utterly proper mama may have helped solve a murder.

That was something I could never tell her. It'd shock the poor woman to no end.

Chapter Thirty-Four

As soon as Mama had driven away, Tori ran into the kitchen. She returned a moment later with a plate of the fried okra and a cup of the Grind's spicy dipping sauce that she'd rescued from the garbage. It was a feast that even my full stomach enjoyed.

Dewey ventured out from behind the chair. His little black nose twitched as he took in the forbidden scent of fried food. Tori smiled at him and tossed him a piece of fried okra, which he gobbled down.

"I'm not sure he should eat that," I said, wondering if I was going to see that okra again . . . on my bed . . . in the middle of the night. "He has a delicate stomach. He's on a special diet."

"According to Mama Eddy, you're on a special diet too. Let him enjoy himself a little."

He settled himself at Tori's feet, licking grease from his paws and purring loudly.

"Just don't give him any more. After living on the street, he panic eats and then throws up. I promise you, it's a mess that you don't want to see," I said.

"Gotcha." Echoing Dewey's movements, she licked her fingers. "This is *the stuff.*"

"It is," I agreed. I ate another forbidden piece of fried okra, dipped in the thick, fatty, high-cholesterol sauce—while only feeling the slightest twinge of guilt about going against my mom's wishes.

"Are you going to tell me what really happened?" Tori pointed a piece of okra toward my scratched face. "You haven't fallen off your bike since you were three years old."

I wasn't sure what to tell her. She probably wouldn't react well to hearing that her newest boyfriend (and potential next husband) was a thief and maybe also a killer. But at the same time Tori was my best friend. If Charlie was a bad apple, it was my duty to warn her.

I supposed the best way to do that was to ease into things.

"Did you give Charlie my phone number?" I asked her.

She chewed the okra she'd just put in her mouth before answering. "Sure did. He said he found something of yours. Did you leave something in his store yesterday when it was flooding?"

"I can't imagine that I did. Has he—?" I started to ask, but she interrupted.

"You still haven't told me what happened on your bike." She used air quotes when she said the word "bike."

"Well, that's the thing. I'm not sure what happened. I think someone was chasing me. I panicked, veered onto a trail, and flipped the bike."

"You think someone was chasing you?" She shot to her feet. Dewey darted behind my chair again. "Who? This is serious! Have you called the police?"

"I did," I said calmly. "Jace took my statement."

"But . . . ?" Tori prompted.

"But I don't have proof. Not really. Just these cuts and a bruised ankle and wrist."

Tori pursed her lips in thought. "But you have an idea who was chasing you, and why, don't you?"

"I do." I closed my eyes. "It was either Charlie or Grandle."

Tori laughed. "That's what you told Jace?" She laughed again. "You're lucky he didn't stuff you into an ambulance and ship you to the state hospital in Columbia for a mental evaluation. Charlie? Sweet, kindhearted Charlie? You think he would chase you? Attack you?"

"I saw him and Grandle breaking into Duggar's house." I kept my eyes closed. I couldn't bear to see the pain I had to be causing her as I told her the truth. She seemed so fond of Charlie. "Just this morning. They noticed that I saw them and shouted at me. When I rode away, I heard a car behind me. I rode even faster and veered into the woods. That's when this happened." I drew a deep breath. "I'm afraid Charlie killed Duggar or he let that friend of his into the library to do the deed for him." Tori didn't speak. I peeled open one eye. "Tori?"

She was standing with her back to me. Her arms were crossed. "I would have expected this from Flossie. She's the one who thinks every guy I date is the scum of the earth."

"I don't think he's —"

"No." She slashed her hand through the air. "No, you just think he's a murderer. That's worse." She turned around. Tears were glittering in her eyes. "I really like him, you know?"

I struggled to my feet and hobbled over to her. We hugged. "I know. I liked him too."

"Of course you did." She mumbled into my shirt. "He's a bibliophile."

With a start of surprise, I pulled out of the hug. "Never heard you use that word before."

"See?" She laughed through her tears. "He was a good influence. You really think he killed Duggar?"

"I don't know. Maybe he didn't kill him, but I think he's involved with what's going on." I reached over and handed her the book. "He gave me this on Friday. He said it was a clue."

"*The Maltese Falcon*? I don't understand."

I sat down and elevated my throbbing ankle before explaining everything I had kept hidden from her up until now, including the scrap of material I found in Dewey's jaw.

"You honestly think Charlie was at Duggar's house to steal a dead man's collection of valuable books? In broad daylight?" Tori scoffed.

"You sound like Jace."

"Well, you have to admit he has a point. It does sound rather crazy."

"What about these texts?" I handed her my phone. "Charlie doesn't have anything of mine. It has to be a ruse to get me to his shop so he can confront me about what I saw."

Tori started typing on my phone, her fingers moving furiously over the screen.

"What are you doing?" I demanded.

"I'm asking him what he has that he wants to give you. I'm surprised you didn't already do it. You're supposed to be the smart one in this friendship."

I tried to grab the phone away from her. But she held it high in the air.

"I don't think I'm smarter than you," I cried.

"Of course you don't. There. It's sent." She tossed me my phone. I stared at the text message, wondering why I hadn't thought of it myself. I mean, it wasn't as if I was going to his shop alone. I was sitting in my house with Tori, asking him an innocent question. What harm was there in that?

A few minutes passed before my phone chirped.

"What does it say?" Tori demanded. She tried to read the screen over my shoulder.

"He says he has my water bottle." Attached to the text was a picture of it sitting on a table in his shop.

"That's the one I gave you."

"I thought I'd lost it on the trail," I said just as my phone chirped again.

"He says you dropped it in front of Duggar's house," Tori said as she read the new text over my shoulder. "That doesn't sound like a man who is trying to hide a crime to me."

Chapter Thirty-Five

I f you knew otherwise, I don't understand why you didn't explain that to Tori," Flossie complained the next morning. The library
had been open for about a half hour. I'd just finished getting Dewey
settled in the basement bookroom and had come upstairs to the café.
Many of the regulars were milling around the new bookless facility like
lost sheep.

"Here's a tablet, Mr. Talbot." I handed one of my favorite retirees
from the lake house district a brand-new reading tablet that residents
could check out. "You'll be able to download your favorite historical
biographies onto it."

"And then what do I do with it?" He grimaced at the thin device.

"You read the books." I smiled at him, putting on a brave face despite the pain I felt for all of my poor lost readers. After he walked away,
I turned back to Flossie.

"I tried to tell her. Tori is smitten. The only person who can change
her mind about Charlie is Charlie himself," I said as I gathered the
teaching materials I kept in the circulation desk's large bottom drawer.

"But he was doing something fishy at Duggar's house yesterday, and I don't trust him."

The Monday morning Mom and Tot program was about to start, and the library was swarming with little ones. Anne looked as if she was about to pull her purple-streaked hair out as she darted here and there, warning the little kids not to touch this keyboard or not to pull on that cord.

Was it wrong of me to find it entertaining?

Probably.

"Charlie texted that he'd return my water bottle today," I said after swallowing my urge to laugh at Anne's discomfort.

"He's coming here?" Flossie blurted out. "And you're going to let him?"

I shushed her and then glanced worriedly toward Mrs. Farnsworth's closed door. She'd come in this morning, growled at both me and Anne, and then closed herself in her office. I didn't want to do anything to upset the poor woman further.

"This is a public building. He said he'll try to arrive during my lunch break." I hadn't discouraged him. Actually, I'd done just the opposite. I'd encouraged him to come. I wanted to see him. I wanted to take a peek at his leg to look for the telltale scratches Dewey had left there. I wanted to catch him in his lie and expose him for the criminal he was.

Okay, I admit it. Yesterday at Duggar's house, he wasn't chasing after me with deadly intent. They were only trying to point out that I'd dropped my water bottle. And yeah, I had gotten hurt because I'd over-reacted. But that didn't mean he was the good guy in this story.

Charlie had warned me to keep as far away from Grandle as possible. Seeing them together was most definitely a red flag.

It still was.

At least the swelling in my ankle and wrist were nearly gone this morning. I barely limped as I walked toward the kids' area, which used to be the fiction section.

"It's time to begin." I waved for the moms and kids to follow me. Anne heaved a loud sigh of relief as the little ones that had been bedeviling her bounded toward the brightly painted room filled with soft cushions, boxes of toys, and, of course, computers. No books.

Yet.

As the librarian in charge of children's programing, I planned to fix that as soon as possible. I might have failed to convince Duggar, who'd been dead set on clearing out every piece of printed material from the library. Whoever took over his position as town manager would see things differently. I would make sure of it.

Flossie rolled alongside me into the new room.

"I'll be done with the children's program in about two hours," I told her. "There's something I need to research before Charlie arrives. Will you be around?"

"I'll be . . ." She hesitated when she saw the fashionably perfect Sissy Philips hurrying toward us with her three tots in tow. Two were three-year-old twin boys and a third, a little girl who had inherited Sissy's dainty, slightly upturned nose, was just learning to walk.

Sissy's platform sandals click-clacked angrily against the terrazzo floors.

"You know where I'll be. Good luck with all those kids," Flossie said before rolling away faster than I'd seen her move in a while.

Sissy, yes, the same high school Sissy who'd stomped over my papers, stopped directly in front of me. She wove this way and that as her little ones tugged on her arms. She looked at me with pleading eyes.

"Has the world gone crazy?" she drawled. "When I asked where the board books were, that new librarian tried to hand my Joey an electronic tablet to use. Is she insane? Didn't y'all hear? Doctors are telling parents to keep our children away from screen time, not that you'd know. You don't have children. I can't set Ashley up in front of a tablet. For one thing, she wouldn't sit still for it. And besides, the last thing I want to be teaching that girl of mine is how to use one of those things. She's already trying to get her hands on my phone enough as it is."

"I know. I know." I held up my hand and said in a calming voice, "We're working on fixing that."

Most of the board books and picture books for our youngest visitors had been shipped off with the books that were sold to a national reseller. Only the older books that were deemed out-of-date or useless were boxed up for the landfill.

Taking books from the boxes that were going to be sold had felt too much like stealing. I would never take money from the library. However, I did manage to salvage some of the older picture books for the secret bookroom. Not that I would tell Sissy that. I wouldn't trust her with Mama Eddy's banana pudding recipe, which wasn't all that good. Sissy hadn't changed since high school. She'd just expanded her gossip range to include the entire population of Cypress.

Even now she was bending toward me to whisper something I was sure I didn't want to know about a fellow member of Cypress society.

"Have you heard about Jace?" Her hot breath tickled my ear.

I jerked away from her. "I'm sure I don't want to hear whatever you have to say."

A tiny lie.

I wanted to know.

Good thing she'd never listened to me. "He's going to lose his job."

"No, he's not. I have to go get set up."

She followed me with those little kids of hers trotting along beside her. "I heard how you think he's been cozying up to you. Just like he did in high school." She tut-tutted.

"He is investigating a crime. I was one of the witnesses." I unfolded an oversized poster board with a photo of a fuzzy caterpillar.

"Did you know he told me that he doesn't think Luke is guilty?" She tut-tutted again.

"He told you? He discussed the case with you?" Why did I not believe her? Oh, yeah, because lying and causing trouble has always been her favorite hobby.

Her grin turned predatory. "You didn't think he's been coming around to visit you because he actually liked you, did you?" She gasped as if in distress.

I rolled my eyes. "Let's all take our seats," I called out. I then turned to whisper to her, "I know why he's been coming around. And it's really none of your business."

"Oh, that's so sad. You really do think he finds you attractive." She shook her head. "He thinks you're guilty." Her voice was too loud. "He's willing to do anything to prove it, because if he doesn't, he's going to be fired for repeating past mistakes and all just because that stupid police chief is starting to think that Jace is actually romantically interested in you, a key witness and former suspect."

"Please, let's take our seats," I said, my voice even louder. A couple of the young mothers were staring at me with their mouths gaping.

"But of course Jace is wrong to waste his time with you," Sissy said, her voice dripping with sarcasm, as she walked away to take a spot near the front of the room next to one of her friends from the high school cheerleading squad. "Even if you'd wanted Duggar dead, it's not like you would have had the courage to do anything about it."

Chapter Thirty-Six

After that bumpy start, the Mom and Tot program went better than I'd expected. Several of the moms who'd been coming to the library program for years now and thought of me like an honorary auntie to their children rushed up afterward to show their support. I helped them navigate the new children's room. I set up a few of the older children on the computers and showed them how to play the educational games. I handed a few of the younger toddlers electronic tablets that Anne had loaded with nothing but picture books.

Everyone seemed happy, even Sissy, who kept looking over at me and smiling in her sly, I'm-better-than-you way.

I smiled back at her. And finger waved.

Without waiting for her reaction, I twirled on my heel and made my exit.

I had a thief to confront.

The first thing I noticed when I returned to the circulation desk was that the light in Mrs. Farnsworth's office had been turned off. In the middle of the day? That was worrying.

"What's going on?" I asked Anne, who had been covering the circulation desk for one of the part-time assistants. I nodded toward Mrs. Farnsworth's office door.

"She came out with her purse and blasted past me like a rocket." She shook her head. "I wonder if she's losing it. She's in her eighties, isn't she? The library is changing. Not just here. Libraries all over the country are changing. Don't you think she needs to retire?"

And put Anne in charge? "No, I can't imagine this place without Mrs. Farnsworth. I don't think anyone can."

Anne refused to back down. "Well, this library is changing, growing. Perhaps the people in charge should change too."

"Do you know where Mrs. Farnsworth has gone or not?" I asked, my voice sharp. I was not going to fight with Anne. Not now. Not today.

"I . . . I think she . . ." Clearly, Anne didn't know where the head librarian had gone or why. And it was just as clear that she hated not knowing something.

I hated not knowing too. I returned the toddler program materials to the bottom desk drawer before marching toward the back stairs. I needed to find Flossie. I'd barely made it a few steps when the noise level in the new café flared. If Mrs. Farnsworth had been here, she would have been shushing like mad.

The loudest of the group were the café employees. They were behind the counter arguing. I stomped over to them. "What's going on?"

Both of them continued shouting at each other and at me.

I shook my head. "I can't listen to you when you're loud like this. Stop arguing and get back to work. When you're ready to talk without drama, you are welcome to come and find me. If you cannot work without the racket, you'll have to go home." The two men didn't answer. They simply stood there gaping at me. "Do you understand me? Get. Back. To. Work."

They nodded in shocked unison and walked to separate ends of the counter. The fact that they'd stopped shouting was progress enough for me.

"Girlfriend." Flossie rolled up to me and swatted my leg. "I've never seen you have so much fire in your belly. What's got you so riled up?"

"Anne suggested that Mrs. Farnsworth was too old and needed to retire." But that wasn't the only thing bothering me.

It was Sissy.

It was Charlie.

It was Tori.

It was Jace making me feel all gushy whenever he brought presents for Dewey.

It was that this murder had made me distrust everyone around me.

I hated it all, and it made me want to lash out at everyone. And yes, that wasn't like me. Lashing out felt as unnatural as creasing a page instead of using a bookmark.

Tears sprang to my eyes. "I hate it when people turn down corners of pages instead of using bookmarks."

"Oh, honey. I have no idea what you're talking about. But don't you apologize for taking charge just now. You are powerful and wonderful, and you're finally showing it."

Then why did I feel so helpless? "Mrs. Farnsworth isn't here. I don't know where she went."

"She went to the police station," Flossie said, her voice soft and soothing.

Mr. Talbot, who was sitting at a nearby table, looked up from the tablet he'd been squinting at. "The mayor showed up. He told us that he'd offered to drive her there himself. But she refused. He said she insisted on going there on her own."

"The mayor?" Was he putting pressure on Mrs. Farnsworth to change her story? Was this his plan to clear his son from the murder charge?

Mr. Talbot rubbed the space between his eyes. "The mayor came in here with a smile that bared all his teeth. The man does that only when he's about to take down an opponent. Gets a charge from playing the political game."

I looked at Flossie. She shrugged. "I didn't see him. I was"—she cleared her throat—"elsewhere." Which I took to mean she was downstairs in the secret bookroom.

She reached into the colorful batik printed bag hanging from her wheelchair and retrieved a biography of Thomas Jefferson. "Is this what you were looking for?" she asked Mr. Talbot as she handed him the book.

"What . . . where did you?" he stammered.

"I'm magic." She grinned. "I'm not giving you the book, mind you. Just letting you borrow it. I'll expect it back in my hands within a few weeks."

He opened the book and thumbed through its pages. "Gracious." A smile crept onto his rather stern face. "Gracious. I didn't think I could read this book on that contraption. Kept going cross-eyed."

Flossie snatched up the tablet and squinted at the screen. "Well, here's the problem." She tapped the screen like she was born using those things. "You had the font set too small."

She tried to hand it back to him. He refused to even look at it. Refused to touch it. "I'm happier with this." He held the book as if it were his firstborn child. "Much happier."

"We aim to please," Flossie said with a wink.

Mr. Talbot moved his chair closer to Flossie. "You know, we really haven't had a chance to talk in a while." His stern voice softened even further. "Have you decided on a color to paint your bedroom? I seem to remember the last time we spoke, you were vacillating between sage green and pale peach."

"Wouldn't you like to know?" Flossie teased.

Mr. Talbot's expression suddenly turned serious again. "Actually, I would."

Was he flirting? With *my* Flossie?

I think he was.

And it didn't look as if Flossie minded.

I walked away, giving the two of them some privacy. That's when I noticed Charlie had entered the café.

Today he wore a light gray suit. He had his coat flung over one arm and the sleeves of his crisply pressed dark purple dress shirt were again rolled up to his elbows.

His gaze met mine. He then nodded toward one of the small recording studio rooms. It happened to be the same one where Luke had been attacked. Did he know it was the same room? Had he chosen it as some kind of warning?

There was only one way to find out. I followed him into the room, but I didn't let him close the door. I stood on the threshold with my arms folded over my chest.

"Let me see your legs," I said.

"My, my, Ms. Becket." He gave me a wry look. "My legs are some of my best assets, but I doubt your best friend would want to share."

"That's not why I want to see them. I know you took Dewey. And returned him. The fact that you returned him is the only thing that's keeping me from doing something rash. Like scratching you myself. But he came home with a ripped dark blue wool material that looked like the blue pants you were wearing yesterday."

His eyes darkened. He took a step toward me. "I did not take your cat."

"Then you shouldn't mind if I take a look at your legs. I doubt Dewey tore your pants without leaving a mark."

"He didn't tear my pants." The look he gave me made the muscles in my legs wobble.

"Prove it," I said, holding my own against his efforts to intimidate me.

"No." He pulled my lost water bottle out of his bag and thrust it at me. "Here. I should have given this to you yesterday, but your bringing that cop with you to meet me and then your accusations of breaking into your home derailed everything, now didn't they?"

"What?" I hugged the water bottle to my chest. "I should have met with you alone? Is that what you had wanted? Well, I'm not that stupid."

"No, I didn't expect you to be alone. And I don't think you're stupid. I simply didn't expect you'd bring that detective. What I wanted to tell you, I didn't want to say in front of the police." He'd lowered his voice. "I was thinking of you and what you're doing here at the library."

"Thinking of me? You're just full of altruistic behavior. Is that what you were doing at Duggar's house? Helping out a poor dead man in need?"

He spread his hands. "I was trying to help."

"Help a killer? Help yourself? Or is that one and the same?"

"You think I killed . . . ?" His brows dipped.

"You tell me. All I know is that I'm starting to feel awfully guilty about not telling the police that you were at the library at the time of Duggar's murder. I think it's time that I come clean about what I was doing in the library and exactly who was there." I closed my eyes for a moment before continuing. "Even if it means I lose everything."

Instead of looking angry or upset, Charlie suddenly looked relieved. "Thank goodness we're on the same page."

"I don't—"

"That's what I wanted to talk to you about yesterday. But you brought that detective with you. I didn't want to say anything in front of him that would get you in trouble. I'm a man of honor, which is why I'm going to talk to the police. I'm going to let them know what I know. I'm going to tell them that they have the wrong man in custody."

"You mean Luke?"

Charlie nodded. "I cannot let him take the blame for a crime he didn't commit."

"You're going to confess?" I felt relieved to hear it, even if it meant he'd have to expose the town's secret bookroom in the process.

"Confess?" He jerked back in surprise. "Why would you think I would kill a town manager I'd never even met?"

"Why else go to the police if not to turn yourself in?" I asked.

"Scores of reasons come to mind. On the morning of the murder, I skirted around both Luke and Mayor Goodvale when I was carrying down boxes Tori had packed. Mayor Goodvale was in the children's and young adult section. And Luke was in the reference section. They weren't together."

"I think that's probably what Mrs. Farnsworth has already told the police. She's the reason why Luke no longer has an alibi. She's the reason he was arrested."

"Yes, I'm sure that's true, but the police are wrong. That's why I need to go talk to that detective friend of yours—"

"He's not my friend," I blurted.

"Well, whatever he is, I need to talk with him."

"Why? Why would telling him the same thing Mrs. Farnsworth has already said change anything? Are you sure you're not doing this because you're angry I accused you of petnapping Dewey?"

His jaw tightened. "I am still upset about that. I didn't break into your house and I didn't take your cat."

"And yet you won't let me look at your leg."

"Your detective already looked at it," he said tightly. "And let me tell you, I didn't appreciate being treated like a common criminal."

"Because you're an uncommon one?" I couldn't stop myself from saying.

"I'm not a criminal." He formed the words slowly. "If not for my affection for Tori, I wouldn't be here right now telling you what I'm going to tell the police. If you don't want to hear me out, fine. I'll go."

He pushed past me to leave the small room.

I touched his arm. "Wait. I want to hear what you have to say."

He gave a sharp nod. "I saw Luke in the reference section of the library. He couldn't have killed Duggar. I wish I saw who did. But I do know this—Luke was on the opposite side of the library at the time of the murder. And so was I. That is what I need to tell the police. And in the process, I'm going to have to tell them about your illicit bookroom." He shook his head. "For such a small town, this one is surprisingly filled to its borders with secrets. And it feels like I've unwittingly become keeper of all of them. It's a burden."

"But because you're an honorable man, you've been keeping silent?"

He nodded. The movement was a stiff, unhappy jerk.

"Just tell me one thing." He owed me at least that much. "What were you doing at Duggar's house with Grandle yesterday?"

"Sorry, Tru. Those darn secrets keep throwing themselves at me."

I wasn't ready to let up. "Were you breaking the law?"

"I wasn't." A weasel of an answer if I'd ever heard one.

"*You* weren't? But Grandle was?"

"I cannot—"

"Yes, yes. I get it. You've become our community secret-keeper. Well, let me tell you something. Your bookish clue hasn't been at all helpful." That wasn't precisely true, was it? I'd called my father last night and had confirmed with him what my mother had told me. It was a first edition and worth a considerable amount of money. "Do you care to spit out what it is you want me to know?"

"I can't." He walked away. "I am sorry, Tru."

"Sorry?" My head started to throb. If it wasn't Luke—and it wasn't Charlie—who pushed over the heavy shelf? Who killed Duggar?

His clue did nothing to help me prove Anne's guilt. Anne wasn't interested in selling the old books.

"What about your promise to protect the secret bookroom?" I couldn't stop myself from calling out. "If you're so good at keeping secrets, why is it so easy to break your word to me?"

He stopped and turned back to me. "I'm not breaking my word. I'm here providing you with fair warning. And you and I both know that going to the police is the right thing to do."

I bit my lower lip. I knew that.

"I don't mean to cause you trouble. Honest."

"You do what you need to do. I can handle it," I said tightly.

"You might be charged with obstruction of justice or withholding evidence," he warned.

Not to mention how I'd lose my position at the library and the books I'd saved. "If that's what you saw, it's what has to be done," I said because it was true.

"Tori is going to flay me alive when she finds out what I've done to you."

I snorted an unhappy laugh. "She will."

He blanched. "Look, I'll wait an hour before I spill my guts to the police. Maybe you should use that time to call that detective of yours and give him a head's up about me. It might make less trouble for you."

It might. But somehow, I doubted it.

Chapter Thirty-Seven

I had an hour (*less* than an hour, really) to prove Anne guilty of murder. It was the only way I could think of to stop Charlie from going to the police. The only way to save the books.

I followed Charlie out of the small recording studio. He turned right toward the front of the library. I turned left toward the steps leading down to the basement.

"It has to be Anne," I said like a mantra as I entered the secret bookroom. Dewey meowed a happy greeting and rubbed against my leg. "It has to be Anne," I told him. I didn't notice that Delanie was standing next to Flossie at the battered old checkout desk, or that the older woman's jaw had dropped open with a look of shock. "We have an hour to prove it." I glanced at my watch. "Make that fifty minutes."

"Slow down there," Flossie said. She glanced over at Delanie and gave a tense laugh. "Tru is always such a kidder. Aren't you, Tru?"

"No, she's not." Delanie straightened. "I won't let you hurt my niece."

"She's not going to hurt anyone, are you, Tru?" Flossie said evenly. She had her phone out on her lap. She tapped frantically on the screen.

"I'm out to uncover the truth," I said.

"About—?" Delanie prompted.

I glanced at my watch again. Time was slipping away. "Duggar's murder."

"I won't let you hurt my niece. She's a good girl."

The other patrons of the secret bookroom were starting to take notice of the drama brewing near the door. A few of them had moved toward us. I was beginning to understand why Mrs. Farnsworth ruled the library with an iron fist.

"What are you going to do to stop me? Expose this place?" I'd lowered my voice to a whisper.

"Perhaps I should," Delanie snapped. "Perhaps I should tell everyone about what you're doing down here. We'll see how long you keep your job. We'll see what actions Police Chief Fisher will take when he learns you've been keeping information that might be vital to a murder investigation from them."

"Delanie Messervey, don't you dare!" one of the patrons shouted.

"This place is a godsend," cried another.

"We won't let you ruin what Ms. Becket has selflessly worked so hard to give back to us!" yelled yet another.

"Shhhhh . . ." I hissed like a snake with a leak. "We'll expose ourselves if we keep shouting."

"You're smiling." Delanie wagged her finger at me. "You're enjoying causing me pain."

I touched a finger to the smile on my lips.

"Don't be daft," Flossie said. "She's smiling because of them. Librarians aren't used to hearing praise. Complaints, aplenty. Queries, all the time. It'd be unnatural if our girl Tru didn't enjoy a few accolades sent her way."

Flossie was wrong. Plenty of Cypress's patrons thanked me. I was smiling because their praise helped lessen the guilt I'd been feeling about setting up this bookroom. I'd broken the rules, rules I'd spent a lifetime following. And yes, not a day went by that I didn't question if I'd made a horrible mistake.

I was about to explain that when Tori burst through the heavy vaulted doors like a raging hurricane. She grabbed my arm and swung me away from where I stood toe-to-toe with Delanie. "Let's take this discussion somewhere private."

Flossie propped a cardboard sign onto the desk that read "Back in 5" and wheeled after us.

Delanie tried to follow, but Flossie blocked her with her wheelchair. "We're on a quest for the truth. If you believe in Anne as fervently as you profess, then you have nothing to worry about."

Delanie harrumphed, but when she saw the determined looks on the faces of the other patrons watching her, she took a step away from us.

"There's a table in the far corner where we can talk," Tori said.

"That works for me," I said. "It's near the filing cabinet where the local documents are filed. We might need to do some research there."

As soon as we'd all settled in around the round table, I filled Tori and Flossie in on what Charlie had told me.

Tori jumped up from her chair. "He can't do that. I'll not let him. He might be good at . . . well, everything, but you're my bestie. I'm not going to let him hurt you."

I put a hand on her arm, stopping her from stomping off in search of her handsome bookseller.

"He's doing what he thinks is right," I said.

"You believe him?" Tori demanded. "Just yesterday you believed him guilty of murder."

"Um . . ." She was right. How had he changed my mind so easily?

"He must have charmed her out of that notion," Flossie said. "We can't take him off our suspect list, despite how good he is at . . . well, everything."

"If he were guilty, why would he go to the police?" I asked, my mind finally working again. "Why would he want to place himself at the scene of the crime? That's why I believe him. He doesn't want to see Luke prosecuted for a crime he didn't commit. I want the same thing."

"But he only gave you an hour to find the killer," Tori said. "That's cruel."

"I don't think he's expecting us to take this up on our own," I pointed out.

"But we are." Flossie checked her watch. "And we only have forty-five minutes now. Tori, sit down. We need to get started."

Tori dropped back into the old wooden chair. "Where do we start?"

My first impulse was to pull out my casebook, but I'd written notes in it that implicated Tori. I couldn't let her see them. "We . . . we need to find a way to prove Anne's guilt. If we do that, the police will release Luke."

Tori nodded. "And Charlie's conscience will be clear."

"Exactly," I said with a smile.

"But why focus on Anne?" Flossie asked.

Because it would break my heart to focus on Tori. "Anne is the killer." She has to be.

Flossie pressed her lips together. Tori looked away.

"Anne has a motive," I reminded them, holding up one finger. "She wanted full credit for the library's transformation, and Duggar wasn't going to share the spotlight with her." I added a second finger to the first one. "She had opportunity. She was working in her office, which was adjacent to the media room. She could easily pop out, do the deed, and then run back into her office, put her headphones on, and claim she hadn't heard anything." I raised a third finger. "Now, all we need to do is find the missing murder weapon in her office. That'll prove that she had the means to commit the crime."

"Forgive me if I'm wrong, but wasn't Duggar crushed by a heavy wooden shelf?" Tori asked. "We're not going to find the shelf in her office. Not when it's still in the media room with the DVDs and VCR tapes back on it."

"Tru isn't looking for that," Flossie scoffed. "She's looking for the hex-head screwdriver that loosened the shelf's bolts."

"Um." Tori wrinkled her nose. "You're saying we ransack Anne's office in search of a missing tool. And when we find it, what do we do? Call your detective?"

"He's not my detective, but yes. That's the plan," I said. I rose from my chair, anxious to get started. "Tori, you could create a diversion, get Anne out of her office. You're good at distracting people. While you're doing that, I will search the office while Flossie keeps watch. And that's how we prove that a stranger to town would have a reason to want Duggar dead."

Both Tori and Flossie stared back at me with owl eyes.

"I know, right? It's diabolical," I said. "It's the perfect murder. No one, save us, suspects Anne. Plus, that explains why the police were so quick to arrest Luke. Everyone thinks the motive is money, not inflating one's ego. Anne is the killer. She has to be."

"Let me search Anne's office," Tori said quietly. "You distract her. I'll go into her office."

"No," I said. "I think my way is better."

Tori stayed seated at the table. Again, she refused to meet my eyes as she shook her head. "Your way is not better," she said softly.

I bit my lower lip, wondering why Tori wanted to get into Anne's office. Did she have a hex-head screwdriver she needed to plant in a desk drawer?

Oh, I hated myself for even thinking that.

Flossie patted my hand. "We can't rush into anything, dear. We can't afford to make any more mistakes."

"We're running out of time," I insisted. "If we're going to do this, we need to do it now."

"Tru," Tori said. "You know I always have your back, right? That includes my never letting you walk out of the bathroom with your skirt tucked into your underwear or toilet paper stuck to your shoe."

"What are you saying?" I demanded.

"You have toilet paper stuck to your shoe."

"What?" I glanced down at my comfortable flats. "No, I don't."

"Not literally." When I didn't catch on to what she was telling me, she added, "Tru, you can't be the one to find the evidence."

"Why not?" Did they think I couldn't handle it? Did they think I was somehow not worthy of being the heroine of my own story?

"Because . . ." Tori started to say but fumbled.

"Because"—Flossie pounced on the opening to say it even louder— "because, dear, your motive to kill Duggar is stronger than Anne's."

My own friends? "How could you?" I whispered.

"Stop it," Tori snapped. "We know you didn't kill anyone."

"*We* know it," Flossie repeated, with emphasis on the word "we." "And that's the problem. The police don't know you like we do. No one does."

"And despite having arrested Luke, the police department is filled with officers who still think me capable of committing the crime," I was forced to concede.

"It would look bad, really bad, if you were the one to find the murder weapon in Anne's office," Flossie said. "All Anne would have to do is tell the police that you put the screwdriver in there, and boom, you'd be in jail instead of Luke."

"Let me search Anne's office, Tru," Tori said. "If the screwdriver is in there, I'll find it."

"No." It was Flossie who objected this time. "You can't do it either."

While I agreed with Flossie that Tori couldn't do it, I wasn't sure why she agreed with me.

"Whyever not?" Tori shot out of her chair again. She propped her fists on her hips. "Go ahead and say it. You don't think I can do it because y'all think I'm not smart enough."

Flossie huffed. "It's not that at all. Out of the three of us, you're probably the most cunning."

"Um . . . thank you?" Tori tilted her head to one side. "But . . . ?"

"Tori, you can't search Anne's office for the same reason Tru can't."

"Because the police will suspect her of the crime?" I asked. Had Flossie come to the same conclusion I had? Was Flossie also worried that Tori had killed Duggar?

"What?" Flossie's brows wrinkled. "No. Why would the police consider Tori a suspect? No one even knows she was at the library that morning."

Tori flashed me a look I didn't know how to interpret before she asked Flossie, "If that's the case, why can't I do it?"

"You're Tru's BFF, have been since preschool. Any evidence you find will appear just as suspect as if Tru had found it herself. Everyone knows how you'd do anything to help your best friend."

"You do have a point." Tori went back to avoiding eye contact again.

"If my plan has that many holes, what do we do?" I asked, feeling more frustrated than ever. "How do we save this place? Or do the two of you think it's hopeless?"

"It's a long shot," Flossie said, patting her chin. "But there's a slim chance something else might work, something that doesn't hinge on the off-chance that the hex-head screwdriver is in Anne's office."

She leaned forward and kept her voice low as she laid out a plan that probably had no chance of succeeding.

Chapter Thirty-Eight

———·———

While Flossie and Tori both worked on setting into motion their part of the plan to get Anne to confess to the crime, I headed toward the circulation desk. Mrs. Farnsworth hurried through the front foyer and skirted the desk without even glancing in my direction. Her eyes looked red, as if she'd been crying.

Alarmed, I followed my crusty boss to her office. I jumped through the doorway before she had a chance to close it.

"I'm not in the mood for whatever you have to say to me," she warned.

I leaned against the door. "I'm worried about you. We all are. Did the mayor pressure you to change your story? To lie to the police?"

The heated look she gave me made me wonder if she was about to transform into a dragon and singe me into a pile of ash. I didn't let her glower intimidate me. Well, not too much. I trembled in my sensible shoes but held my ground.

"We're worried about you," I repeated. "You're an important member of the library and the community. Please, let me help you."

She huffed. I cringed, half expecting her to breathe actual fire. Amazingly, she didn't.

She sat down, steepled her fingers, and sighed. "He told me that I had no choice."

"You mean the mayor?" I said.

The pearls gracing her neck trembled. "He was worried. He told me that it had turned into a life-and-death situation. He told me that blood would be on my hands if I didn't do what he needed me to do."

"Because Grandle attacked Luke?"

She looked up at me in surprise. "You know about that?"

"I know about the debts Luke was running from. I know Grandle followed him to Cypress to collect."

She shook her head. "The mayor will be distressed to know his son's troubles are common knowledge. He's worked so hard to keep them quiet."

"That's why he wanted his son locked away behind bars, isn't it? You went to the police the day after Luke's attack," I said as the pieces started to fall into place. I hadn't spent enough time thinking about Mrs. Farnsworth's role in this mystery. I'd been too focused on Anne. And that had been a mistake. "Mayor Goodvale was worried about his son's safety, wasn't he? He pressured you into destroying their alibis."

After Luke was in jail, the mayor had assured everyone of his son's innocence. He'd seemed almost pleased that his son was in jail because he *was* pleased.

Mrs. Farnsworth's watched me. Her brows crinkled. "How do you know this?"

"It only makes sense." My heart beat a little faster. "I'd initially thought the mayor was coercing you to change your story in order to clear Luke of the murder charge. But that wasn't the case. He'd coerced you to lie about seeing Luke. He wanted his son safely behind bars because he needed to keep his son safe from Grandle."

Mrs. Farnsworth nodded. "Grandle, what a name. After Luke was attacked, Marvin was convinced his son's life was in danger." She drew in a long, slow breath. "They didn't have the money to pay him."

"I get that. What I don't understand is how the mayor convinced you to lie about something so important." Mrs. Farnsworth placed honesty on the same sacred shelf as rule-following. It was a strict personal code she not only expected of others but also lived by every day of her life.

"The reason isn't important." Her voice cracked.

"Isn't it?" I asked.

"No." She said that one word with such finality, I didn't dare press her. "And even though I followed the mayor's orders and went to the police just now and told them that I was mistaken, that I hadn't seen Luke near the media room a few moments before Duggar's death, it didn't matter. Fisher refused to drop the charges against Luke. He said they didn't need my eyewitness testimony, that they were building a rock-solid case against Luke." She sniffled. "I should have never lied in the first place. This wouldn't have happened if I had simply refused to be blackmailed by—"

"What did the mayor have over you?" It shocked me to imagine that someone as straitlaced as Mrs. Farnsworth could be blackmailed. What secrets could she possibly have?

Mrs. Farnsworth merely shook her head. "Marvin is going to be furious."

"This is not your fault." How dare the mayor put her in such a position! "And why would he want his son out of jail? Grandle is still in town. Still a threat. I saw him just yesterday."

With Charlie.

At Duggar's house.

Mayor Goodvale didn't have the money to pay off Grandle, but perhaps the old books at Duggar's house would serve as a substantial down payment. Heck, for all I knew, the sale of the books Duggar had spent a lifetime collecting would pay off Luke's debts completely.

"I don't know." Mrs. Farnsworth bit off the words. "Marvin hasn't exactly confided in me."

"No, I don't suppose he would." Charlie had sworn to me that he wasn't robbing Duggar's house. Perhaps he didn't realize that the mayor wasn't inheriting Duggar's collection. Perhaps the mayor had convinced Charlie that by removing the books from Duggar's house, he was helping settle Duggar's estate. Or perhaps Charlie was lying to me.

I didn't know the answer. And it really didn't matter.

What mattered right now was catching the killer.

Anne?

"Don't worry," I told Mrs. Farnsworth. "One way or the other, Luke will be cleared of the murder charges and out of jail before the end of the day." I simply hoped the secret bookroom would still be a secret when the sun set over Lake Marion.

"How do you—?" she started to ask.

"I just know it's going to happen," I said as I opened the door. "And if things don't work out how I hope they will, I want you to know that I did what I did because I love this library and this town. I'm not sorry."

Mrs. Farnsworth shot to her feet. "Tru!" she cried. "You didn't!"

I didn't have time to disabuse her of the conclusion she'd jumped to. I had a killer to catch and, gracious, very little time to do it.

Chapter Thirty-Nine

Luke desperately needed money.

Duggar understood the value of old books. *The library had been packed with them.*

And Mayor Goodvale was clearly prepared to go to any length to protect his son.

I hurried through the library, searching for Tori and Flossie. I had my phone out and was texting Tori as I headed toward Anne's office. I didn't notice the large man coming toward me until I knocked into him.

"Whoa there, little girl." The man caught my arms. "Where's the fire?"

"Uh . . . um . . . Detective Ellerbe. I'm so glad to see you." The detective reminded me of a well-used paperback novel, creased and tattered around the edges. The cover bulging slightly. But behind his tired exterior and thick mustache, intelligence shone in his eyes. "I didn't think you'd still be in town, I mean, after Luke's arrest."

"Just tying up a few loose ends," he said. His mustache quivered. "Why are you glad to see me?"

"Well, it saves me from having to make a phone call to the police department."

One eyebrow rose. "Yes?"

"There's a man in town by the name of Grandle. I'm pretty sure he attacked Luke the other day."

That single eyebrow remained elevated. "Pretty sure?"

"Luke owes him money. And he is a dangerous man."

"Is that so? Do you have any proof of this?"

"Proof?" That was the trouble. I didn't have proof of anything. "Can't you talk to Grandle? Get him to confess? I suspect he's been paid off, or at least given enough money that he won't hurt Luke again. Which means you need to stop him before he leaves town."

Ellerbe put his hand on my shoulder. "I heard what happened yesterday and that you thought you saw trouble out at the late town manager's house. Look, you've been through a terrible shock. Everyone who was at the library the morning Duggar died has. It's only normal that your mind will start making up stories to explain how such a bad thing could happen in a town like Cypress."

"I'm not making this up," I argued.

"I know it seems real to you."

"Because it is." And, obviously, I wasn't going to make any headway with him. I might have kept trying, but the baristas in the café had started shouting at each other again. "Excuse me," I said to Ellerbe. "I need to handle that."

He gave me a knowing nod before heading toward Mrs. Farnsworth's office. I walked briskly in the opposite direction, toward the café, where it sounded like a war was about to erupt. There was a loud crash. A thunderclap of shattering glass.

And then—silence.

I sprinted the last several yards to the café.

As it turned out, I didn't need to run. Tori was standing behind the counter. She'd put herself physically between the two argumentative baristas. Her arms were outstretched, her face red with anger.

"Go home, Hansen," she growled. "Mop up that mess, Brantley." She held up a finger. "And I don't want to hear a word from either of you."

"But . . . but—"

"Not a word." Tori's eyes flashed fire. "I already covered for you once." She held up her still-bandaged hand.

"You hurt your hand because of these two?" I demanded as I came skidding to a stop at the counter. "Why didn't you tell me?"

Tori jerked her hand behind her. "Don't sneak up on me like that!"

"You've been doing my job, Tori?" I was in charge of managing the new café. "You should have told me." It would have saved me hours of worry.

"I know these two jerks. Hansen, I said go. Get out of here."

The young man looked to me for guidance. "You heard her," I said.

With slumped shoulders, he headed for the exit.

"And you, Brantley. The library doesn't pay you to stand around slack-jawed."

The other young man grumbled as he went to fetch a mop from the maintenance room.

Tori shook her head. "They're good kids, but they cannot work together. Like ever. If anyone had asked me, I would have told them."

"Duggar hired them." Without consulting anyone.

"Stole them from me, you mean? I would never schedule those two numbskulls for the same shift at Perks. The way they act when they're together would make a preacher cuss."

"But we didn't know that. You got between them on opening day? And got hurt? Is that what happened to your hand?" She really should have told me.

"It's just a scratch."

"Not just a scratch." I pointed to the white bandage still wrapped around her hand and wrist.

She shrugged. "Like I said, they're good kids. I hoped they'd be able to work things out, since they both seemed excited about working for the library. Charlie came running when I called to tell him I was bleeding all over your opening ceremonies. He got me patched up. That man of mine has some wicked skills." She waggled her brows, making what she'd said sound naughty.

I smiled. "Do tell." I wanted to hear all, but then I remembered the ticking clock. "I mean, later. Right now we need to change our plans. I think I'm wrong about Anne."

"Oh, I'm so glad you finally came to your senses. It was so hard to keep supporting you as you kept insisting we go down that wrong path."

"It might not have been the wrong path," I started to argue, but we didn't have time for that. "Regardless, text Charlie and buy us some time. I'll need at least another hour."

Tori pulled out her phone, but before she sent the text, she looked up at me again. "You don't still suspect I kicked Duggar's bucket for him?" she asked quietly.

"What?" My face immediately started to flame.

"Hello? We've been friends since preschool. I always know what you're thinking. And that, you have to know, hurt my feelings to no end."

"I was wrong," I wasn't too proud to admit.

"Yeah? You think?" she said. "Well, if I'm not the root of all evil in Cypress, who do you think killed Duggar? Please don't tell me our culprit is Santa Claus or Flossie."

"Not Santa Claus. But perhaps as unbelievable. Mayor Goodvale." I held up a hand before she could object. "I know. I know. It sounds crazy."

She shook her head. "No. Not really. Charlie said he saw Luke at the time of the murder. And his father was nowhere around. And yet, the mayor lied and used his son as an alibi. He wouldn't have done that unless he felt he needed an alibi."

Tori came around to the front of the café counter when Brantley returned with a mop to clean up the mess. "You don't need to have two baristas working at the same time, Tru. Brantley and Hansen are both more than capable of handling this small counter service by themselves."

Duggar had been the one to set up the library café schedule for the first month. He'd told Mrs. Farnsworth that the changes to the library were too big and too important to leave the scheduling in the hands of librarians inexperienced in the real world of business. I wished he were still alive so he could see for himself that he wasn't nearly as perfect as he thought he was.

"I get that the mayor had the opportunity. What I don't understand is why would he kill his own town manager?" Tori asked as we left the café. "Those two men were as close as brothers."

"They were. But it's because of the books." We walked toward the reading room. "Duggar knew all along that those old volumes had more value than Mrs. Farnsworth or I had ever imagined. For me, the value of the books was found in their content. Keeping those books readily available to the residents of Cypress is worth more than money to me. I'd never really thought of them as investments or assets that could be sold."

"But we're talking about the mayor, not Duggar. Do you think Duggar found out about the mayor's plans to sell the discarded books and tried to stop him?" Tori asked. "Is that why the mayor turned on his friend?"

"No." My gut tightened. "No, the mayor might be charismatic, but we all know he's not that smart, and he's especially not book smart. He wouldn't know a first edition from an anniversary reprint."

"Then why would he . . . ?" Her eyes grew wide. Her tan complexion paled. She pressed her fingers to her lips. "No. No, that can't be the reason."

"The reason for what?" Jace asked. I spun around to find him standing in the reading room's entrance with a tiny toy squirrel dangling from his fingers.

"Dude, get yourself a cat already," Tori said with a nervous laugh. She brushed against Jace as she left the reading room. "I'm going to find Flossie and tell her about our change of plans."

"Don't forget to text Charlie," I called after her in my whispery, librarian voice.

"The reason for what?" Jace asked again as soon as we were alone. He took a step toward me. "What was Tori talking about? What's going on?"

I pinched my lips together before finally saying, "Nothing, really. Dewey will love that. You did buy it for him? Or are you—as Tori suggested—planning on adopting a cat of your own?"

"I don't think my dog would appreciate it if I brought home competition."

"You have a dog?" I didn't know why that news surprised me. I knew practically nothing about him.

He gave a rueful smile. "I'd introduce you to her sometime, but I think she'd see you as competition too. Bonnie has an awfully jealous nature."

"Bonnie?" I pictured a large pit bull with a round, kind face but also with jaws that could smash bone.

He nodded. "I was a beat cop when I adopted her. My partner and I picked her up in a back alley in Queens. Even though she was half-starved and in serious need of a bath—that dog stank to high heaven—she tore into the both of us like a beast in a horror flick by the time I finally managed to push her into the back seat of our squad car. She ripped a hole in the seat on the drive to the animal shelter. The shelter worker took one look at her snarling in the squad car and blanched. That's when I learned that not all dogs make it to the adoption floor. The vicious ones are . . ." He cleared his throat. "Well, I didn't have the heart to let that happen to her. Not after everything we'd been through to get her off the street. So, I got back into the car and drove her to my apartment. It took an entire package of hot dogs, but my partner and I finally managed to lure her out without sustaining any more bites. She's been with me ever since."

I tried to overlay the image of a young cop saving a vicious dog with the image of the high school boy who had trampled my heart and stolen my work. But no matter how hard I tried, those two images wouldn't mesh. "You're not the boy I tutored," I said.

He swore softly before saying, "I hope not. I think back on my high school 'glory days' and cringe. I didn't like who I was then, and remembering that boy, I like him even less."

"He was a royal jerk," I said in agreement.

"Especially to you. I am sorry, Tru, that I stole from you. I'm sorry that I hurt you. In high school, I'd become someone I thought my friends wanted me to be. It took leaving Cypress and years of spending time alone to grow into someone I didn't hate. I'm still working on that last part." He dredged his fingers through his hair. "And I can't believe I just said that."

I touched his hand. "I don't hate you, if that means anything."

He drew a long, slow breath. And I held my own, waiting to hear what he might say next, expecting this to turn into one of those grand moments that happened at the end of the best romance novels, the endings that left me with tears flooding down my cheeks.

He stroked my cheek. I melted into his touch. My eyes started to close. It was all so, so romantic. Sissy was wrong. He wasn't using me. We had a real connection. One that maybe could grow into something—

"Hmm," Jace purred, his voice deep and sexy. "Since you're feeling all gushy toward me, why don't you tell me what's going on. What's the big secret you've been keeping from me?"

I hadn't expected him to say that. Nor had I expected feeling so tempted to tell him everything.

Chapter Forty

It's the mayor," I blurted.

Jace schooled his features, becoming as unreadable as a blank page. "The mayor," he parroted back.

"I know it sounds crazy." And when the entire story came out, it was going to sound like Duggar's death was my fault. I never meant for anyone to get hurt. I only wanted to save the books. "I already told Detective Ellerbe about Grandle, and he reminded me how I'm seeing things that aren't real. But I assure you, this is real."

"Okay." Jace's features remained frustratingly inscrutable. "Tell me what you think our esteemed mayor is up to."

I drew a steadying breath. I needed to do this. "Marvin Goodvale killed Duggar." I held up my hand before he could say anything. "The mayor and town manager have always worked closely together. Duggar, I've since learned, is a collector of rare and expensive books. He knew the value of the books in this library better than perhaps anyone in town—save for our new bookstore owner. And yet, he planned to send those old books to the landfill? Or so he'd told us.

"Now add Luke to the equation. He returns to Cypress buried under a pile of debt and a dangerous debt collector nipping at his heels. We all know that everyone in Cypress is as poor as church mice. Even the mayor."

"He has his lake cabin. That must be worth something. The land values on the lake have been skyrocketing ever since the folks in Columbia and Charlotte discovered us," Jace pointed out.

"Yes, but he owns that house with his two brothers." Everyone in town knew that. "Perhaps they're not willing to sell. And even if he could force a sale, I doubt that would be enough money to cover Luke's debts, which appear to be vast."

Jace didn't look convinced. "A few old books can't be worth even one-third of the value of a house."

"That's what I thought at first too. The books were valuable to me. As books." As lifelines for a depressed teen. "I hadn't ever considered the monetary value the books might have. But the more I've researched the subject, the more I've learned that some of the books in our collection are worth thousands of dollars." I swallowed over a lump of guilt in my throat. "I think when you add up the value of the entire collection, it might be worth close to a small fortune."

Jace seemed to chew on that information. "Yes, but what does that have to do with Duggar's murder?"

"The mayor and Duggar couldn't just walk in and take the books from the library. No, that wouldn't do at all. For one thing, the alarms at the door would go off if they tried to steal them. And I'm talking about dozens of books in the collection, not just one or two, that they would have to take. The two of them would have to get the books legally out of the town's holding before they could sell them. Otherwise, they'd be stealing from the town. Duggar could have upgraded the library while keeping the printed books. There's room for the books. But he didn't. He made certain that those books—books he had to know were valuable—would be disposed of."

"That's an interesting theory, but it's still not a motive for murder," he said. "If what you're saying is true, it sounds as if the mayor and town manager were working together."

"Yes, I think they were working together. You have in evidence a sheet of paper from Charlie's store providing an estimate of some of those books."

"You know I can't—"

"I know. I know you cannot discuss that. I'm not asking you to. I'm simply providing supporting information for my argument."

He crossed his arms. "Go on. You think their partnership fell apart because one of them got greedy?"

"Um . . . something like that." I tried to tell him about the secret bookroom and how I'd removed the books that they were planning to sell. I tried to tell him that the mayor, after discovering that the books they'd planned to sell were missing from the boxes, had suspected Duggar of double-crossing him and had killed his best friend in a fit of anger. Even after Duggar's death, the mayor had continued to search the boxes for those books I'd taken. I'd witnessed him digging through the boxes myself. But what came out of my mouth was, "I think the mayor was worried that Duggar might try to keep the books instead of selling them. And he killed him to keep that from happening."

Not a lie. I did think Mayor Goodvale had blamed Duggar when he couldn't find the books we'd moved downstairs to the vault. And when Duggar denied knowing where the books were, the mayor lost it. In a rage, he killed Duggar.

That was why the mayor had lied about his alibi. (He needed one.) That was why someone had broken into Charlie's bookstore. (The mayor was on a desperate search for the missing books.) That was why someone had broken into my house. (The mayor had heard that I was loaning out old library books and had suspected I'd stashed the books somewhere in my home.)

If I hadn't started the secret bookroom, Duggar would still be alive.

I drew in a ragged breath. "Um . . . Luke isn't guilty. His father is." And me.

I was also guilty.

I needed to tell Jace.

I needed to come clean about my role in the murder.

"I . . . I—" I stuttered.

"Yes, Tru?" Jace leaned toward me, his expression looking so kind, so earnest. Still, I trembled at the thought of telling him about my role in Duggar's death.

"Tru!" Tori hurried into the room. Her voice was too loud. Her eyes were wide with a look of panic. "You need to get downstairs. Now."

"What's going on?" Jace asked, his voice just as loud as Tori's.

"Book business," Tori nearly shouted.

I shushed them both. "We can finish this later," I told Jace softly before following Tori out of the reading room. I had to jog to keep up with her.

Jace had started to follow but was waylaid by Detective Ellerbe, who looked awfully concerned about something.

"I wasn't able to stop Flossie's plan," Tori whispered. "And now Anne is downstairs poking around outside the vault and is as angry as a bear."

"Anne? But she isn't the killer, is she?"

"I don't know. Flossie is trying to calm her down, but I'm scared."

We made it down the stairs and into the basement in record time. Anne was pacing in front of the vault doors. Flossie had parked herself in front of them, her hands firm on the wheels of her wheelchair.

As soon as Anne spotted us, she rushed toward me. "You!" she shouted. "I knew you did it!" She jabbed a finger toward the vault doors. "I'm not going to let you get away with it."

She whirled back around toward Flossie. "Let me pass. You have no right to stop me. I work here. You don't."

"Anne," I said, my voice much calmer than I felt. "What's going on?"

"I . . . I heard that you have it." Her voice trembled.

"It?" Not *them*? Not the books?

"In there!" She thrust her finger at the vault doors again. "You hid it in there!"

"What are you talking about?" I asked.

She gave Flossie's wheelchair a mighty shove.

"Hey!" Flossie cried. The wheelchair teetered on two wheels, but Flossie quickly shifted her balance and managed to keep it from flipping over on its side. At the same time Tori rushed to the vault door and threw her arms wide to block Anne.

"It's Dewey," I said quickly. "I'm keeping him in there. If you open the doors, he'll rush out and run upstairs and start chewing on your wires."

That seemed to do the trick.

"If there's something in there that you need me to get, I'll get it for you," I told her.

"It's the screwdriver," Flossie said and gave me a meaningful look. "She wants the screwdriver you found this morning. The one that was used to loosen the bolts on the shelf that killed Duggar."

"The missing murder weapon?" I asked as I turned back to Anne.

Tori had warned me that she hadn't been able to stop the plan, the plan that none of us had expected to work. Flossie was going to tell everyone that I'd found the missing hex-head screwdriver and that I'd put it in the basement until I had a chance to hand it over to the police for them to dust for fingerprints. Anne, we figured, would panic and come running to the basement to get the screwdriver.

But our suspicions had shifted to the mayor. He had to be the one who had killed Duggar, right? Not Anne. Unless . . .

"Wait a minute. You killed Duggar?" I asked Anne. "I mean, I had thought you might have killed him because you wanted the credit for the work you'd been doing at the library and he was going to claim he was the mastermind behind the renovations. But then the evidence pointed—"

"I didn't kill him! You did!" she shouted.

"Please, don't shout. This is a library. Even down here," came my automatic response. "If you didn't kill him, why in the world would you come looking for the screwdriver?"

"Because I didn't want to let you get away with it!" she shouted, though her voice wasn't quite as loud as before. "I'm not going to let you get away with murder. And I'm certainly not going to let you frame me for the crime." She held out her hand. "Give it to me."

"The screwdriver?" I asked dumbly. Of course that was what she wanted. "I don't have it."

She tilted her head to one side. "I don't understand."

"You don't?" Tori said, her voice dripping with fake sympathy. She sounded just as catty as Sissy. "And everyone has been telling us how smart you are. Oh, dear. Were they wrong?"

"I don't—" Anne started to say again.

"It's simple, really," Tori explained. "We put out word that Tru found the screwdriver and is handing it over to the police. And then we waited for the killer to come running down here to reveal herself."

"But I didn't kill anyone!" Anne cried.

"Then you should have been smart enough to keep your nose out of our business," Tori said in a patronizing tone.

Anne stabbed her finger toward the vault doors again. "But there's something fishy going on in there."

Dewey, bless him, meowed loud enough to be heard through the thick doors.

"You're . . . you're really keeping your cat in there?" Anne stammered.

"Please, don't tell Mrs. Farnsworth," I begged. "He can't do any harm in that room. It's an empty storage room. He's miserable when I keep him home."

Anne's brows wrinkled as she continued to stare at the double doors. "But why do patrons keep coming down here?"

"To visit Dewey, of course," Flossie explained as if it were the most obvious thing in the world. She maneuvered toward the platform lift she used to get her wheelchair from floor to floor in the library. "Well, clearly our plan to entrap the killer flopped. Anne, could you show me how the 3D printers work?"

"Really?" Anne's eyes lit up. "You really want to see the printers? No one has asked to see those printers."

"Honey, I want to hear about everything," Flossie called over her shoulder.

"I'd better check on Brantley in the café." Tori followed in Flossie's wake, heading toward the stairs.

"That's not your job." I started to chase after my friend, but Dewey meowed again so plaintively that the sound froze my muscles.

My little kitty never meowed like that. He needed something.

I opened the vault door to check on him. Like the naughty kitty that he could be, Dewey scuttled between my legs, nearly knocking me down as he rushed out into the basement hallway.

"Dewey!" I whisper-yelled. What was that kitty up to now?

At least he wasn't darting toward the stairs. With the library as full as it was right now, his appearance upstairs would be a disaster. Still, I needed to catch him. I chased him as he skittered along the wall and around a corner in the large maze of a basement. He came to a sudden stop at the back door, the exact door where the two of us first met on that fateful night nearly two weeks ago. He scratched at it.

"I'm not opening the door," I told him. "I'm not letting you run loose through town. It's not safe out there."

Dewey glanced at me and then scratched at the door again.

"It's not safe," I repeated, as if that would change my stubborn kitty's mind. The words had barely left my mouth when the basement door swung open. And in walked Mayor Goodvale.

"Ah, Miss Becket," he said and flashed his slick politician's smile. "Just the librarian I was looking for."

Chapter Forty-One

Mayor Goodvale remembered my name. He hadn't even hesitated. That had to be a first for him. I doubted it was a good omen.

"Mayor," I said. Dewey backed away from the door. He squatted low and growled like a bobcat. "What can I do for you?" I reached into my pocket for my phone. I needed to call for help.

"For starters, you can keep your hands where I can see them." His smile never wavered, which unnerved me. He took a step toward me. He let go of the metal basement door. It slammed closed with a bang behind him.

I pulled my hand from my pocket and backed away from the mayor. Dewey stuck by me. His small body pressed against my leg. "How did you get in here? That door is always locked."

"Darling, did you forget I'm the mayor? I have the keys to the city. Literally. At least when it comes to the public buildings."

"Ah. That must be convenient."

"It is." He took another step toward me. "Now, let's have a little chat, shall we?"

"About what?" I could shout, if I needed to. There was a library filled with people upstairs. Jace was upstairs with a gun. So was Detective Ellerbe. I wasn't in danger. Not really.

If I did start shouting for help, the mayor could easily deny he was threatening me. I'd end up looking like a fool. But I supposed I'd rather look like a fool than end up hurt or dead.

"People have been talking about you," he said, still wearing that false smile of his. "They're calling you a human library. They're saying that you're lending out books. Old books. Books that should have been packed up and sent to the landfill."

I swallowed over a lump in my throat. "Most of the residents want books they can hold in their hands, not tablets. Duggar was making a mistake."

"No, it wasn't a mistake!" Dewey hissed at the mayor's clipped tone. "Duggar knew exactly what he was doing."

"And I ruined his plans." Feeling braver, I put my hand on my hip. "And I ruined your plans as well. I know what you did. I didn't at first, but I finally figured things out. I now know why Duggar had insisted those books be taken away. The two of you planned to sell them and keep the money for yourselves."

"That's not quite what we'd planned." The mayor slowly shook his head. "Duggar wanted to keep some of the books. I planned to sell the others."

"To help your son," I supplied.

He huffed in frustration. "Not at first. But then Luke came home. *Ran* home, more like. That boy of mine wasn't prepared for life outside Cypress. He certainly wasn't prepared to take a job where he made so much money. He thought the cash flow would never run out. He didn't understand that even if his paycheck was large, he still needed to live within his means. They say he can't stop shopping, those head doctors my wife sent him to. I don't know if that's true, but he's always clicking on links online, unable to pass up what he calls 'the perfect deal.'"

He took another step toward me. Dewey let out a sharp, feral meow. Before I could stop him, my skinny kitty darted down the hallway and around a corner toward the staircase that led up to the main library. Without even thinking about it, I started to run after him before he got us into even more trouble.

The mayor grabbed my arm. "I'm not done with you, darling."

My shoulders dropped, not because I was afraid for my life, but because I was afraid Dewey would get caught upstairs. "I suppose not. What do you want from me?"

"Everything." His smile disappeared. "I want everything you took from me."

A fresh wave of guilt washed over me. My lungs tightened with the crushing weight of it, leaving me feeling as if I needed to gasp for air. "You killed Duggar because the books you'd planned to sell weren't in the boxes."

I didn't push that shelf over on Duggar, but I felt just as responsible.

The mayor's grip on my arm tightened. "It . . . it was an accident. I didn't mean to hurt him. He . . . he was like a brother to me. But . . . but the books . . ."

"Were gone," I finished for him when his voice broke. Tears filled my eyes. "And Luke's life was in danger. I am so sorry. I didn't know."

His grip tightened even more. "You should be sorry. This is your fault."

His words gutted me. I was only trying to do the right thing.

"You need to make this right," he said. "First, you're going to tell me where you hid the books. They're not at Duggar's house. They're not at your house. Where are they?"

"Was that what Charlie and Grandle were doing at Duggar's house? They were looking for the books?" But they left with boxes.

"I gave that bookseller the spare key I kept for Duggar. He easily found enough moldy books at Duggar's to pay off Luke's debts. Can you believe that? Duggar was hoarding a fortune on those shelves in his living room. Grandle seemed satisfied. And the murder charge against Luke was going to be dropped. Mrs. Farnsworth was seeing to that."

"Um, she said the police—" I tried to tell him.

"But then Charlie called and said that he couldn't sell the books until he had proof that Duggar had willed them to me. He has them set aside. And Grandle is back out there, demanding his money or blood will be spilled."

"But Duggar didn't leave the books to you in his will." And Charlie had proved once again that he was a decent guy. I owed him (and Tori) an apology.

"I know that!" the mayor snapped. "Seemed like a cursed inconvenient time for that bookseller to get a conscience. He'd have gotten a cut of the sales, you know. It would have set him up right nice with his new business. But, no, he has to have papers proving provenance or some sort of nonsense before he'll get Luke the money he needs. His morals are going to get my boy killed."

"I am sorry about Luke's troubles." I truly was.

"You'll be even more sorry if you don't hand over the books." He gave my body a violent shake.

I held up my hands. "Wait a minute. Let me get this straight. You thought those books Charlie had taken from Duggar's house would cover Luke's debts, and yet you still broke into my house to search for the library books?"

"They're not yours to keep," he growled in my ear.

"And when you couldn't find the books, you kidnapped Dewey?"

"Kidnapped who?" the mayor spat.

"Dewey. My cat."

"That beast at your house? It attacked me and ran out the front door when I tried to kick him."

"You kicked my cat?" I twisted out of his grip and started to swing at him. "He's a defenseless little animal. How dare you hurt him!"

"Wait a minute." He threw up his hands and deflected most of my flaying blows. "I'm the victim here. Your cat attacked me. You stole from me. *Me!*" The mayor kept his hands in front of his face. "Just tell me where you put the library books."

"No!" I started to run down the hallway following the path Dewey had taken in the basement's maze of hallways. I moved as if I'd just spotted my favorite author signing books at the American Library Association's annual conference. (Believe me, that's fast.) I wasn't simply running away from him and the threat he posed. I was also running from my guilt.

The mayor cursed and chased after me. But my legs were longer, stronger. He had no chance of catching up.

Until I stopped at the base of the stairs.

I stopped so abruptly the mayor slammed into my back.

"You're lying." I whirled around to face him. I shook my finger under his nose. "You didn't blow up in a fit of rage and accidentally kill your friend. The bolts securing the shelf to the floor had been removed. It was the only shelf in the entire library missing them. I know. I looked. You removed the bolts because you planned to kill him. You planned to take all of the books—and all of the money—for yourself."

Duggar's death wasn't my fault.

"No." He tried to grab me. Somehow I managed to keep out of his reach. "No. That's not—"

"It is what happened. The library's hex-head screwdriver, the screwdriver used to remove the bolts, is still missing. I wonder if the police searched your place, would they find it? Or did you dispose of it? Did you dispose of the bolts too?"

"You don't understand," the mayor whined. "Luke's life was in danger. I had to do something drastic to save him."

"By killing your best friend? Why didn't you explain the situation to Duggar? Why didn't you try to work something out? Wouldn't that have been better than murder?"

"I tried. He wouldn't listen to reason. Those books . . ." He slashed an angry hand through the air. "Duggar didn't care about the money. He said those books were worth more than money to him. He wanted to put those stupid things on his shelf in his personal library so he could look at them, admire them. Can you believe that?"

"He's a monster," I ground out, and truly meant it. Not because Duggar wouldn't help out a friend in need, although that was rather deplorable. But because the town manager had planned to take those old books from a public library and hoard them for his own pleasure. The books in the library belonged to everyone. They were meant to be read and shared. Their very availability made the community a richer place. Duggar, of all people, should have understood that.

"I'm glad you agree that I had no choice. He had to die. And now you must realize how desperate I am. Take me to those books." The mayor's mouth puckered. He looked as if he'd tasted my Aunt Sal's pumpkin pie. There was something seriously wrong with the mix of spices that dear woman used.

"If I have the books and I took you to them, what happens then?" I demanded. "Do we go our separate ways, keeping each other's secrets?"

His mouth tightened even more. He wore the same look people got when they were too polite for their own good and had let Aunt Sal talk them into taking a second bite of her infamous pie. "Take me to the books."

"What is one more murder?" I murmured. "It's not like I'm anyone important. You usually cannot even remember my name."

"Oh, I remember now. I'll always remember you. You're Becket's girl and a cursed thorn in my side. Get moving."

I held my ground. He might look at me and see a mouse. He might think he could bully me into handing over those books he wanted to sell and then submissively do nothing while he killed me. Luckily for me, he was wrong.

I wasn't going to take him to my secret bookroom, not when I could scream for help. I whispered a silent apology to Mrs. Farnsworth. Drew in a deep breath. And—

"Tru? What's going on?" Jace's sharp voice came from directly behind me.

Before I could answer, Mayor Goodvale pounced. He grabbed my right arm and spun me around, using my body as a shield between him and Jace. He'd twisted my arm behind my back with such force, I was afraid bones might snap.

Jace reacted just as quickly. He'd drawn his gun and had aimed the deadly weapon at the center of my chest. I'd never felt so vulnerable in my life. I prayed this wasn't going to be the last emotion I'd ever experience, because it sucked.

"Thank goodness you're here, Detective. You know I never believed what others said about you. I never believed the whispers saying you couldn't be trusted." The mayor's grip tightened. He pressed what I assumed was the missing hex-head screwdriver into my hand and squeezed my fingers (which were turning numb) around its handle. "I caught Ms. Becket in an attempt to move vital evidence, evidence that proves she killed my friend Duggar."

He then sniffled and heaved a ragged breath. Was the mayor crying?

"I loved that man like a brother." His voice cracked. "She took him from me."

Jace lowered his gun. "That is disappointing. Was hoping it'd go another way." He shrugged. That's when I noticed Dewey standing by the detective's side. My little brown and black tabby rubbed against his leg in one of those deep kitty hugs. "But what can I say? She's been our lead suspect all along." He tucked his gun back into its holster and pulled out his handcuffs. Dewey's green eyes appeared to glitter at the sight of it. "Well, there's only one thing that needs to be done now. I'll take her in."

The mayor's grip tightened even more. My right arm screamed in pain. He caught the screwdriver as it slipped from my now useless hand. He pressed the point of it into my side. "Actually, son, go fetch the chief.

I want this done all official-like. Can't have her getting off because we didn't cross all our *t*'s."

"I can call him once I get the scene secured." He reached for me. "Hand her over."

"Son." The mayor sighed. "She killed my friend. Give me a few minutes with her."

Jace stared at me for a long while before he gave a short, brisk nod and turned away.

"*What?*" I wheezed through the pain searing up and down my arm. Was he serious? "*You . . . you're going to leave me here? With him?*"

Jace didn't turn back. He didn't slow his step. Just like when we were in high school, he was going to walk away as if he didn't know me. I didn't know why I was surprised.

Dewey stayed. He sat down and started to wash a paw.

Did no one care about me? Not even my cat?

"Now that we're alone," the mayor breathed in my ear. He poked me in the side with the screwdriver. Its point was sharp. "How about you save yourself a world of pain and take me to the—"

His grip on my arm suddenly went slack. He started to pitch forward. Unable to catch myself in time, I tumbled forward too. Dewey gave a startled yelp and jumped out of the way a moment before I landed face first on the concrete floor with the mayor on top of me.

"Get him off her," I heard Jace order just as someone rolled the unconscious mayor off my back. I eased up onto my elbows to find both Jace and Charlie frowning down at me.

"I didn't kill Duggar," I told them.

"Don't be daft. We know you didn't," Charlie said.

"Did you really think I'd walk away and leave you to the mayor's whims?" Jace sounded insulted. "What kind of cop do you think I am? Even if I thought you were guilty, I wouldn't do that. But I also couldn't attack him from the front. Not when he had that knife to your side."

"A-a-a—*knife?*" I stammered. It wasn't a screwdriver he was poking me with, but a knife? I saw it lying on the ground next to the unconscious mayor. It was a big bowie knife. There was one like it in my backyard shed. Had the mayor taken it during the break-in?

"Your nose is bleeding." Jace tossed his handcuffs to Charlie before helping me scramble to my feet. He took a crisp cotton handkerchief from the mayor's suit pocket and handed to me.

"Um, thanks." I pressed the handkerchief to the stinging scraped skin on my nose.

From the ground beside me, the mayor groaned. "Son, you're making a huge mistake. You'll never work in law enforcement again."

Jace ignored him. "Do you need me to call for medical care?" He ran his hands up and down my arms and along my side. "He didn't break anything, did he? He didn't stab you?"

"No." I stepped back from his gentle touch and picked up Dewey. My nerves were still badly shaken from thinking Jace had left me in the mayor's sick clutches. I needed to use my kitty as a shield between us. "I don't understand what's going on. What made you suddenly start to believe me?"

"I've always believed you, Tru." Jace scratched Dewey's soft head. "This little guy, however, deserves all the credit for saving you. When he ran up to me in the reading room, I knew there was something seriously wrong. He led me to the basement stairs, where I overheard you talking with the mayor, which in itself wasn't suspicious. So I didn't say anything or make myself known. But I'd never seen Dewey so agitated. He kept clawing at my leg, as if he were trying to tell me to do something specific. Always trust a cat's instincts, Tru. They're smarter than we are. I listened to your cat and grabbed the first person I could find as backup before going back downstairs." He nodded toward Charlie.

"I'd come back to the library after I received a troubling text from Tori," Charlie said. "It was filled with threats. Next thing I knew, I was being called on to be a hero. I got the key from Mrs. Farnsworth and sneaked in through the basement back door."

"Mrs. Farnsworth entrusted you with the key?" First she gave it to Jace and now she'd handed it over to Charlie?

"What can I say?" Charlie smiled. "I'm a charming guy. Women trust me."

The mayor had been spouting threats all this time. But suddenly his tone changed. "Ah. There you are. Arrest these miscreants. They've conspired against me, Miss Becket threatened me with a knife, and they killed the town manager."

Detective Ellerbe looked at me and then at Charlie. His gaze finally stopped at Jace. "Read me into the situation, Detective."

Jace gave a brief summary of the events. "In short, Mayor Goodvale killed the town manager. As I came down the stairs, I heard him as he confessed to the crime to Ms. Becket."

"And I recorded it," Charlie interjected. He held up his phone.

And that was that.

It was over.

Chapter Forty-Two

She's in shock," Flossie said.

"She needs coffee. Strong coffee," Tori said.

"For once, I agree with you," Flossie replied.

I heard them talking. I felt their comforting hands petting my back. I wasn't in shock. At least I didn't think I was. The police had escorted Mayor Goodvale to the station. I'd given a statement to Detective Ellerbe. He was the one who'd suggested I go upstairs and get something from the café. He was the one who'd told me to find my friends.

Jace had pried Dewey from my arms moments before I'd climbed the stairs. He promised to take good care of my "hero kitty." That was kind of him.

"It wasn't my fault." I whispered the one thought that kept circling and circling in my mind. *It wasn't my fault.*

"Of course it isn't. What happened after we left?" Tori pulled me into the circle of her arms. "Charlie marched right past me. He said he'd call. But he didn't kiss me or smile or anything. He's either upset, or I'm losing my allure. Tell me I'm not losing my touch when it comes to men."

"Stop making this about you," Flossie fussed. "This is about Tru."

"Charlie was heading to the police station, I think," I said, my face buried in Tori's peasant blouse. "He recorded the mayor's confession on his phone."

"Let go of her, Tori, so I can hug her. You're always such a hog."

"Says the woman who doesn't let anyone touch her computer," Tori shot back.

I hugged Tori tightly and then bent down and wrapped my arms around Flossie. "The two of you are gems. I love you both more than anything in the world. And I'm fine. I simply felt overwhelmed for a moment. It's over. And Duggar's death wasn't my fault." I drew a steadying breath. "The two of you are right about one thing. I can use that coffee."

The library café not only served coffee but also sold a selection of freshly baked pastries. I ordered my coffee black and a bear claw so sweet and gooey that Mama would lecture me for a solid week if she saw me eating it.

But it was over. And the secret bookroom was safe.

That was the part I still had a hard time believing.

"That was a stupid, brave thing you did at the library," Jace said when I answered my door that evening. Dewey was at the screen door in a flash, meowing for me to open it for his new best buddy.

"Thank you," I said.

"It wasn't a compliment. You should have run away. You should have shouted for help. You could have gotten yourself killed."

I tilted my head. "Is that why you're here? You came to scold me?"

"I came here to—" He dragged his fingers through his hair. "Are you going to let me in before your cat rips a hole in the door?"

I pushed open the door and stepped out of the way so he could come in because he was right. Dewey was about to rip a cat-sized hole in my screen door.

"I was never in danger," I told him. "I was about to shout for help when you barged in."

"Tru, Tru, Tru, you took too big of a risk. He had a knife." Jace shook his head. "This isn't how police investigations work. It's not about the big confession at the end. We gather evidence, we build cases, and yes, it often ends up muddy. But in the end, if we're lucky, justice is served."

"I'd run out of time. I couldn't wait for the police to handle things." Not with Charlie about to run to the police and expose us all.

"What do you mean, you'd run out of time?"

"Nothing. Just a slip of the tongue. Next time, I'll try to trust the system."

"And me." He took a step closer and put his hands on my hips. "I want you to know that you can trust me, Tru. If you ever find yourself in trouble like this again, come to me. Let me help you."

My cat was tracing figure eights around both Jace's and my legs, as if trying to join the two of us together in some kind of secret cat ceremony. Plus, Jace had believed in me; at least he had in the end. And he had taken excellent care of Dewey, sneaking him out through the basement door without Mrs. Farnsworth learning I'd brought him to the library and personally bringing him home.

Despite all that, I had to be honest. Trusting Jace was going to take some work.

He seemed to understand my hesitation. His hands slipped from my hips. "I'm glad you're okay, Tru. I came by to also let you know that the state police picked up Grandle about an hour ago. Luke is now willing to testify that Grandle attacked him. That moneylender isn't getting out of jail anytime soon."

"That's good to know. Maybe he and the mayor can bunk together."

"The facts are piling up against the mayor. Much of the evidence we had thought we'd traced to Luke traces to his father just as easily. And with his confession, the district attorney won't have any trouble building a case against him. But there is one thing that's troubling us, Tru. The mayor keeps trying to implicate you. He's saying you stole library books. You wouldn't happen to know anything about that, would you?"

I bit my lower lip. "I would never steal from the library."

"That's what I told them. Now, get some rest. You deserve it." He started toward the door but stopped abruptly and turned back to me. "And Tru, I know you still have a secret. I'm okay with that. We all have secrets we feel like we need to keep."

I closed the door and leaned against it. A bubbly feeling of happiness brought a smile to my lips. *Oh, boy, he doesn't know the half of it.*

Secrets seemed to be as popular as sweet tea here under the shade of our ancient bald cypresses. Thankfully, the residents of our tranquil town had no reason to fret. A small but dedicated team had devoted their lives to protect them.

Librarians were adventurers. Librarians were warriors. Librarians were superheroes dressed in plain clothes. Beware, villains. You don't stand a chance against one of us.

Acknowledgments

Oh boy, launching a new series is terrifying. It's like jumping off a cliff and hoping that by some miracle you know how to fly. Luckily, I have an awesome support system (including you) that serves as my wings. This library series has been in my heart in some form or other ever since my high school days. I'm grateful to my amazing editor at Berkley, Michelle Vega, and my super awesome agent, Jill Marsal, for encouraging me to write *The Broken Spine*.

To my writing buddies—especially and not exclusively: Dru Ann Love, Paula Benson, Nicole Seitz, Amanda Berry, Ann Chaney, Nina Bruhns, Catherine Bruns, and Shari Randall—thank you for being there, for the cheers, the plotting advice, the scene ideas, and the fact-checking. I love you all and miss you.

A special round of thanks goes to a couple of library friends (warriors) who helped with the research of this book. Leslie Koller, a digital/emerging technologies librarian, listened as I talked through the plot with her, answered all my silly questions, and gave all kinds of guidance on topics from new technologies to rare and collectible books. Frankie

Lea Hannan, assistant branch manager at my local library, provided some wonderful insights after the tai chi classes she'd teach in the library's meeting room. I bet you never knew I was quietly plotting murders during those classes!

Heartfelt thanks go to my super supportive family, especially to Jim, who gave me time to write even when time seemed scarce (plus let me buy a puppy), and Avery, who is and will always be my joy. I love you all dearly.

Finally, to my readers, especially those who have stuck with me, who attend my book signings, who write me emails, who send encouraging messages on Facebook, and who leave reviews. I hope my words inspire, keep you guessing, and make you smile. You are the best readers a writer could ever hope for. Thank you.